THE Painter
of Time

THE Painter *of* Time

MATTHEW O'CONNELL

STATION
SQUARE
MEDIA

New York, New York

THE PAINTER OF TIME

Copyright © 2015 by Matthew O'Connell
Published by Station Square Media
16 West 23rd Street, 4th Floor
New York, NY 10010

This novel is a work of fiction. Any references to real people, events, establishments, organizations, or locales are intended only to give the fiction a sense of reality and authenticity, and are used fictitiously. All other names, characters, places, and incidents portrayed in this book are the product of the author's imagination.

Editorial: Write to Sell Your Book, LLC
Cover Design: Kathi Dunn
Interior Design: Karen Hudson
Production Management: Janet Spencer King

Printed in the United States of America for Worldwide Distribution.
ISBN: 978-0-9966693-3-7

Electronic editions:
Mobi ISBN: 978-0-9966693-4-4
Epub ISBN: 978-0-9966693-5-1

First Edition
10 9 8 7 6 5 4 3 2 1

—To Mari, my soul mate and best friend—

Acknowledgments

I'd like to specifically thank Kevin Klinvex, Gary Weitzman, Dennis Doverspike, my wife Mari, and everyone who read earlier versions and shared their insights, suggestions and most importantly provided positive feedback and encouragement.

Many thanks to Kathi Dunn for her beautiful cover design and to Annie Nichol for her outstanding attention to detail and grammatical fluency in reviewing the manuscript.

Finally, I owe special thanks to my editor, Diane O'Connell (no relation), who has helped me develop as a writer and taught me to understand the real craft of writing. Her straightforward feedback and ideas were and are invaluable to me.

❧ Chapter 1 ❧
New York, June 2009

The brush moved gently. Firmly. With a confidence belying generations of experience. His breathing was rhythmic, deliberate, but not forced. His attention was at once on the painting and at the same time on the horizon, the distant past—lost in thought, an active meditation. He focused on his brush strokes, long and smooth, careful not to hold his breath, at least not for very long. Sometimes when he was deep in a painting and concentrating on tiny details he would forget to breathe, so as to keep his hand steady. But it was a bad habit. If he did that too much or for too long, he'd get light headed and, in rare cases, he'd even passed out. No, it was important to match your breath to your brush strokes. Like yoga, but with a brush in your hand.

He stopped and laid the brush down, sat back and studied the painting. *Is that how it was or am I trying to improve what was there?* The cherubic child reached up for his mother's face. The plain face of the mother holding her young child looked off to the side and downward as if she were watching a dog playing in the grass. Why didn't she look directly at her young son, just as he looked at her? Would a mother look this way? Were the eyes correctly positioned or had time distorted their view? He quieted his mind and thought back, trying to remember how it had originally looked, or at least how the painter had intended it to look. It was a common problem he ran into, almost daily. His job was to restore, to conserve. To bring back the glory of what was. How had it looked before time, the elements, and neglect had taken their toll? His job was not to improve, not to fix errors that most people, even art critics and historians, never saw but that stood out to him like a nose ring on the Mona Lisa. Such was his job. Restore. Don't improve and definitely don't detract from what was there in the first place.

1

He stepped away from the painting and looked at it from a short distance. He could see the shimmer of the new paint, but other than that you wouldn't have known it had been touched up just moments before. That was the plan. *Enough for now,* he thought. He carefully cleaned his brushes with turpentine. He smiled softly as he performed the routine task that he had completed thousands, perhaps millions of times. Routines were one of the world's hidden joys. Like washing your face in a basin of warm water, with fragrant soap, scented with lavender from the fields of Provence and drying it with a plush, clean towel. Even the pungent smell of turpentine and linseed oil used to clean the paint from brushes was a timeless smell that you would never confuse with any other, like pine needles and fresh cut grass. Weren't these the things that made life rich, made it worth living? *Indeed they were,* he thought.

He stretched, trying to work out the kinks that come from sitting and focusing intently for three hours at a time, and from the accumulation of a lifetime of painting. He took several deep, long restorative breaths, hoping that the increased oxygen flow would shake off his fatigue.

He walked slowly to one of the stone benches in the Medieval, cloistered garden. It was warm, with creamy, titanium white clouds slowly making their way across the cobalt blue summer sky. He took out his lunch from his well-worn leather satchel. A thermos of Earl Grey tea, carefully mixed with milk and sugar, a tomato and cucumber sandwich on white bread with the crusts carefully trimmed. He rarely sat with anyone else. Solitude was underrated as far as he was concerned. Besides, it was hard for him to carry on small talk. Who do you like on *Idol?* Have you seen the mouse chasing the dog on YouTube? He was never sure how to answer. He wasn't even sure what they were talking about most of time. Fortunately, most of the other restorers were introverts and tended to keep to themselves as well.

Anthony never thought of himself as a loner. In fact, he really wasn't. Introspective and thoughtful, an observer as opposed to a wallflower, but more than anything, tired. He wasn't bored with life per se, but he was certainly tired of the ever-flowing stream of transient nonsense that made up the vast majority of people's lives. It wasn't that he was trying to be an intellectual snob, trying to figure out the existential nature of being, the reason for our existence, a higher purpose or anything like that. He was guided more by John Maynard Keynes's observation that, "In the long run, we die." That seemed to sum it all up. It was hard to keep up with the revolving, predictably mundane nature of what most people found to be important.

He looked around the garden. It was June and the trees were full and heavy with deep, Windsor green leaves. Fortunately, there was a nice breeze blowing. Summer in New York could be awfully hot and humid, to the point where drawing in a full breath was a Herculean effort. It sat on you, pushing your lungs downward and taunting them to take in the saturated air almost bursting with moisture. Those months were still ahead of him. June was a great month in most of the places he had lived. The cold of winter was a distant memory and the rains of spring had left everything vibrantly green, colorful and lush. It wasn't the hottest month of the summer and anyway, after the rain and cold, a little heat was more than welcome. Every season had its upside, but June was definitely a good time of year.

A small Japanese maple that had recently been planted in the far corner of the garden caught his eye, its delicate leaves seeming to float in the air. It wasn't the beauty of the tree that caught his attention, but that it was out of place. This particular species should not be in a Medieval European garden. It was as if this sapling had somehow snuck in unnoticed into a place it knew it did not belong but was gamely trying to fit in, unseen. He smiled to himself and hoped that no one else would recognize that this tiny tree shouldn't be here, and that it would be allowed to flourish in its own right, hidden in a quiet corner.

He finished the last bite of his sandwich and sipped what was left of the warm, sweet tea in his stainless steel cup. He closed his eyes and felt the soft summer breeze, heard the sparrows chirping and smelled the fresh green of early summer. He allowed himself to be absorbed in that moment, a brief glimpse of near perfection in a constantly moving world that was far from perfect.

Chapter 2

Mackenzie stood at the top of the staircase and looked at the paintings that studded the walls. Not just this wall, but almost every wall of the house. Some she had done as a girl, some as a young adult. There were a few that she was proud of, that probably could rightly hang in anyone's house. Some, mostly the early ones, were paintings that had sentimental value and would only be hung in the home of a parent, a reminder of days gone by. She cringed as she looked at some of the paintings that had brought her so much praise in junior high. She was an aspiring artist then, filled with talent and potential. Since then she had painted much better works than these, works that she was truly proud of, but which were stacked in a corner now somewhere in the attic. She'd have to talk with her father about some rearrangements. But for him, this wasn't a place to exhibit art; it was a place that brought back memories. A photo album of sorts. This one just happened to hang on the walls. She didn't want to take that away from him, but she also wanted him to know that she wasn't that same fourteen-year-old girl who won the art prize at the local junior high. She wanted him to see her for who she was now, and not just the girl he remembered. It would be a challenge, but not an altogether unpleasant one.

It was early, but the house was already bright with sunlight streaming in through the large wood framed windows on the first floor. It reflected off the parquet floor and accentuated the contrast between the royal blue walls and the crisp white framing. That was her mom's touch. Her mother knew how to make the house seem chic but also homey. Even though it was in the South Bronx, it always reminded Mackenzie of one of those quaint cedar shake houses on Cape Cod, or at least somewhere on the Long Island Sound.

The distinctly magical smell of bacon mixed with freshly brewed coffee had caught her attention when she stepped out of the shower fifteen minutes ago and had speeded her descent to the dining room. Her dad was an early riser. Always had been. He was also a big fan of a solid breakfast. Typical mornings in her house consisted of some combination of bacon or breakfast sausage with eggs, pancakes or French toast, and sometimes hash browns or home fries on the side. Occasionally her mom had succeeded in convincing her father to eat something with a bit more fiber and a bit less fat, but not often. To him, bagels and cream cheese was health food. Getting him to toss on a tomato and a sweet onion along with some smoked salmon was a major victory. Beyond that, you were pushing your luck.

"Kenz, you up?" she heard her father's distinct baritone call up from the kitchen. It was the same voice she heard almost every day growing up. Like most kids, she had tried to squeeze the last few precious minutes of sleep every morning before school.

Ironically, her mother was the one who had died of cancer before she turned sixty; the pharmacist who knew what was in everything and made sure that her family avoided overly processed food, even when the term "processed food" wasn't yet in vogue. The one who watched her weight and exercised before exercising had become popular. As is often the case, she was the one whom cancer decided to take in its steely grip and refuse to let go. Her father, the cheeseburger-eating police detective who eyed vegetables with suspicion was the one who looked like a man twenty years his junior.

Mackenzie made her way into the tiny kitchen where her dad was finishing up the eggs.

"Mornin', Dad. Smells good." She poured herself a cup of black coffee and took her first sip of the morning. Coffee smelled better than it tasted, she thought, but it sure did taste good, especially the first cup in the morning.

"Hey, Kenz. I wanted to make sure that you got off to a good start for your first day in the real world." Then, in his best Groucho Marx voice, he added, "Even if fixing old paintings is only on the fringe of the real world," and laughed. "Not sure what you ate in college but I can't think of a better way to hit the ground runnin' than some bacon, eggs and coffee. You want one egg or two?"

"Let's go with two this morning. Any toast?" she asked but she already knew the answer. Of course there would be toast, probably sourdough, but possibly pumpernickel or rye.

"Yep, I got a couple slices ready to go, can you press the button for me?" he nodded towards the toaster.

"Sure. What have we got today?"

"I picked up some sourdough at Rubin's around the corner. It looked good."

As they worked their way through breakfast, her dad looked over at the Siamese cat curled up on the dining room chair next to Mackenzie.

"Seems like Octagon, or whatever his name is, has made himself at home pretty quickly. I thought cats take time to warm up to new places."

"Octavius," she corrected him, knowing full well that seasoned detectives don't forget names easily. "I think he likes it here. He probably smells me. In any case, cooking bacon probably helped bring him out of his shell." She gently stroked his back as he sat in a tight curl. He started to lick her hand with that sandpaper tongue all cats possess. It burned, but she knew he was expressing some form of affection and didn't want to punish him for that so she endured the pain.

"I hope he enjoys the smell, because there sure as hell isn't going to be a lot leftover to eat. I wonder if I should dab a bit of bacon fat on that canned stuff that he eats."

"Dad, I buy premium cat food because it's supposed to be more nutritional for him. I don't think he needs any bacon fat added."

"You sound like your mother. But it's probably better that I don't give him any. Once he gets a taste for it he'll be climbing all over the counter when I'm cooking, and he'll start snubbing his nose at your fancy canned food."

She knew that under that gruff exterior lay a pussycat with a heart of gold. Her dad and Octavius had a lot in common, she thought. Both gave the illusion that they wanted to be alone, and both made a lot of noise when they were bothered, but when all was said and done they enjoyed the company of someone else, whether it be person or cat. She knew that the two of them would be close friends in no time, if it hadn't happened already.

"So what time do you have to be there this morning? The I-95 can get pretty backed up this time of day. You should leave yourself at least an extra fifteen minutes."

"I know, Dad. I don't have to be there until nine so I have plenty of time." Sometimes she wondered if her dad thought she was sixteen as opposed to twenty-six. "Somehow, you know I did find a way to make it to class on time every day for the past six years." She had just finished up her masters in fine arts from NYU and had moved back in with her father to save some money. She also felt bad for him puttering alone in the house now that her mother had passed. In fact, half Mackenzie's stuff was still in boxes upstairs.

"School and work are different. You miss a class and you grab the notes from someone else. You miss work and they soon find a way to get someone who actually wants to come to work."

"I know. Dad, I won't be late. It shouldn't take that long to get there. I did a dry run of the route a couple of times. If everything goes well, it only takes fifteen minutes, but I'm allowing for at least a half an hour. I've got plenty of time." Unlike many places in New York City, it was much easier just to drive to the Cloisters from their house in the Bronx. It was less than six miles, but because of the way the trains ran it would take over an hour to get there via the subway. It was great being back with her father, and it sure helped out with expenses, but she wondered if she was going to be able to get used to the constant parental oversight. She knew it was based on love, but still, it was a bit annoying.

"You nervous, Kenz?" asked her dad as he sat across from her.

"No," she lied. "Why?"

"'Cause one of the things you do when you're nervous is fold things. You've folded your napkin back and forth for the past five minutes. I thought you might be making one of those origami birds or something."

She smiled and looked down at her napkin that showed a spider web of creasing. "Pretty good, detective."

"You'd have to be an idiot not to be a bit nervous for your first day. It's perfectly natural. It's a new job, a new place, new people, the whole nine yards. You're gonna do great. You always do. Just don't be late."

"Thanks, Dad. Don't worry, I'll be there on time." Even though she craved independence, she liked the fact that her dad watched out for her.

Joseph Ferrara knew his daughter almost as well as she knew herself, and maybe in some ways more so. He always had, which gave her comfort. It meant she wasn't alone.

❧ Chapter 3 ❧

Trying to follow her father's advice of, "Act like you belong, without being a cocky know-it-all," Mackenzie strolled as confidently as she could into the main hall of the Cloisters and told the receptionist that she was there for her first day of work in the objects conservation department. She wondered if new experiences like this would ever stop feeling like the first day at a new school. *Doesn't that terrifying feeling in the pit of your stomach go away once you become an adult?* As far as she was concerned, it hadn't disappeared yet. The receptionist welcomed her and told her to wait while she rang someone in that department to take her through.

About two minutes passed before a smartly dressed man with sandy blond hair and steel blue eyes emerged from behind one of the thick granite walls to greet her. With his muted, chestnut brown suit, a periwinkle blue dress shirt with a deep gold woven silk tie, he reminded her of the American blue bloods that frequented uptown Manhattan. They wore tailored suits with a casual ease accented with a touch of boredom. Dr. Simon Davidson was the conservator in charge at the Met. She had met him several times during her internship two years ago, as well as during her job interview for this position.

"Mackenzie, it is wonderful to have you on board full time. Welcome to the Cloisters," he said with delight.

"Thank you Dr. Davidson," she replied, "I wasn't expecting the conservator in charge to be here to greet me on my first day."

"Nonsense, I wouldn't have it any other way. By the way, Dr. Davidson is only for interns. Please call me Simon," he said and escorted Mackenzie casually through the main hall and into the Romanesque hall. "We don't bring on many new conservators, so I always want to be on hand for their first day, help them get settled and all."

9

"I've only been here a few times and I actually never saw the center during my internship. I only worked at the main building," replied Mackenzie as they continued forward.

"Yes, occasionally we have interns here at the Cloisters, but because the center at the Met is so much larger, that's where most of the internships are located. Are you familiar with the history of the Cloisters?"

"Well, I've read about it and I visited it once while at NYU, but I'm certainly no expert."

"Tell me what you know while we walk and I'll fill in on any gaps," he said.

Okay, here we go, she thought. *I've only been here three minutes and I already have my first oral exam!* Fortunately, Mackenzie prided herself on being meticulous, and had researched the history of the buildings.

"From what I've read, the Cloisters is a branch of the Met devoted to the art and architecture of medieval Europe, dating from the twelfth through the fifteenth century. The building, as well as the cloistered gardens, is made up of five medieval French cloisters that were disassembled and then reassembled here in Fort Tryon Park between 1934 and 1938. The cloistered gardens are populated with plants that would have been prevalent in Medieval Europe." She paused, waiting to see if this would suffice. She had a habit of data dumping when put in situations like this, though she was trying to break it if possible.

Simon grunted as they continued down the hallway. She decided to add a bit more to her description.

"I also recall that the museum and the adjacent park were created from an endowment by John D. Rockefeller, Jr., who also donated most of his private collection. Not only did Mr. Rockefeller buy the land for the Cloisters, he also purchased several hundred acres of the New Jersey Palisades on the other side of the Hudson River and donated them to the state of New Jersey to help preserve the view of the museum." She paused again, wondering if that would satisfy Simon.

"Very impressive," nodded Simon. "I expected that you would have done your homework. That's one of the things that impressed us about you."

Phew, she thought. *I'm glad I did my homework, too!* She would have hated to blow the first question asked of her. She wondered if she should have mentioned that the Cloisters held over five thousand pieces of artwork in its collection. She decided to keep that information handy just in case Simon asked.

They made their way to a wooden doorway secured with a modern security system that Simon opened by swiping his ID card. "I have an ID card waiting for you at your desk."

They walked through a small hallway, down a flight of stairs, through a large set of doors and into a large, well-lit modern room with a series of workstations on wheels. *My gosh!* she thought, *this is like a playground for restorers.* Three large crescent-shaped lunette windows let in steady light from the west. Overhead fixtures with daylight-balanced fluorescent tubes evened out the lighting. The cork flooring and stained oak laboratory cabinets were designed to mimic the original look and feel of the Cloisters offices of the 1930s. These contrasted nicely with the ultramodern X-ray radiography system for object imaging, the Zeiss Axioplan modular microscope and Zeiss Stemi steromicroscope, both connected to a series of MacPro computers and digital imaging cameras.

Six people worked at various workstations in the large room. There were two paintings, both of which seemed to be thirteenth century French gothic, and a small gold-and jewel-encrusted cross under restoration at three separate stations. Near a large window two people leaned closely toward computer screens. Another individual carefully reviewed what appeared to be an old manuscript propped up and supported on one of the work stations. All of them were focused so intently on their work that they didn't look up when Simon and Mackenzie entered the room.

From Mackenzie's standpoint, coming in relatively unnoticed was a blessing. She hated drawing attention to herself, especially on days like today. Would they accept her? After all, she was only in her mid-twenties and most of these people looked like they had been doing this for twenty years or more. She worried that she'd say something stupid and sound like an idiot or, even worse, try to sound really smart and come across like a freshly minted know-it-all. What did Simon think of her? She didn't want him to question his decision to hire her. She knew that this was a great position and that there had been a lot of qualified candidates. Why had he chosen her over all of them? She always felt like this in new settings, with new people.

She had worked with conservators for a while now and knew that they tended to be very focused individuals that some might call shy, aloof or even detached. She didn't think of herself as shy or aloof, but she did enjoy the quiet, the smell of the turpentine, the glues and oil paints, and the ability to get lost in what you were doing for hours at a time. She didn't interpret the lack of reaction as rude or standoffish. It was exactly what she had expected. Everything she had hoped for.

Simon apparently knew how Mackenzie felt and proceeded to explain, leaning towards her in a clear tone that was a bit louder than a library whisper, like the commentary at a golf tournament. "I'll introduce you to each of them later and you'll have time to get to know and work with them all, I'm sure. They're a very diligent and hard working group, and they all love their work. I think you're going to learn a lot and enjoy working with them."

He proceeded to give her a short account of the various individuals working in the room.

"That man with the somewhat graying beard in the white polo shirt and jeans is Charles van Arden. He works almost exclusively on reliquaries, especially crosses, chalices, and the like. He's also very good with paper products, vellum, parchment, and old books. He's a bit brusque when you first meet him, but he's really a teddy bear when you get to know him. Are you a Yankee fan?" asked Simon.

"My dad is an avid Yankees fan and he started taking me to games when I was about six. So, yes, I guess you could say that I'm a fan," replied Mackenzie somewhat sheepishly.

"Well, Charles is a diehard fan. I'm surprised he doesn't wear pinstripes to work. Ask him about going to see Mickey Mantle when he was a boy and you two will get along fine."

Mackenzie nodded. Sounded just like her father. He and Charles would probably have plenty of stories to share over a couple of beers.

Simon directed their focus to the next workstation where a petite woman sat. Mackenzie guessed that she was probably in her late forties, but could easily have been older. Her dark brown hair was pulled into a tight ponytail and held in place with a delicate blue satin ribbon. Her skin was smooth and very light brown, like an acorn. She wore a cream-colored short sleeve blouse that was tucked into a pair of black slacks and a simple pair of canvas slip-ons that matched her blouse. In front of her was a portrait of what looked to be a Venetian merchant, probably from the fifteenth century.

"That," Simon continued, "is Ariadne Estrada. She works predominantly on early Renaissance oil paintings, although she'll dabble in some other mediums on occasion. She is also a leading expert on authentication. We get a lot of work coming through here from various auction houses and she takes almost all of them. She's very thorough and you two will hit it off quickly. A word of warning: she has pretty strong opinions on things and doesn't enjoy being disagreed with. Fortunately, she's right most of the time," Simon paused and smiled, "just ask her."

Mackenzie tried not to laugh out loud.

"That painting looks Venetian," she nodded towards the large canvas in front of Ariadne.

"Yes, good eye. It's a Gozzoli from 1453. It's a painting of a wealthy merchant who commissioned a portrait of himself, which, as you know, was quite common amongst wealthy Venetians at the time," replied Simon without hesitation. "There's a fair amount of sun damage and a great deal of oxidation. Several of the original colors have washed out due to overexposure. We just got that in about a week ago and started working on it."

"The same Gozzoli who painted the *Journey of the Magi* fresco for the Medici?"

"One and the same," replied Simon.

He led her slowly around the room and made informal introductions, engaging in some small talk with each person without interrupting the other restorers, who remained focused on their work. While she didn't particularly enjoy meeting new people or being thrust into new situations, she'd learned to deal with them and usually did all right. She always remembered what her father had told her before her first day of high school when she could barely make it out of her room: "You often can't control what happens to you," he had said, "but you can control how you respond to it."

Simon led Mackenzie to the final workstation, which was just to their left.

"Mackenzie Ferrara, I'd like to introduce you to Anthony Bataglia," Simon said in front of a thin, olive-skinned man who appeared to her to be in his early thirties. He was sitting in front of a large wooden panel with a paintbrush and multicolored palette. He was slightly built but at the same time seemed to have a sinewy strength that you see in lightweight fighters or distance runners. He wore a white cotton shirt with the sleeves rolled up just below his elbow, tucked into a faded pair of jeans with worn-out knees. She figured that he had worn them out himself because he didn't look like the type of guy who went to the store and bought distressed jeans. He had a full head of dark brown, almost black hair that seemed to flow effortlessly. It was neatly kept but his bangs hung well over his forehead, which he had parted and pulled back slightly.

He stood and reached a delicate hand out to Mackenzie. "It's a pleasure to have you with us." His eyes were green and they looked deeply into Mackenzie's as he greeted her. They were captivating, almost hypnotic, like they were looking through her.

"The pleasure is mine," said Mackenzie, somewhat breathlessly, wondering if he had this effect on every woman he met.

She looked at the panel that Anthony had been working on and had to steady herself. "Is that Lippi's *Madonna with Child*?" she asked, shocked to be two feet away from the fifteenth century masterpiece, not mounted on a museum wall but on an easel.

"It is," replied Anthony calmly with a hint of an Italian accent. "I'm impressed that you were able to identify it so quickly. Most people are not that familiar with Lippi."

Mackenzie smiled, still somewhat awestruck by the painting as well her introduction to Anthony. "Well, most people didn't write their master's thesis about late fifteenth century Florentine artists. I've always been impressed with Lippi, and this is one of my all time favorite paintings. I thought it was at the National Museum in Washington."

"It was," said Simon, "but it needed some work and Anthony is perhaps the world's foremost restorer of medieval Italian tempera paintings." He leaned forward slightly to look more closely at the painting and then continued. "We made a deal with them. Anthony restores the painting, and we get to display it at the Cloisters for two years. What's two years for a painting that is over five hundred years old?"

"I hope to finish soon," said Anthony, returning to his stool and grabbing his brush.

"Please," said Mackenzie quickly, "I'm sorry to have interrupted you. I'm a little overwhelmed by being this close to the painting."

Anthony turned a slow glance to her and said calmly, "I think you will like it even more when the restoration is finished. There is still much to do to get it back to how it was originally painted by the artist."

"I can't wait!" said Mackenzie, hoping that she didn't sound like a schoolgirl who was just asked out by the starting quarterback.

As Simon and Mackenzie walked away she whispered to Simon, "He seems so young, and yet he's restoring a fifteenth century masterpiece."

Simon smiled at her with a knowing look. "I know, he looks like he's only a few years out of graduate school but he's here with us as a master conservator who comes with impeccable credentials and a personal recommendation from the director of the Ufizzi himself." He turned to Mackenzie. "I know the word genius is tossed around freely these days, but I have never met a better painter."

"You mean as a restorer?" Mackenzie clarified.

"No, I mean I've never met a finer artist," corrected Simon. "In all honesty, I don't really know why he is a restorer. He should be painting masterworks on his own. His understanding of light, of what the artist was truly trying to say is something you can't teach. It's a gift." Simon stopped and looked at Mackenzie and said quietly. "Everyone here is very good at what they do. You will learn a lot from each person. But whenever you can work with Anthony, do it. If you are as good as I think you are, you will learn the most from him."

She hoped she wouldn't have to wait long to work with him, although she wasn't sure how she'd respond if he looked at her the way he did today. She actually thought she heard her knees knock together when he shook her hand. Hopefully, he hadn't noticed. She hadn't expected to meet such an incredibly handsome man at the Cloisters. The fact that he was also a phenomenal painter pushed her over the edge. Her experience with restorers at the Met had left her with an image of a group of crusty, self-absorbed introverts who made librarians seem like game show hosts.

❧ Chapter 4 ❧

Mackenzie stood to Anthony's side and focused a beam of light onto the painting laid out on the workbench in front of them. Anthony gazed fixedly under the large circular magnifying glass at the painting lying flat and secure on the worktable.

One of Berlinghiero Berlinghieri's greatest works, *Madonna and Child*, painted in 1231, rested snuggly in a white cushioned mat on the workbench. Despite being widely considered Lucca's greatest artists and one of the greatest of the late pre-Renaissance Byzantine artists of Italy, only about half a dozen of Berlinghiero's works remained. The graceful, flowing blue robes of the Madonna along with her furrowed brow, the pouting lips and the pleading expression of her eyes, created a timelessly mournful expression.

Like almost all pre-Renaissance paintings, the Christ Child's head was proportionately that of an adult. He and his mother stared off into the distance towards some unseen object or person to the left of the painting. The dramatically long sinewy fingers of the Madonna pointed towards the Christ Child, drawing attention to him. He in turn raised his right hand, specifically his index and middle finger in benediction. On the back side of both of the Madonna's hands the artist had used an abstract, almost leaf-like pattern to indicate that this image was from another world. Both mother and child had two-dimensional circular halos around their heads, as opposed to above them, as would be the norm in later paintings. As with most Byzantine icons, the background was gold leaf, to indicate the grandeur and majesty of the individuals in the painting.

"A little more to the left. Focus in on her right elbow," Anthony directed. "Good. Do you see that?" he asked, pulling back from the large magnifying glass so Mackenzie could look.

Mackenzie looked intently through the glass.

"It looks like the paint is flaking away in the lower left corner, right at her elbow. There's also some discoloration there, where it has faded compared to the paint around it."

"Exactly," agreed Anthony. "Why do you think that is the case?"

"I don't know. It looks like it's a bit thicker there than in some of the other places," noted Mackenzie.

"What about the brushstrokes? Notice anything?"

"Yes," she paused. "They seem wider and straighter than the others around them."

"What does that tell you?" he prodded.

She pulled back from the table and looked at Anthony.

"It looks like someone tried to repair this area but didn't do a very good job."

He nodded, "Do you know why it is flaking?"

"Well," reasoned Mackenzie, trying to come up with the right answer on the spot. "It would seem that the paint isn't binding correctly to the medium for whatever reason."

"It is not for *whatever* reason," corrected Anthony. "There is a very *specific* reason why the paint is not binding and is now starting to pull away. Any ideas?"

She racked her brain for a plausible reason.

"My guess is that the restorer failed to clean up or prepare the original surface adequately and therefore ended up with a poor medium for the paint to adhere." She looked at him with the confident feeling of having aced the final.

Anthony looked at her impassively.

"While that is a good textbook answer and in fact may have something to do with this situation, it is not the root cause of the problem." He directed her to look through the magnifying glass again. "Whether or not the previous restorer prepared the surface adequately or not is irrelevant because his effort was doomed before he ever picked up his brush." He continued while Mackenzie focused her attention on the right arm of the Madonna, at the elbow.

"This painting was completed in 1231 in Lucca, Italy. The only binding medium used in Europe at that time was tempera, and specifically egg tempera. Notice the very fine crosshatch pattern of the brushstrokes in the rest of the painting. Look at the rest of her arm and her fingers. The pigment sits in the tempera and is applied in very thin layers. It was almost three hundred years before oil-based paints were introduced into Europe from Afghanistan and Asia Minor. What our previous restorer has attempted to do, either because of haste, convenience or ignorance, is to touch up a tempera-based painting with oil-based paint. You can see that the brushstrokes are smoother and the paint is thicker in that area, which I think we will find in other problem areas of this painting as well. Oil is a much easier medium to work with than tempera and leads to smooth, thick brushstrokes. This would be like touching up an oil painting with acrylic today. It may be fine for fifty or even a hundred years but eventually the oil will start pulling away from the egg base, just like we see here."

Rain pounded against the windows from the summer storm raging above them. It created a type of white noise that quieted and insulated everything. Although there were half a dozen other restorers working on projects all around them, to her it seemed as if they were alone in their subterranean lair. Their ancient panel, painted by an Italian master over seven hundred years ago, was the only thing that existed in the world, or at least the only thing that mattered. If someone had asked her at that moment where she was, the day or the time, she would have been hard pressed to give an answer.

"But why would a restorer use oil instead of tempera?" she asked while continuing to look through the glass at the painting.

"Like I said, either because he was in a hurry or lazy, he did not know how to mix tempera-based paints, or because he did not know any better. Remember, the science of restoration is relatively new, especially compared with seven-hundred-year-old paintings. There were a lot of well-intentioned artists who tried to restore classical masterpieces without thinking about the history of the materials used in the original or what implication mixing mediums might have on the painting."

Mackenzie pulled away from the magnifying glass and turned to Anthony, who had been staring at her. She blushed slightly. "So what is our plan for correcting this?" she asked, trying to sound as professional and detached as she could.

Anthony sat down on his stool, pressed the palms of his hands together with the tips of the fingers resting under his chin and his elbows on his knees and took a few breaths.

"The plan is pretty straightforward. We are going to go over every inch of this painting using the magnifying glass and you are going to record every irregularity and apparent defect, whether it was caused by a flawed restoration process, sunlight, moisture, or just plain aging. I want you to take copious and detailed notes on everything we find. I want your descriptions to detail exactly where on the painting the defect existed, what the problem is, and what was the likely cause."

Mackenzie nodded and began to write notes down on a pad she had on the workbench.

Anthony continued talking while he looked upwards towards the ceiling as opposed to looking directly at Mackenzie. *He's probably told apprentices this same thing about a hundred times,* she thought as he continued.

"After that, we are going to do the same thing using infrared light. That should help us identify anything we might be missing on the surface and will definitely help determine whether the problem was with the original work itself or from a subsequent restoration. You are responsible for making sure that everything is logged and documented in the permanent file. We will take photos of everything and include it in the documentation."

He placed the palms of his hands on his knees and looked directly at her with a slight smile that caused tiny crease lines to form on the outer corners of his eyes. *God, this guy is handsome,* she couldn't help thinking.

"Then we will set about correcting what needs to be fixed. We have a good couple of weeks ahead of us before we start doing any of that, though. Tell me," Anthony continued, "have you ever mixed raw pigments with egg yolk to make tempera paint?"

"No," responded Mackenzie. This was not the time and certainly not the person to try to impress by saying she could do something that she couldn't. "I've always used off-the-shelf oils or acrylics when I painted."

Anthony nodded, seeming pleased. "Good. Then you have not had a chance to pick up any bad habits."

He redirected his gaze into the magnifying glass and focused his attention to the upper left hand corner of the painting.

"Let us get started. I want you to write down everything I say about the painting. In fact, if you want to use a recorder for now that might be best. You can type it all up later. We are going to start in the upper left and work our way across from left to right, top to bottom. I will want you to confirm everything I find once I go through it, just to make sure that I am not missing something."

Mackenzie pulled a small hand held digital recorder out of her work drawer and directed it towards Anthony. She felt like a reporter at a news conference trying to get that key tidbit of information that would later help her write her story.

His observations were crisp and exact, almost surgical. It reminded her of watching autopsies on TV where the coroner would describe the most gruesome details of the deceased in a detached, clinical manner. But there was also something more human about how Anthony approached this. He was clear and focused, but he wasn't detached. He was engaged and intent on identifying every flaw, every mistake, so that they could bring this work of art back to life. He was less a coroner describing a cadaver than a surgeon preparing to save a severely injured patient. She felt that there was compassion, a deep sensitivity in his observations that made them feel more personal, almost intimate. It was obvious to her that this painting was somehow special to him. Maybe that's what made him such a good restorer.

❦ Chapter 5 ❧
Lucca, Italy, August 1231

Despite the mid-morning heat, the inside of the studio walls remained comfortable, almost cool. Beams of steady light streamed in from the windows. Iron tripods, each holding five wax candles, were placed throughout the room, providing additional light. Although it was only a single room, the studio itself was quite large. Poplar wood panels of various lengths and widths were stacked four and five-deep against the walls, arranged in stacks according to their color, which reflected their progress in the seasoning process.

Berlinghiero Berlinghieri was joined in his studio by his three sons, Marco, the youngest, who was just ten, Barone, who was fourteen, and Bonaventura, his oldest son who was just about to turn twenty. Berlinghiero was putting the final touches on his painting, *Madonna and Child*, which was commissioned by the bishop of Lucca and would be the focal point of the newly renovated church of San Giovanni. He was pleased with how the colors came out as well as the general look and feel of the painting itself and hoped the bishop would feel the same way.

Berlinghiero sat down next to Marco, who was hard at work grinding azurite with a mortar and pestle. He worked quietly and with a focused attention. At last Marco stopped and showed the bowl to his father. Berlinghiero ran the deep blue grains through his fingers.

"This is close," he said, "but still a bit too coarse. This is too rough to use as a pigment. It will not stick to the surface. A little bit more and it should be ready to wash. There is a very fine balance. If you grind too much, then it will become too pale in color. I want this deep azure blue color to hold." He handed the pestle back to Marco and watched him continue to grind away diligently. After a few more minutes he stopped and held the pestle in front of his father.

"What do you think?" Berlinghiero asked without touching the azurite. Marco looked down at the pestle again and ran the grains through his fingers.

"I think that this is the right consistency, Father. Not too fine. It is still a dark blue, but the grains are less coarse." He said this with the unquestioned confidence of a ten-year-old boy.

"It looks good to me too. Now, get it washed and graded." Berlinghiero stood up, as Marco made his way to the barrel of water in the corner. After minerals such as azurite were ground to the proper consistency, they were washed in clean water to remove whatever mud and other impurities still remained. The impurities tended to float to the top, leaving the minerals at the bottom. They would then be divided into different grades based on size and color, ready to use as pigments. The process was similar for most minerals, from malachite and celadonite, which were used for various shades of green to yellow ochre and lapis lazuli. Marco was a good student and learned quickly. He probably had the most potential of all his sons. He relished his father's approval and worked hard to get it.

Berlinghiero walked over to his middle son, Barone, who stood in front of several easels supporting large wooden panels varying in size from four to six feet tall. The poplar that grew in the region served as an effective medium on which to paint. Although inexpensive and abundant in that area, the wood was soft and tended to warp. It needed to be treated to help strengthen the wood and to hold the paint. These panels had been dried, or seasoned, in a warm, dry area for over two months.

Barone was applying the first coat of *size*, a glue made from animal skins. This would be a long, detailed process that would later involve laying a piece of linen soaked in water over the front of the panel to conceal any surface flaws, such as knots or nicks. Over this, coats of gesso, a mixture of gypsum and animal glue, would be applied before the panel would be ready for preliminary drawings.

"How are these coming?" Berlinghiero asked, standing beside Barone.

Barone looked perplexed, "I do not know, Father." He motioned towards three large planks to his left. "These keep warping. They were fine before I put on the first coat of size and then they started warping from the center."

"Take them down and put them outside for another two weeks. Let us see what happens. We might need to cut them down and use them for smaller paintings. These others look good, though. They look ready to apply the linen."

"I was going to put one more coat of glue on them first," responded Barone in a serious tone. Barone was quiet, meticulous, and thoughtful. He was more of a perfectionist than either of his brothers, or even Berlinghiero himself, for that matter.

Berlinghiero held up one of the planks, turning it sideways, and looked at the surface from different angles before setting it down.

"That sounds good. But do not put too much on it before you start with the linen or they might start cracking. I think they are ready now, but one more coat will not hurt," added Berlinghiero. He knew that Barone always wanted things to be perfect but he also needed him to keep moving forward with his work. Barone was meticulous. He was also slow.

Berlinghiero made his way to a large wooden table with various manuscripts and books strewn on its surface. Most of these were copies of paintings and pattern books that provided examples of faces, hands, feet, and other shapes that artists used to make their paintings. There were sable hairbrushes of various sizes, styles, and shapes in leather pouches on the table and hanging on the nearby easels. His eldest son, Bonaventura, was making notes on a piece of parchment.

Berlinghiero had recently secured an important commission for Bonaventura, his first commission as the primary artist. He had high hopes for Bonaventura to become a great artist, even though Bonaventura often lacked the drive of either of his brothers. In preparation for the new work, he had sent Bonaventura to interview the monks in Assisi about the life of Saint Francis.

"Tell me more about what you learned from your conversation with the monks. What type of man was this newly Sainted Francesco?" asked Berlinghiero.

Bonaventura looked at the notes he had made during his conversation with the Prior in the monastery in the hills of Assisi the previous week.

"He was a very interesting man, born to a wealthy family in Assisi. His father, Pietro, was a cloth merchant who was very fond of France. In fact, he was originally baptized Giovanni Bernardone, but his father renamed him Francesco to help demonstrate his love of France and to hopefully pass along that love to his son."

Berlinghiero listened while he straightened out the patterns on the table. Bonaventura could be such a slob when he worked.

"As a young adult, he spent most of his time drinking and carousing with a group of young people, of which he appeared to be the group leader. Like his father, he also fell in love with France, mostly the songs, the romance and particularly the troubadours who wandered through Europe. He became wealthy working in his father's business.

"Like many wealthy men he dreamed of becoming a nobleman. He joined Assisi when they attacked the nearby town of Perugia. It was not a successful fight for Assisi, though, and they were defeated. Because of his wealth, he was captured and held for ransom. He spent almost a full year in a dungeon. After his father paid the ransom, he went back to partying with his friends."

"Up to this point he does not sound like anything more than a spoiled, rich brat," grunted Berlinghiero.

Bonaventura was used to his father's blunt comments. "He still dreamed of becoming a nobleman and decided that the quickest way to do that would be to go on Crusade. He had a beautiful suit of armor, inlaid with gold, made for himself and his horse. He started on his way and had only ridden one day from Assisi when he had a dream in which God told him that he had it wrong and that he should return home. His return was not greeted fondly by the people of Assisi. He was laughed at, called a coward by the villagers, and raged at by his father for wasting so much money on his suit of armor. He was twenty five years old when this happened."

Berlinghiero grew impatient. "Please tell me this gets better because I am starting to question why you are even painting this person." Bonaventura had been blessed with the gift of patience, thought Berlinghiero, or so his wife constantly told him. Unfortunately, as far as he was concerned, his patience manifested itself in procrastination and an inability to get to the point. Patience may be a virtue, Berlinghiero thought, but it did not help one get work done.

"Yes, Father, it does," defended Bonaventura. "He began praying for long periods of time and often snuck away to a cave in the hillside where he cried to God to forgive his sins. One day, when he was riding in the countryside, he came face to face with a leper. He was of course repelled by the sight and smell of the leper but nonetheless leapt from his horse and kissed the leper's hand. The leper returned his kiss and Francis was filled with joy. As he rode off, he turned to look at the leper one last time, but even though he had only gone several paces, the leper had disappeared. He saw this as a test from God, and one that he had passed.

"While he was praying at the ancient church at San Damiano, he heard Christ on the cross talk to him and say, 'Fix my church.' He thought that the Lord meant the physical church itself, which had fallen into disrepair over the centuries. He sold cloth from his father's company to repair the church. Francis's father was furious with him and dragged him in front of the bishop.

"The bishop was kind to Francis and told him that he needed to return the money and that God would provide."

Berlinghiero couldn't help himself. "Now I know the story must be fiction. I have yet to meet a bishop who willingly gave any money back to anyone."

Bonaventura continued, undeterred. "Francis renounced his father right there in front of the crowd. He went off into the frigid woods where he was beaten and robbed of his clothes. He spent the next several months begging for stones to rebuild San Damiano church with his own hands."

Berlinghiero sat back and laughed. "It sounds like he might have become a man of God, but he does not sound like a very good son. All his father did was provide him with a wonderful life, money, and a good career. I can see why he was so unhappy! I assume he did a number of good works after that to justify his Sainthood. They do not usually make you a Saint for wasting other people's money and spending your life drinking and womanizing. If they did, then every father in Lucca would have at least one Saint in his house."

Bonaventura couldn't help himself and laughed as well. "Of course, Father. The Saint went on to live a very pious life and gathered a large following. They are even called the 'Franciscans'. There was an interesting story about a wolf that was killing people in the village when they were out in the fields. The villagers wanted to hunt down and kill the wolf. But Saint Francis went to the wolf and talked to him about changing his ways. The wolf ended up becoming a pet of the village and the townspeople fed him and he helped protect the village. He was also known as a healer and helped cripples walk, blind men see, and also preached to the poor and ill. Apparently he was blessed at the end of his life with the Stigmata," said Bonaventura.

"The Stigmata. So he had the wounds of Christ on the cross. That is significant. It is something that needs to be highlighted," said Berlinghiero. "Make a note of that."

Bonaventura grudgingly nodded his agreement. "I was not thinking of making it a focal point but perhaps you are right. At the very end of his life, he went blind. He kept on preaching and people flocked around him. He died in 1226 when he was forty-six years old. Pope Innocent III, who actually met Saint Francis, canonized him two years after his death."

"Well, the part about talking with wolves and other animals still seems a lot more plausible than the bishop giving back the money," said Berlinghiero. "Did the monks tell you anything else about the Saint or about what they wanted to see in the painting?"

"They said that we need to tell the story of the Saint. They wanted to emphasize that this was a very Holy man who gave his life to God and lived a pure life that emulated the Savior."

Berlinghiero sat back, crossed his arms, nodded his head a few times, and asked, "Given that, what are your thoughts?"

"Well," replied Bonaventura, "I am not exactly sure. There are about twelve scenes that I could paint about the Saint's life. I was thinking of placing a large image of Saint Francis in the center of the painting surrounded by the various stories. The problem I have is that I think twelve stories may be too many. What do you think, Father?"

Berlinghiero crossed his hands behind his head and looked at the dark wooden beams and plaster on the ceiling of the workshop. He thought quietly for a few moments, taking in what his son had said. There was never just one way to make a painting, but some approaches clearly were better than others. He knew that their choice would be critical to the success of the painting. After a few moments he started sketching roughly on a blank sheet of parchment.

"It is critical that the Saint be the central image of the painting. This will be an icon for the church. That provides a wonderful focal point for the work. That should be the most important image on the painting. Everything else is there to support that image," said Berlinghiero with confidence, drawing a large circle in the center where he thought the Saint should go. "I agree with you, twelve stories is too many. The central image is what people will see and remember. It is what *sells* the painting. If you have too many individual stories around that, then you will either need to make the stories very small or reduce the size of the icon. Neither one of those is a very good idea."

"I agree, Father. To keep the icon as the focal point we should have no more than six separate stories," said Bonaventura enthusiastically. "Three on each side of the icon, one on top of the other is what I think will work best."

"That seems about right." Berlinghiero drew six circles, three on each side of the Saint, on the parchment. He nodded approvingly at the layout. He loved symmetry. *This will work well,* he thought. "Have you thought about how you will present the image in terms of color schemes?"

"That is another challenge," replied Bonaventura with concern. "If this were anyone else, I would use bold colors, with gold leaf as a background. I was going to use your mosaic on the church of San Frediano as a reference point. But Saint Francis preached about giving up worldly goods. He gave away all of his money and lived an incredibly humble life. I do not know if gold leaf and bold colors are the correct approach for such a man."

Berlinghiero sat back and smiled. He was pleased that his son was thinking about such things in considering how to create his painting. This was the sign of a true artist, and yet it was also naive. He reflected back to when he was younger and only thought about art for the sake of art. Nothing else mattered to him, not money, not fame, nothing, except the sheer truth and purity of art and being an artist. Recently, he had come to realize that you needed to paint what people wanted if you were to be successful. He needed to pass those insights along to his sons if they were ever going to be famous artists and bring glory to the Berlinghieri name.

"My son, your thinking is well founded. I understand your dilemma. But let me share with you what I have learned about painting grand monuments and icons like this for the church. This icon that you are painting will be the central point on the altar in the first church erected specifically to honor Saint Francis. Do you think that they will erect a small, humble chapel to honor this Saint? No, they will erect a monumental edifice to glorify his memory and his teachings. The church may preach about the virtues of humble poverty, but have you ever seen a bishop wearing rags or a modest cathedral?"

"No, Father, I have not. Cathedrals are the grandest and most beautiful buildings in any village I have ever been to."

"Exactly," continued Berlinghiero. "When people go to church, they want to be in awe. They want to know that their God is truly great and powerful. A great and powerful God would want to be worshipped in a magnificent manner. Anything less and you raise the risk of offending the Lord. So even though our Savior Jesus Christ lived a life of poverty and humility, we worship him in the greatest possible buildings, with glorious paintings gilded with gold. This is no different with our newest saint. Saint Francis needs to be remembered as a great man and the people will only see him that way if you depict him with the level of glory used for other Saints. Anything less than that would call into question his Sainthood."

Berlinghiero stopped, and motioned to his other sons to come closer. They sat at the table with Bonaventura and turned towards their father.

"Keep in mind, my sons, that we are artists. This is the noblest profession of them all and we are blessed to have these talents as well as the opportunity to display them. The mosaic I made on the facade of San Frediano will live on for centuries after I am gone. People in future generations will look upon it, admire its beauty, be moved by its grandeur, just like the people in Lucca today. Art is immortal. To a lesser extent, the artist himself is immortal. When people from Rome or Florence or Venice, perhaps even from France, come to Pescia five hundred years from now, they will see Bonaventura's altarpiece. They will marvel at its beauty, be moved just like we all are when we see great art. They will know that Bonaventura Berlinghieri painted that piece. Your name and, most importantly, your art will live on for hundreds, perhaps thousands of years. They will not know that Bonaventura was just a young man trying to decide what to paint. They will know that you were a great painter and the names of all Berlinghieris will be honored. That, my sons, is what God has chosen for us." He paused. "And we will not let Him down."

"But also remember this because it is equally and perhaps more important," continued Berlinghiero. "You need to paint what others want to buy. You need to know your audience. Art is wonderful in and of itself. But it only becomes worth the effort when you can actually sell it to someone."

His sons nodded their understanding. Nonetheless, while Bonaventura would never contradict his father in front of his younger brothers, on this point he disagreed. Art, to him, was a true expression of life, of God's hand. It was divine and sacred. Whether it sold well or not was not the question as far as he was concerned. Being a true artist was what appealed to him. Whether he became rich and famous was irrelevant.

His father hadn't always been this way, lamented Bonaventura. He had always preached the value of being a true artist, of pursuing purity. That was before he became famous after painting the façade of San Frediano. That had propelled him to the top of the Luccan art world. He met with royalty, with bishops and cardinals. He was the toast of the city and he relished every minute of it. His coffers were fuller than they had ever been and yet, at least in the opinion of his eldest son, his soul was emptier than ever. Somehow, fame had changed him and, as far as Bonaventura was concerned, it was not a change for the better.

❧ Chapter 6 ❧

J oe Ferrara sat at the dining room table with papers spread out in neat stacks. They consisted of copies of old files, interviews with witnesses, phone records, forensic reports, and forensic accounting records covering Stephen Thompson's tax returns and business records over a ten-year period. Joe poured through files that he had been through dozens if not hundreds of times before, making notes on a yellow legal pad. His reading glasses were perched on the bridge of his nose and there was a cup of lukewarm coffee in front of him. Octavius was curled up quietly on the corner of the table, asleep in the warmth of the late afternoon summer sun. He had spent the first five minutes of his interaction with Joe walking all over the papers and knocking anything loose on the table, paper clips, pens, erasers, pencils and the like onto the floor, each time followed by a groan from Joe, typically accompanied by a *Jesus Christ, O!* and being lifted, and occasionally swatted, off the table and onto the floor. Octavius had either grown bored with the knock-everything-off-the-table game or realized that he would soon find himself locked in a bedroom and moved over to a cozy resting spot.

On October 25, 2004, at approximately 6:12 p.m., a blue Ford F-150 SuperCrew, had exploded into a ball of fire in the driveway of 57 Sunset Trail in the Bronx, New York. In the truck at the time was Maureen Thompson, age forty-three, her daughter Laura, age eight, and son Timothy, age six. They died almost instantly. The father, Stephen Thompson, forty-four, had been in the house at the time of the explosion.

Joseph Ferrara was then a Detective First Class stationed in NYPD's 45th precinct. He had finished work for the day, but lived less than ten minutes away and responded to the call. By the time he had arrived, paramedics were on the scene as well as a fire engine, eight police cars with a crime scene investigation unit, and an FBI task force was on their way. In post 9/11 New

31

York City, responses to bombings were immediate and aggressive. When he arrived on the scene, Joe Ferrara, as the senior detective on site, took over the crime scene and ultimately took the lead on the investigation.

Neighbors were questioned about suspicious behaviors leading up to the explosion. Stephen Thompson, who was in shock at the time of the incident and in need of medical assistance, was questioned extensively over the coming weeks. While he was never considered a primary suspect, detective Ferrara and his colleagues always thought that the bomb had been intended for Stephen rather than his wife and children. They also thought that he knew more about why he was a target than he ever admitted. As expected, the CSI unit eventually found trace amounts of a C4 explosive at the crime scene.

Joe Ferrara had spent the previous eight years working as part of an organized crime task force, which worked in conjunction, and occasionally at odds with, the FBI. After 9/11, the FBI's organized crime units were thinned dramatically to refocus on anti-terrorism. During the 1980s and 1990s, the FBI's efforts had dramatically impacted all five mafia families in New York, putting hundreds of associates, including multiple mob bosses, underbosses, capos, and soldiers for each family in prison for long, often lifetime prison terms. While the five families were devastated and disorganized, they were not dead. As the FBI reallocated their resources, the families gradually started rebuilding their ranks. *Cockroaches survive*, was a phrase that Joe's Captain had used.

Joe was convinced that this was a mafia related homicide and not an act of terrorism, which many in the department and the city believed. Stephen Thompson was the owner of a chain of car washes throughout the Bronx, twelve at the time of the crime. His business was highly profitable, too profitable, in fact. While they were never able to prove fraud, it seemed likely that some type of money laundering was going on behind the scenes of these establishments. Stephen Thompson never caved under questioning, even though they dug up phone records tying him to known associates from the Genovese crime family. He was a cool customer who claimed that he had no idea that those individuals were associated with the mafia. He was just a businessman trying to run a successful small business. He didn't know why anyone would want to target him or his family in such a manner.

There were a number of leads that Joe and his team had pursued, but all turned out to be dead ends. After two years the case was filed as a cold case, officially unsolved but still open. Despite moving on to other crimes that required his attention, the Thompson case stuck with Joe Ferrara. Some cases just wouldn't leave. That was one of the curses of being a detective for almost thirty years. Your job as a detective was to piece together clues and solve mysteries. Some were easy while others tested you in every way possible. In the end, most cases were solved. Some remained open but eventually expired because of the statute of limitations associated with the crime. Because this was considered a homicide, there was no statute of limitations, but nonetheless it remained, like many murders, unsolved. He knew deep down that Stephen Thompson knew who did it and why, but he wasn't talking and there was no way to force his hand.

The sound of a car rolling into the driveway broke the relative silence, but not enough for Octavius to stir. Moments later Mackenzie entered through the kitchen door.

"Hey Dad, I'm home."

Joe raised his head from his work without turning around, "Hey Kenz. How was your day?"

Mackenzie opened up the refrigerator, grabbed a bottle of lemon Snapple, and sat down at the end of the table. Octavius lazily looked up with half-closed eyes, opened his mouth and eked out an *"Awww"* to welcome her home. She rubbed the bottom of his chin as he raised his head to facilitate the massage.

"Any luck with the Thompson case?"

"No, unfortunately, the same old shit," responded Joe grumpily. "I know that bastard was involved one way or another, but there's still no way to directly tie him to it or to make him talk."

"Well," said Mackenzie, taking a sip, "you have to admit that at this point there's not a lot of incentive in it for him to talk. They already killed his family. He still has his businesses, and whatever threat was made is in the past. He's still alive, so somehow or other he's either made amends for his transgressions or they're leaving him alone."

"These people don't just decide to leave you alone. He's still hooked up somehow. He's smart and he's got balls, I'll give him that. I'd still like to nail him and the people who did this before I leave this earth."

"As always, Dad, I wish you luck. But remember what you've told me—sometimes the past should stay right where it is and let us go on with our lives."

"I said it's a good philosophy. I didn't say that I necessarily believed in it," Joe said with a laugh. "Hey, I got some steaks at Rizzo's today. Thought we'd fire up the grill and even throw on some eggplant and zucchini to go with them. What d'ya think?"

"Jeez, Dad, sounds like you're turning into a vegan on me." They both laughed.

He turned back to the papers in front of him, making more notes on a dog-eared legal pad. These would be added to the countless notes accumulated over the past several years that still hadn't gotten him closer to catching the bastard. But Joe would catch him—he knew he would.

❧ Chapter 7 ❧
Lucca, Italy, April 1232

I t was just past six in the morning and the sun's rays were starting to bathe the studio in early morning light. The rains from the previous night had left the air clean and fresh and the roads muddy. Such was spring in Lucca.

Berlinghiero sat alone in his studio. Bonaventura had been in a funk for the past two weeks and Berlinghiero was trying to figure out how to reach his eldest son. He was probably just nervous about the unveiling coming up at the end of the month. Everyone dealt with stress differently, thought Berlinghiero. In Berlinghiero's case, it made him a bit more frantic, worried about small details, and convinced that something was either missing or going to go wrong. It rarely did, but it pushed him to work harder. It also made him a little hard to be around. Berlinghiero's wife, Ilaria, tried to cook his favorite dishes when he was feeling stressed and generally avoided anything that would upset him.

Bonaventura was different. He wasn't frantic at all. In fact he seemed to retreat from the world into a protective shell. For Berlinghiero, it was simply *un cattivo umore*, a bad mood. Bonaventura seemed uninspired, lacking his normal energy. This was to be his moment in the sun, his time to shine. At times it was all Berlinghiero could do not to grab his son by the shoulders and shake him until he finally woke up.

Ilaria told him to give Bonaventura time, that he was a different man than his father, with aspirations of his own, which might not involve following in his father's footsteps. But Berlinghiero had gone out of his way to ensure this opportunity for his son. He had put his reputation on the line and called in numerous favors that he had accumulated over the past decade. His own father had never done anything like this, not because he hadn't wanted to, but because he was simply a poor merchant who was not in a position to influence powerful men like the bishop. Artists throughout Tuscany had all wanted this commission. It was not only prestigious—it was profitable. This was just the type of commission that, if done correctly, could set up a young artist for a prosperous career. As the unveiling grew closer, Bonaventura acted less like the up-and-coming artist his father knew he could be and more like a spoiled child of privilege.

He knew that if he asked Bonaventura what was wrong, he would simply respond, "Nothing, Father," and then continue plodding along like a man in mourning. His painting was exceptional. It would be a huge success. Berlinghiero had an excellent eye and knew what people, especially influential people, wanted to see. He had worked closely with Bonaventura to ensure that his painting had all the right elements. It was sure to be a success.

† † †

The Via Fillungo led to the Piazza San Frediano and then to the church of the same name. The church, and the piazza as well, were named after a sixth century bishop of Lucca. Frediano had originally built the church and dedicated it to St. Vincent, a martyr from Zaragoza, Spain. When Frediano was buried in the church, it was renamed Saints Frediano and Vincenzo. Over the years the church had grown in stature and the prior of San Frediano was afforded equal status to that of a bishop.

It was a large Romanesque basilica. The most striking feature of the church was the enormous golden mosaic of *The Ascension of Christ the Saviour* over the entrance that had been created by Berlinghiero himself. The Byzantine style mosaic itself was massive, almost twenty-four feet wide and thirty feet high. On a background of brilliant gold sat Jesus, dressed in flowing blue robes, on a red throne. On his left and right were angels wearing graceful green and violet robes with deep green and purple wings. Beneath Jesus and the angels stood the twelve apostles, the entire mosaic bathed in vivid colors. For obvious reasons the church had long been the Berlinghieris' favorite.

Sunday services at San Frediano were typically well attended, but today the congregation was especially large. In addition to a considerable number of worshippers, a dedicated group of both Benedictine and Franciscan monks were also in attendance because this was to be followed by a formal unveiling ceremony and banquet for Bonaventura's panel honoring

Saint Francis.

The panel itself was standing on the right side of the altar, covered with a shimmering red silk sheet. When the mass ended, the congregation exited the church and milled about in the large piazza outside. Inside, church workers readied it for the unveiling ceremony. They closed the large, intricately carved wood screen, or *tramezzo*, which divided the chancel or altar area from the nave where the congregation sat. In this way, the church was transformed into a large ornately decorated meeting hall.

It was not uncommon for the church to be used for more secular gatherings such as town meetings or guild meetings. The church not only provided one of the largest enclosed places for people to meet, but its construction was funded largely by contributions made by guild members and other citizens. It served as an integral part of the community.

The choice of San Frediano for today's ceremony was in many ways more out of convenience as well as respect to Berlinghiero himself. After all, the church in which it would formally reside, San Francesco in Pescia, was not yet complete. The altarpiece would therefore reside at San Frediano for the next several years until another formal ceremony could be held in Pescia.

Berlinghiero always enjoyed unveiling ceremonies, now even more than when he was a young artist. Back then he was so nervous, hoping that people would find his painting to be worthwhile, that he couldn't enjoy the splendor of the whole event. Now, having established himself as the premier artist in Lucca, he carried a quiet confidence that gave him perspective. He was able to look around, to appreciate the spectacle of richly dressed nobility and merchants mingling with high-ranking church officials. It was an opportunity for everyone in the community, or at least the wealthy ones, to connect with old friends, meet new ones, share the latest news of the day, much of which was nothing more than gossip. Nonetheless, it was a feast day. People turned out in mass and there was great festivity. By this point in his life he knew that most of the people were less interested in the artistic value of the piece being unveiled than about whom they were able to talk with and be seen with, but he didn't care. He, and now his son Bonaventura, were why such events were possible. Despite the superficial nature of the whole gala, at its core was a work of art. That, if nothing else, was something that they could control.

Preparations were finished and the congregation was ushered back into the church. Bonaventura stood just in front of the altar area to the left of his still covered panel. He looked uncomfortable with all of the attention directed towards him. He was used to the quiet of the studio, not the stage. Next to him were several wealthy benefactors who had helped finance the painting. On the right side of the panel stood the local prior as well as a bishop from Pescia, two Franciscans in brown robes and a Benedictine monk.

After several minutes of introduction and explanation by the prior, who loved being at the center of such events, they were ready to unveil the artwork. As was the artist's honor, Bonaventura took hold of a silk tie at the bottom of the sheet and, with a nod from the bishop, pulled firmly. The cloth fell gracefully to the floor in red shimmering folds. The massive panel with its brilliant gold leaf illuminated the front of the church, giving off what would later be recounted by observers as a "divine aura." The entire audience took in a collective breath and stared in wonder at the beauty of the panel and the figure of St. Francis at its center. The silence was broken by applause that came first from the bishops and then from the rest of the congregation. The applause rolled through the basilica. There were shouts of joy and *bravo*, unbecoming of a church service but quite appropriate at an unveiling. People made the sign of the cross and bowed their heads. Somewhere in the back a woman swooned and was caught by the man next to her. Bonaventura peered out at the audience, bowing slightly, as his father had instructed him.

Berlinghiero looked around him and took in the entire spectacle with great pleasure. Well-wishers shook his hand, kissed his cheeks, and patted his shoulder in congratulations. The adulation was, of course, directed at his son and he absorbed it, as would any proud father.

The congregation was invited by the bishop to come closer and see the painting in more detail. The pews emptied rapidly as lines formed to make their way to the altar and view the icon up close. A throng of people moved towards the painting and to Bonaventura as well. He was soon surrounded by a crowd of admirers. They were quick to shake his hand and express how much the painting moved them and did service to the saint. He accepted their thanks while at the same time looking ill at ease. Berlinghiero couldn't help but feel for Bonaventura. He knew what it was like to have strangers grasping at you like they were trying to touch the relics of a dead saint. He originally hated the feeling. It scared him. He grew to accept it, although it was never comfortable for him. He imagined that Bonaventura would never get used to it. He was a shy boy who was happy to stand in his father's shadow. But now he was the one casting the shadow, leaving no place for him to hide.

After the crowds left, Berlinghiero stood alone by Bonaventura's side next to the panel.

"This was a huge success!" he exclaimed with his hand on his son's shoulder. "You need to relish days like this. Your name will now be famous as will this panel. The offers for new paintings will start rolling in and you will be able to set your price."

Bonaventura, still looking lost, said, "Thank you, Father, I am glad that you are happy." He paused a bit, biting his lower lip, trying to find the right words. "But I do not paint to make money or to be famous. That became even clearer to me today. This ceremony seemed hollow to me because this was really the painting you wanted to paint, not the one I wanted to. I painted it as you instructed and you were correct, it was received very well, probably more than any painting I would have done on my own."

Berlinghiero could not believe his ears. This should have been one of the happiest moments of his son's life and yet he acted like he was at a funeral rather than a celebration. But he knew Bonaventura. He was dutiful but he was also dark. He was never truly happy with anything. Fame and fortune were something that would take him a while to embrace.

"Bonaventura, you are talking nonsense," interrupted Berlinghiero. "This is your painting and the adoration is for you, not for me. You will be a famous painter because of this and you will carry on the Berlinghieri name with pride."

At his father's words, Bonaventura looked down at his hands that were folded in front of him and then looked up at his father.

"I understand that, Father, and I will always do everything in my power to bring honor to our family name. But being wealthy or becoming famous is not why I paint."

"Then why in the world do you paint?" he asked his son.

"Because I *love* to paint. I love creating something beautiful that did not exist before. I love taking what I see and making it come to life. When I paint, I feel alive. I feel happy. If people like what I have painted, that is wonderful. But if I feel that I painted something to the best of my ability, then I am content. Whether people like it or not is out of my control at that point."

Ah, so that was it, thought Berlinghiero, *the guilt of the true artist who feels that commercial success must mean that you have traded your soul for a bag of gold.*

"Of course, that is one of the great things about art, to create something new and original. I understand that and feel the same way. But people obviously love your work. They will have banquets for you. Bishops and noblemen will seek you out. They will praise your work and call you a master. You will be famous throughout Tuscany. Certainly, you cannot ignore that there are benefits to being well received."

Bonaventura listened closely to his father's words with reddened eyes. He had heard these same words many times.

"I am happy that my work has been received positively by people, and I hope that it is seen positively hundreds of years from now. But those external factors are why I am *allowed* to paint, not *why* I paint. If I am afforded a good income for myself and my family because people like my work, then I will be eternally thankful. But being an artist must be something personal, something you feel. I do not know how else to say this, Father, but I need to paint. If I could not paint, I would fade away and cease to be who I am. Being a painter defines my existence."

Berlinghiero listened to his son and saw the pain in his face. Bonaventura had always been loyal to him and obeyed him without question. Had he steered him astray? Had he pushed him down a path that he would not have chosen on his own? All Berlinghiero wanted was success for his sons. Was that wrong? How could a father be blamed for wanting his sons to be successful, to have more than their father? What was true art after all? Being a true and pure artist was a noble concept, but at some point you still needed to feed your family and make a name for yourself. Bonaventura would understand in time. He was sure of it.

❧ Chapter 8 ❧

Mackenzie and her father sat at the kitchen table. A bowl of mixed green salad sat in the center alongside a rectangular casserole dish with bubbly hot goulash, one of her father's favorite dishes. She had convinced him that it would be a good idea to have the side salad even though his goulash "Already had a bunch of vegetables in it." It was a small victory on the road to healthy eating that she knew would have made her mom proud. She had to admit that she loved coming home to hot casseroles, even in the summer. It reminded her of growing up when one of her parents, usually her mom, would have been responsible for dinner. They always ate together. It was part of who they were as a family and something she cherished.

While her mother was alive, her father's cooking had consisted of hamburgers, meatloaf, spaghetti and meatballs, the occasional steak, and goulash. Since he took over full time cooking duty following her mom's passing, he had broadened his repertoire, but not by much. Mackenzie had a glass of red wine and her father had a cold can of Budweiser. Octavius had already eaten his canned food for the evening and was now curled up in one of the kitchen chairs. He seemed to enjoy evening meals with the family as well.

"I was talking with Tom Lombardi down the street today," her father said, after finishing a mouthful of goulash. He had eaten about three pieces of lettuce to satisfy Mackenzie and was into his third helping of "real food." "He asked how you were doing and I told him that you were working at the Cloisters as a restorer. He said, 'Wow Joe, that's top end in that field.' I told him I didn't really know what the hell you did but it had something to do with fixing old paintings. He said that there are probably about ten places in the whole world that restore paintings on the level that they do at the Cloisters." He paused and took a sip from his Bud. "Didn't know he knew anything about art or art restoration. Sort of caught me by surprise. But then, hell, he's drunk half the time anyway, so I'm not sure what to make of it. Anyway, he was pretty impressed."

Mackenzie smiled to herself while she listened to her dad. She knew how satisfied that comment from Mr. Lombardi must have made him. Her dad didn't brag about his daughter because that would be like bragging about himself, and he certainly never did that. This was his way of telling her how proud he was of her.

"Yeah, the Cloisters is one of the top conservatories in the world and in terms of Middle Ages artwork from Europe, it's probably number one or number two." She was careful not to boast because he wouldn't approve of it.

"So you've been there for two months. How are things going? You settling in all right?"

"Yeah, I'm working with some people that just totally blow me away and the artwork that we get to work on is incredible. I'm working on a famous Italian artwork from the thirteenth century right now."

They ate quietly for a while. It was always like this when they ate together. Sporadic conversation mixed in with focused eating.

"Sounds pretty good, I guess. Thirteenth century's pretty old," said her father after making it through most of his plate of goulash.

"Yes and no," admitted Mackenzie. "When I say that I'm restoring a thirteenth century painting, I should really say that I'm serving as the personal assistant to the person who's restoring it."

"And who's actually doing the work, that you were just about to take credit for?" asked her father with a smile without looking up from his plate.

"His name is Anthony and he's Italian. He looks to be in his early thirties, but he's so worldly and knowledgeable that he seems like he's at least twenty years older. He's an incredible artist, and not particularly bad looking either." Mackenzie couldn't help but giggle when she said this.

"Ah, looks like you have fallen for the charms of the sophisticated European man. Tell me more of this Don Juan, or should I say Don Giovanni."

"His name is Anthony Bataglia. He's here on loan from the Ufizzi. He only works on Italian paintings between 1200 and 1500, but for that particular niche, he's considered one of the best in the world, if not *the* best. Seriously, we get museums all around the world to loan us priceless works of art just so that he can restore them."

"I can see why you're enjoying your work. What a name, Anthony Bataglia. You sure he's not *Cosa Nostra* or anything, right? Maybe he goes by Little Tony Bats and does some cleanup work for Tony Soprano."

"You're funny. Anyway, he is so experienced at these types of restorations that I've spent the past two months taking notes, helping him mix pigment with egg yolks, and cleaning his brushes in turpentine. That's pretty much what I am at this point, a painter's helper. Heck, I'm not even sure I'm that good at doing those things," continued Mackenzie, sounding dejected.

"Kenz, you've only been doing this for two months!" encouraged her father. "You didn't think they were going to hand you a thirteenth century painting and just say, 'Fix it,' did you?"

"I guess not," she said, frowning and taking a bite of salad. "I just thought I'd be doing more than mixing paints and cleaning brushes. Do you know that we've spent three weeks, eight hours a day, just mixing paints and testing them out on canvas surfaces to see how they will look? The first week was terrible. No matter how I mixed it, he hated it. Too thin, too thick, too pasty, too dark, too light. I thought I would die."

"Boo hoo," chided her father. "Listen to yourself. You said this guy is one of the tops in the field, maybe the top. He's giving you a chance to learn his craft, and you're bitching about it. Three weeks is nothing when you consider you're trying to match the color and texture of a seven hundred year old painting with something you mix up today. I'm surprised it only took that long."

"I know, you're right," Mackenzie grudgingly admitted. "I think my problem is that I was trying to impress him and in reality I'm just an extra thumb. He could have mixed all of it up by himself in a day or so and been done with the damn thing already. I'm just holding him back."

"Well, you're probably right about that," nodded Joe.

"Nice! Thanks for your support," Mackenzie laughed. Her dad always knew how to bring her back to reality.

"But he must like you or think there's something there, or he wouldn't spend the time working with you. You should see that as the compliment it really is. Maybe he likes you, ever think of that?"

"I'm not sure that he thinks of me that way."

"You want me to slip him a note during recess and see if he likes you?" asked her father, snickering. "Seriously, if you like the guy and you want to see if likes you, you need to slowly raise the heat a bit and see how he reacts. If he's interested in you, he should respond in kind. I've never known Italian guys to miss those types of cues."

Her father finished off his plate of goulash, pushed his chair back from the table and took a big swig from his beer. It always amazed Mackenzie that a man with the eating habits of a truck driver could have such good insights into human behavior.

❧ Chapter 9 ❧

Anthony and Mackenzie put the finishing touches on the Berlinghiero restoration and she subsequently found herself with nothing to work on. Mackenzie was anxious to keep moving forward, to learn more, and to hopefully *do* more. Grinding pigments had been a real learning experience, and watching Anthony work was a treat. But she felt like she was doing just that, watching. Fortunately, the first person she reached out to, Ariadne, was working on an authentication project and said she'd be happy to have Mackenzie help out. Authentication was more investigative work than restoration, which appealed to her inner detective. At least she wouldn't have to grind pigments for a while.

The two of them sat in front of a late fifteenth century wood panel. The painting depicted a bearded man, likely a saint, given his halo, dressed in green with a red cape holding a gold chalice filled with snakes. He appeared to be blessing a dour yet attractive woman dressed in black robes and ermine cuffs, indicating royalty, who was kneeling with her hands held together in prayer. Behind them was a castle on a lake set in rolling fields studded with trees. It was in excellent condition. This was definitely not in need of any restoration. The colors were vivid and the images were sharp.

"The Cloisters is in the midst of buying this and several other pieces from the estate of a wealthy family from Avignon in the south of France. They've asked me to authenticate this and two other pieces before they finalize the deal," Ariadne explained to Mackenzie as they looked over the painting, which sat on an easel in the corner of the workroom, where most of the sophisticated equipment was kept. Mackenzie hadn't spent much time in this part of the workshop. It was tucked away from most of the other restorers in what was almost a cave-like alcove with little natural light. Several moveable floor lamps provided most of the light, allowing the restorer more control over how much and what type of light was directed at the artwork in question.

"Do you have any idea what they're looking to pay for this?" asked Mackenzie.

"No, at least not for any individual painting. The entire block is probably in the ten to fifteen million dollar range," replied Ariadne.

"I can see why they want to get them authenticated."

"So, what do you know about authentication? Have you ever worked on an authentication before?" probed Ariadne.

"I had one class on it at NYU, nothing too serious. I'm familiar with the major ways that people go about looking for forgeries, but I've never had any experience actually doing it. I'm sort of excited to see how you do it."

Ariadne sat on one of the cushioned stools next to the painting and motioned for Mackenzie to have a seat as well.

"Okay," Ariadne sighed. "Let me give you a quick overview of what we're trying to accomplish here. If you've heard it before, let me know." Mackenzie got the distinct impression that Ariadne saw her as more of a burden than an asset.

"Forgery is a very specialized craft. It's as much about being an artist as it is about being a con man. Good technique is critical, but there is a lot of psychology that comes into play in any successful forgery. Forging old masters is getting very difficult, but not impossible. The main reason is that a lot of people, people whom one would expect to know better, don't bother seeking out the experts and getting a piece of artwork tested using proper scientific methods." Mackenzie picked up a note of disdain in her voice directed at those individuals who failed to take advantage of experts such as Ariadne.

"Let's assume that there is a painting by a famous artist, a Velázquez, for instance, that has been hanging in the Prado for seventy five years. Back then, there weren't particularly good scientific analyses to help detect forgeries. So while the museum would be able to pull up the painting's provenance or its pedigree, there would be no guarantee that the painting as well as the documentation wasn't fake. If that painting that has been sitting on the walls of the Prado for seventy five years comes on the open market, say at a Christie's auction, it's more likely that it would not be subjected to rigorous testing to confirm that it was really a Velázquez as opposed to a forgery."

Mackenzie jumped in, "You mean it *would* be tested."

"No," corrected Ariadne. "It most likely *would not* be tested. There's too much money and reputation at stake. The Prado would not pay the money to have it tested. Testing would either confirm what everyone already assumes, that it's the real thing, in which case they really haven't gained anything and they spent a lot of money. But if it turns out to be a forgery, then not only does the painting become effectively worthless, the reputation of the Prado's entire collection is called into question. It's a no-win scenario for them."

"But it's probably a reasonable risk, right? I mean, if it's been sitting in the Prado for that long, it's probably been viewed and evaluated by dozens, if not hundreds of art critics and Velázquez scholars. If it really was a forgery, it would have been found out years ago, wouldn't it?" asked Mackenzie skeptically.

Ariadne shook her head. "One of the greatest forgery teams in history, John Drewe and John Myatt, were able to forge approximately two hundred paintings of mid-tier artists, such as Giacometti, Millet, Georges Braque, and Ben Nicholson, to name a few, for prices ranging from $40,000 to over $250,000 each. Myatt was the artist, but the real mastermind behind the plan was Drewe. He realized early on that the documentation of the painting's history, from owner to owner—in other words, its provenance—was just as important, if not more important than the painting itself. If you could show direct and credible evidence of the painting's history, then no one would question the painting itself. That's where Drewe's real genius showed."

Ariadne was becoming a bit more animated. Mackenzie got the feeling that while Ariadne was obviously not in favor of forgery, she held a grudging respect for the people who were able to pull them off. Perhaps catching them at their game was part of the thrill of this whole painstaking process.

"For the price of two forged paintings that he donated to a fundraising auction, he was able to gain full access to the archives of some of London's greatest museums, including the National Art Library and the Victoria and Albert Museum. With access to the records themselves, he went about inserting new pages with photos of Myatt's forgeries along with fake provenances into the museum's record books. So should a gallery or a collector wish to research a particular painting, namely one of the forgeries that Myatt had made, Drewe would recommend that they look to the National Art Library archives in order to feel comfortable with the lineage and authenticity of the paintings. This all happened in the 1980s and 1990s. We're not talking about ancient history here. Even today with internet access to these archives, you are still making the assumption that the information in the archives is legitimate. All the internet has really done is provide broader and faster access to potentially bogus information."

Mackenzie nodded. "Actually, I remember reading about them in class. I remember thinking at the time how easy it was to pass off a forgery as long as you had the proper documentation."

"Also, even if you do use the latest technology and analyses to determine the authenticity of a piece of artwork, it's not as clear cut as you imagine. For instance, with dendrochronology, we can tell the exact year that someone felled the tree that was used to make the panel for a painting. But if someone were able to get hold of some original panels or planks from the right time period and then completely strip and paint over them, they would pass that test with flying colors. That's one of the problems with dendrochronology and why we use IR spectroscopic analysis more often."

"Wouldn't an X-ray be able to detect that it was painted over?" asked Mackenzie.

"Not really," said Ariadne. Mackenzie could tell that Ariadne was fascinated by this whole subject and probably didn't get a lot of opportunities to talk about it in this much detail. She was tempted to start taking notes, but decided to just pay attention instead. "You run into the same problem with X-rays, Wood's light, microscopic analysis, ultraviolet, infrared and autoradiography studies. If the forger has been careful and hasn't used paints from the local art supply store to paint a Rembrandt, then he might be able to pass all of the scientific tests. Science really works best at flagging the most glaring irregularities, like twentieth century paint on an eighteenth century painting. Having said all that, it's getting much harder to pass off a newly created work as something significantly older." Ariadne paused and took a sip of bottled water before continuing. She had wrapped the bottle in a paper napkin so that her hands didn't get wet. Even sipping water she looked casually elegant, thought Mackenzie. She wondered if she had been raised in a wealthy family or just had impeccable manners.

"Art historians and connoisseurs aren't immune either. Van Meegeren, perhaps the most famous forger of all time, sold fake Vermeers for millions of dollars to buyers as sophisticated as Andrew Carnegie and Hermann Goering. Not only that, he was so good that he accomplished such successful ruses by fooling the top art experts of the day. His paintings hung in the top galleries in Europe and the U.S., including the Louvre and the Met. In fact, his *Christ in Emmaus* was hailed by experts as perhaps the greatest Vermeer of all."

"Yes," exclaimed Mackenzie, sharing in Ariadne's excitement. "I remember seeing some of his paintings and some were amazing, while some of them that passed as Vermeers were horrible. Anyone looking at them now would see in a second that they aren't Vermeers."

"Don't be so sure," said Ariadne with a sly smile, waggling her finger. "If I told you that those Vermeers had been sitting in the Louvre for the past century and they were considered to be some of his greatest works, you would already be biased to see them in a certain light. Sometimes it's the most sophisticated art connoisseurs that are the most likely to be taken advantage of, precisely because they don't think that they could be taken advantage of."

Mackenzie had to agree. Her father had told her as much years earlier. He had basically explained it as everyone can be suckered, and rich people are more likely to be suckers because they're convinced they can't be suckered.

"At the end of the day, there's still a great deal of speculation involved in authenticating a piece of art. The best that we can say after all of the tests and the reasoned analysis by someone familiar with that genre and time period is that the documentation, the scientific tests, the general style of the artist, etc., would strongly suggest that it is an original. In other words, there is nothing to suggest that it is *not* an original. But that doesn't mean that it *is* an original."

"What about the piece you're currently working on? Where do you stand at this point?" Mackenzie asked, looking at the painting in front of them.

"Good question," replied Ariadne, gesturing towards the panel. Mackenzie was again caught by the elegance of her movements. The hands of most artists she knew, including her own, tended to be worn and stained because of the chemicals they used for cleaning brushes. But Ariadne's hands were supple and exquisitely manicured. She moved with a genteel grace that gave off an air of wealth and refinement.

"Here's where I am so far in terms of the process. I've X-rayed it, and the underlying panel is clean. It wasn't painted over anything else. Also, it doesn't appear that the painting has been touched up, which is impressive because it's in great shape, as you can see. Someone took very good care of it, kept it out of direct sunlight, didn't expose it to large swings in temperature and humidity."

"But couldn't that be a red flag for you?" suggested Mackenzie. "What I mean is that this painting dates from 1492 or thereabout. There is no discoloration, no significant fading. The red and green of St. John's tunic and cape are stunning. There's almost no craquelure either."

Craquelure is the formal name of the delicate, shallow network of crisscrossing cracks that appear on most old paintings. Craquelure occurs because oil paintings are multilayered, combining thin layers of glue, followed by gesso, typically made from glue and chalk, a priming layer of oil and then subsequent layers of oil paints, to get the right hues and shades. A final layer of varnish, maybe from tree resin, is applied to protect the painting. Over time, with slight changes in humidity, temperature, etc., canvas, as well as wood, expands and contracts, putting more strain on the underlying layers of sealer, primer, glue, paint and resin, and then small hairline cracks begin to emerge.

"Very good. You're right, there is no craquelure. Why might that be?" probed Ariadne.

"Well," Mackenzie paused and thought about the question. "I can only think of two reasons. One would be that the painting isn't nearly as old as it is purported to be, in which case it's a forgery. The second would be that it is done completely in tempera." She smiled confidently. "The painting I was working on with Anthony was in tempera and he said they don't show craquelure."

"Ah yes, the talented and charming Mr. Bataglia," responded Ariadne with a discernible edge to her tone. "I'm sure you're learning a great deal from him."

Mackenzie wasn't sure what Ariadne meant by that, but there was a definite chill attached to that last statement. Was Ariadne jealous of her working with Anthony?

"Yes, he's been amazing to work with," replied Mackenzie matter-of-factly. "Is there anything about him that you want to share? I take it that you're not a big fan of his."

Ariadne shook her head and gently held up her left hand in protest. "No, no, of course not." She paused, seeming to choose her words carefully, and then continued. "There's just something odd about him that raises questions in my mind. Maybe I've been spending too much time searching for forgeries, but he makes my radar go up and I don't really know why."

"Anything specific that makes you suspicious?" asked Mackenzie, clearly taken aback by Ariadne's impression of Anthony.

"Nothing in particular," admitted Ariadne, looking around the workshop to make sure none of the other restorers could hear her. Fortunately, they were off in a far corner and many of the other workers were either done for the day or engrossed in their own work far at the other end of the room. Anthony was off today, his work area clean and free of any sign of habitation. "But sometimes," she said quietly, "when something or someone seems too perfect, it makes me wonder." She looked up at Mackenzie and smiled conspiratorially. "But he is awfully good looking, I have to give him that."

Mackenzie smiled at Ariadne, but she was left feeling uncomfortable. Ariadne's tone had shifted from professorial to downright snarky when she referred to Anthony. Maybe there was something in their past that led her to negativity. She thought it best not to pursue it at this point but made a mental note to dig into it later.

"In any case," continued Ariadne, focusing back on the artwork in front of them, "you're right. This painting was done entirely in tempera, which doesn't experience craquelure to the same extent as oil and varnish. It also makes dating it extremely easy because the tempera base they used at that time was almost entirely made up of egg yolk and water. An organic compound like egg yolk is ideal for analysis. I took a tiny small sample from the corner and had it tested using an infrared spectrophotometer. This one comes back right in the appropriate time period, 1485 to 1495. This painting was supposedly painted in 1492, the same year Columbus discovered America, so that analysis supports its age, at least."

"You mentioned the wood panel itself and that you don't use dendrochronology much anymore. Why not?" Mackenzie asked, looking at her notes.

"Like I said, that's a good method for some things, like dating wood in ships. Dendrochronology can tell you not only the year that a tree was felled, but it can pretty much tell you where, right down to the specific forest. But a smart forger can get their hands on an old plank."

Ariadne paused and leafed through a stack of manila folders on the workbench. She pulled one folder out from the stack and took out two sheets of computer printouts with lines that looked like icicles dripping from the top of the page.

"Take a look at these," said Ariadne with a note of mild excitement. "These are two analyses using the IR spectroscope. The one on the left is of the surface layer of the wood from this painting and the one on the right is from the wood on the inside of the plank. Do you notice anything?" She laid the two sheets on the table in front of Mackenzie.

Mackenzie had never seen an IR spectroscope analysis before, although she was familiar with the general theory. They looked very similar to each other but several of the downward spikes differed between the two reports. "I don't know, they look pretty similar, but there are some differences," she replied meekly, not wanting to sound like a complete idiot.

Ariadne nodded in agreement. She pointed to three clear differences in the depth and width of the icicles. "In an older painting the profile of the surface will be much different because it has been exposed to the elements more than the inside of the plank. If it's just an old plank that was recently painted, then the two profiles will appear identical."

"Clever," admitted Mackenzie. "It sounds like you've pretty much wrapped this up."

"Not quite," cautioned Ariadne. "We can say with great certainty that the wood panel is the right age, and that the paint used is also the right age. So we're pretty good there. What science can't tell us is who painted it. For that we need some more subjective analyses.

"This painting was supposedly painted by the Master of Moulins. He was a very prolific painter at that point in time and, although his true identity isn't known, we think that he was either Jean Perreal, the official painter of Charles VIII and Margaret of Austria, or that he was actually the Flemish painter Jean Hay. What you and I are going to do is sift through every painting we can find that is attributed to this artist, analyze their structure, style, use of color and brushwork and compare it to this one."

"We have another Master of Moulins here, don't we?" asked Mackenzie eagerly.

"Yes, we have one here and there are two others at the Met," replied Ariadne. "I'm going to review those personally. I want you to go through everything you can find online and do a similar analysis. Let's see what we come up with. I'll give you the same notes template I use for analyzing the paintings and we can compare notes in a couple of days."

Mackenzie was so excited she squirmed in her seat. "Sounds like a great plan. Would you mind if I shadowed you while you reviewed the one here at the Cloisters so I can get a feel for how you approach it?" Mackenzie asked timidly.

"Of course," responded Ariadne. "I'd welcome another set of eyes on these. No matter how many times I do these and how confident I am in my findings, there's always a part of me that wonders if someone was able to slip something past me. The hacks are easy to find. But the real master forgers are meticulous and they're clever. You have to be on constant guard because even if you're looking for them, they can fool you."

Mackenzie saw that glint in Ariadne's eyes again that seemed to tell her that she begrudgingly respected the great forgers. Her dad had told her many times that most criminals were idiots and, if left to their own devices, they would get themselves caught. It was the criminal geniuses that posed the most danger, and also the most challenge. In thirty years on the force he said he had only run into three, but those three were the ones he thought of most, and ultimately held in the highest esteem.

❧ Chapter 10 ❧

Mackenzie looked up casually from her magazine and was surprised to see Anthony standing next to her desk. She hadn't heard him coming and wasn't sure how long he had been there. It was a pleasant surprise but it was also a bit unnerving. She had just finished working on the authentication project with Ariadne and had some down time until a new project came her way. She spent it reading about the latest developments on image enhancement and restoration in the *Journal of Conservation and Museum Studies*.

"Good morning, Mackenzie. I am sorry if I startled you. You seem engrossed in your studies."

Mackenzie looked down at her journal and then at Anthony, trying not to blush. "It's nothing important. I was just trying to catch up on some reading that I'm behind on."

"I was not sure if you had any availability, but I have a new project that I thought you might be interested in working on with me." He paused, and smiled. "Assuming the last project was not too painful an experience."

Mackenzie actually had mixed emotions. On the one hand, she enjoyed working with Anthony, and she always learned an awful lot. At the same time, working with him could be excruciating. She thought her father was demanding but he was a pushover compared with Anthony. She always thought of herself as a perfectionist but Anthony was borderline clinical. He was an unyielding and relentless taskmaster, not just for her, but for himself as well. Signing up to work with him was like re-upping for boot camp. But she figured it was probably worth it, or at least it was worth it most of the time.

"I'd love to," she said hiding any misgivings. "I just finished up a project with Ariadne. I'm all yours!" She hoped that hadn't come across like a schoolgirl with a crush, like it sounded in her head. She also wondered what he would say when she mentioned Ariadne's name. Clearly Ariadne was not a huge Anthony Bataglia fan. Mackenzie was curious to see if he shared those feelings.

"Wonderful, meet me here tomorrow morning at 9 a.m. sharp." He turned and calmly walked away. It seemed that either he didn't really care about Ariadne one way or another, or he did and definitely didn't want to talk about it.

The next morning they met just before nine. They made their way through the hallway and to the elevator.

"Are you going to tell me what the project is or are you going to keep me guessing?" she finally asked.

Anthony smiled. "I am not trying to be secretive, but I think that being surprised is an under-appreciated emotion. Do you not agree?"

"Just as long as that surprise doesn't involve spiders falling from the ceiling or crazy men tapping me on the shoulder in the street at night, then yeah, I do like surprises."

"Well, you know this is an old building. I cannot guarantee that there are no spiders lurking in the rafters just waiting to drop onto you. But I think this will be a pleasant surprise, no arachnids or crazy men."

When the elevator door opened, there was a man standing behind a dolly that held a large wooden box, which Mackenzie knew was the way that paintings, especially rare, expensive, old ones were transported.

"Thank you, Thomas, I can take it from here," said Anthony to the man.

"Certainly, Mr. Bataglia. I'll just need your signature here," responded the man as he handed Anthony an electronic pad for him to sign.

Once the artwork had been signed for and transferred over to Anthony, they headed back to the elevator with the painting on the dolly. When they arrived back at the lower level, they slowly wheeled their precious cargo to an empty table that Anthony had cleared off and prepared earlier. Takeshi, the Japanese restorer, and Ariadne saw them and came over to help lift the crate onto the table. While it was large and bulky, it wasn't particularly heavy, especially for four people. It was best practice to have more people than necessary involved whenever artwork was being lifted, flipped over, moved, etc.

Better to have one extra hand than one too few. Dropping a five-hundred-year-old painting was not something that anyone would forgive or want to live with.

They slowly made their way through the uncrating process. For Mackenzie, it was like opening a present on Christmas morning. She had always peeled away the paper delicately, taking off the cellophane tape so slowly that it wouldn't tear the wrapping paper, folding the paper neatly before attacking the box itself.

Eventually they had made their way through the outside crate to the more form-fitted, customized cedar box and then through the wrapping and padding material that actually surrounded the painting itself. All of the conservators in the room came over to watch as Anthony peeled off the final layers to reveal the artwork below. They were all art lovers and artists in their own right, so of course they loved moments like this. It was one of the most exhilarating moments in time in what was often a slow and tedious, although rewarding, job.

The painting itself was wrapped in a thin opaque protective paper that had been sealed. They could see that there was a painting underneath it but you couldn't make out much beyond that. Anthony turned to Mackenzie. "The honor is yours, Miss Ferrara."

Mackenzie was nervous, but she was also very excited. She carefully pulled on both sides of the seam and a piece of art emerged before their eyes.

It wasn't a large painting, about 171/2" x 28". It was held in a wooden frame embossed with gold leaf. Despite its age, the colors were spectacular. The striking gold leaf background contrasted beautifully with the vivid reds, greens and gold of the figures in the scene. There was clearly some fading and modest blistering on the right hand side, which was likely the reason for it being sent to them.

The left side was dominated by two figures, both angels, along with a figure in the upper left corner who appeared to be a representation of the adult Jesus or potentially a representation of God. On the right side stood a solitary figure, Mary, the eventual mother of Jesus, dressed in dark green robes.

The angel in front of Mary wore a long rose colored silk robe with a lime green lining over a gold long sleeve tunic. His wings were striped green, rose, and gold. The three-dimensionality of the folds in his robes demonstrated the growing sophistication of late pre-Renaissance painters. The second angel, who knelt slightly behind the first, wore a bright red robe with a forest green collar. His wings were green and gold.

There were clear, laser-like rays of light coming from the mouth and hands of the undefined being in the upper left hand corner, who wore a pink robe and appeared to emerge from a dark green opening in the gold leaf sky.

Mary sat with an open book on her lap in a dark green hooded robe inside a white and gold wood frame enclosure, much like a flat roofed gazebo. The walls of the gazebo were lined with a green and red flower pattern. Mary sat on a red platform patterned with green squares.

It was beautiful, Mackenzie thought. It had that ethereal, otherworldly quality that late, pre-Renaissance and early Renaissance artwork possessed. Somehow it was magical, like Botticelli's *Birth of Venus*.

After carefully setting the painting on the worktable, Anthony turned to Mackenzie.

"I do not mean to put you on the spot, but as the newest member of the group it is only fitting for a bit of professional hazing. Do you recognize this painting?"

Mackenzie looked closely, deep into analysis mode. Clearly it was the annunciation, but the annunciation was one of the most frequent topics in all of Christian art and had been covered by the greatest artists of all time, from Botticelli to Caravaggio and Da Vinci. The earliest appearance dated to fourth century frescoes. This, however, was definitely much later than the fourth century.

She studied the work a bit more before making her guess. She had performed this same exercise dozens of times in art history classes. It wasn't uncommon to be put on the hot seat in front of the class and asked to identify a painting or a painter. In fact, she didn't mind it at all because she tended to be quite good at it. Her father had nurtured her deductive reasoning skills from a very early age.

After about forty-five seconds of careful perusal of the entire piece, she was fairly sure of her answer, but she wanted to toss out a few possibilities as backups, just in case.

"I'm going to say that it is a fourteenth century work, which removes Fra Angelico, who painted primarily in the fifteenth century. I would guess that it is either by Simone Martini or Bernardo Daddi, who both painted an annunciation scene between 1330 and 1340." She paused and looked at Anthony. "I'm going to go with Daddi."

Anthony nodded approvingly.

"Very nice analysis. You are right that Martini's work is very similar to this and was painted at almost the same time, in 1335. But Martini's annunciation is a large triptych while this is obviously not. Therefore your very educated guess of Daddi is correct. Are there any other observations about the painting that you would like to share?"

Emboldened by his compliment, Mackenzie nodded in the affirmative. At last, she thought, perhaps this was her chance to show him that she actually did know something.

"Yes, in fact there are some very interesting points about this painting that are common to most annunciation scenes, especially those of the pre-Renaissance." She looked at it again and began talking to no one in particular.

"According to the gospel of Luke, the archangel Gabriel was sent by God to inform Mary that she had been chosen above all women to be the mother of the savior of the world, Jesus Christ. Gabriel is represented here as the angel in front of Mary. You can see that he holds a lily branch, which represents the eternal purity of the Virgin Mary. Gabriel was sent to the town of Galilee, to a virgin betrothed to a man named Joseph, of the house of David. He came upon Mary who was reading a book in her courtyard, and said to her, 'Ave, gratia plena. Dominus tecum.' 'Hail, full of grace; the Lord is with thee.'

"The angel behind Gabriel is Mary's guardian angel. The figure in the upper left is the adult Jesus, who points to Mary signaling that she has been chosen as his mother. There is a small green Seraph, one of the caretakers of God's throne.'

She pointed out several additional features to the group, who listened intently.

"You'll notice that there is a clear distinction between the gold leaf on the left hand side from that of the right, where Mary sits. There's no gold leaf at all on the right side. This is a remnant of the classical Byzantine separation of heaven, the divine, from the secular earth. Later Renaissance painters, including Giotto, would move away from this distinction of the divine and the secular.

"Very astute observations," admitted Anthony. Mackenzie tried not to blush at his praise, but she knew she probably was in spite of herself.

Anthony continued. "There is an interesting feature of this particular painting that has probably been lost over time. Gabriel holds a lily flower, which is the classical representation of purity, and which appears in almost all subsequent annunciation scenes. But the lily flower, or fleurs-de-lis, was also the heraldic symbol of Florence at the time. If this had been painted by an artist from Siena, Gabriel would have held an olive branch, which would have represented Siena," Anthony added and then turned to Mackenzie.

"Well, Miss Ferrara, let us get started on this. We need to get it X-rayed, scoped and documented to see what needs to be done."

"I'll get everything set up," replied Mackenzie, still feeling the excitement of the moment. He had actually said the word *astute* about her comments. Thank goodness she had studied hard in school. It was times like these that made those sleepless nights sipping stale coffee and eating packets of twenty-five-cent ramen noodles seem worthwhile.

But why did she care so much what this man thought about her, especially about her intellect, pondered Mackenzie as she started on her preparations. Was it because she doubted herself? Didn't everyone? He was too young to be a father figure, and besides, she already had a very well established father figure. No, this was different. She worked hard to please her father. He had always wanted her to follow in his footsteps and become a detective. He had taught her how to think like a detective, how to dissect complex problems into small pieces and then assemble those pieces into a solution. But being a detective wasn't really what she wanted to do. She was good at solving problems, she knew that. She was also good at art, maybe not good enough to make a living as an artist, but good nonetheless. Maybe she wanted Anthony's respect because he was himself respected in the field she had chosen for herself. It meant validation of the career choices she had made. Perhaps it was because he didn't give out praise easily, or at least that was what she had been told by the other restorers. Maybe it was part of all of those things, and possibly something more.

❧ Chapter 11 ❧
Florence, Italy, September 1312

I
t was that time of day when afternoon and evening challenge each other for supremacy. Afternoon had lost all but its last remnants of heat and raw energy while evening had not yet truly emerged with its calming darkness. The day's heat had quickly subsided and calmness settled on the bustling city. Merchants still hawked their wares to the ever-diminishing passersby. Smells of garlic, olive oil, fish, grilled meats, and sautéing vegetables filled the air. Of course mingled in with those more pleasant aromas were the acrid smells of horse manure, rotting garbage, and open sewage.

Bernardo Daddi sat at a corner table in a small *enotecca,* locked in conversation with another man. In front of them on the table were two silver chalices of red wine, a plate of bright green olives, and a platter of warm crusty Tuscan bread, along with a ceramic bowl of pungent freshly pressed olive oil. To the other patrons, they were simply two well-to-do gentlemen, relaxing after a day of work with a simple antipasti and some refreshment before dinner. To those who knew better, they were two of that city's and, indeed, the entire city-state of Florence's most renowned artists. Daddi's companion was an older man, dressed in forest green stockings, a deep blue tunic with a flowing crimson cape. He was the city's most well known artist. His name was Giotto di Bondone, but his fame was such that those who knew him, or knew of him, simply called him Giotto. In years to come he would take over the design and construction of the *duomo,* the largest cathedral in all of Italy and, at that time, the world.

Daddi, a young man in his early thirties, was quickly gaining renown among the city's art community, and was himself a disciple of the great Giotto.

But as they sat there, they were simply two men discussing their trade.

"It is still too Byzantine. It is two-dimensional and lifeless. You have to move forward in order to grow," said Giotto as he bit into a green olive dripping with oil and fresh rosemary.

"You keep saying that, but the modern paintings lack the grandeur, the splendor of their predecessors. They are not worthy of the honor bestowed on those masterpieces. The masses want to be awed and inspired, not just to look at images of things they see every day," protested Daddi.

"Do not get me wrong, my friend," said Giotto calmly, as he took a deep pull of his wine. "Those artists are indeed masters in their own rights. They have brought us beauty and reverence. When I look at the altarpiece in Pescia by Berlinghieri, I am humbled." Giotto paused. "The first time I saw the way he painted the Saint in such grandeur, I was almost brought to tears. I felt the same way when I looked upon the work of his father, Berlinghiero, who was clearly the superior artist. His *Madonna and Child* influenced artists for the past fifty years." Giotto poured off the remainder of the carafe of wine, took another long sip, and slowly chewed on an olive and moved the pit with his tongue. "But, Bernardo, we must move on. While I love the works of the Byzantine masters, they create awe through their use of colors, not by reflecting reality. I was awed, yes, but I also knew that it was not what I wanted to paint. Look closely and you will see that all of the faces, everyone in those paintings are the same." He waved over the server to bring them more bread and wine, both of which he dug into eagerly.

"Of course they are," countered Daddi, sipping his wine at a decidedly slower pace than his master. "They were painted based on style books. Everyone used them. The faces themselves were not important. They are just elements of the overall effect of the painting. Just like gold leaf is an element, the indigo, the angels above the saint, the intricate borders, each thing onto itself is just part of the whole. The overall effect and how it makes the observer feel is what is important."

"Of course, that is true. But if all the pieces make up the overall effect, why not make all of the individual pieces as good as they can be? Why not give life and emotion to each of the individuals in the painting? Why not make them seem real, lifelike? Does that detract from the overall effect of the painting?" Giotto tore off a large piece of the thick crusted, rustic bread and plunged it into the bowl of pungent olive oil, and then threw the whole chunk into his mouth and chewed voraciously as the viscous oil dripped from his lips. He took a deep pull of his wine and wiped his mouth with the back of his hand and continued.

"Look at what they were doing in Rome, and Greece well before the Byzantine artists. They were able to capture human emotion better than any of us and that was centuries, no, millennia ago." He slapped his hand down on the table excitedly, which elicited stares from several of the patrons. "We need to bring back emotion, reality. That is what stirs the hearts of men." He tapped his heart with his fist to bring home the point.

Daddi sat back in his chair and took a long pull from his chalice. He nodded to Giotto, and to himself. Daddi felt like a wise child who has been exposed to a new truth that had shattered and disrupted his comfortable world. He knew it to be true. Whether he truly understood it or not, he knew that what he had heard was the truth and that what he had believed before then was wrong, or if not wrong, then incomplete. He needed time to assimilate this new information into his worldview. He never stopped being impressed with Giotto's insights, nor by his seemingly endless ability to drink copious amounts of wine and remain cogent. Most mortals would have dropped by this point, but Daddi knew that Giotto was just warming up.

"My friend, I am happy to call you master," said Daddi.

Giotto smiled and chewed on another olive.

"I am happy to be called master by a friend such as you. You are wise beyond your years. Do not take what I say as the truth. Take it as an idea, a perspective. We are scholars, men who see the world and try to understand it. Our gift is the ability to capture what we see and translate it into something spectacular." Giotto drained his cup and refilled his and Daddi's from the silver carafe on the table. He cut off a chunk of cheese and stuffed it in his mouth before continuing.

"Keep in mind, my young friend," he said, aggressively chewing the cheese, "while we are of course artists, we are also businessmen. Fortunately for us, our trade doesn't involve anything as mundane as peddling linen or fava beans, but nonetheless, we do not exist on an island. If I thought that painting in the Byzantine style was the road to fame and fortune I would take it up tomorrow. But it is not. Those days have passed. Luckily for me, the way I prefer to paint is currently in vogue and therefore I am richly rewarded for what comes naturally to me. You need to find a style that works for you while also being attractive to those with money to pay for it. Otherwise, you will find yourself wasting your time painting things that no one wants."

Daddi looked at the ceiling and smiled. He'd heard those exact words years earlier, although at the time he was the dispenser of that advice and not the recipient. Giotto was definitely opinionated, he thought, and incredibly arrogant as well. Be he was also right more often than not, which made the first two qualities tolerable.

❧ Chapter 12 ❧

*A*vuncular, *that would be a good description*, thought Mackenzie. *So would crusty, and perhaps even thorny.* She had been working with Charles van Arden on restoring a reliquary cross for the past week and found him to be all of those things, usually in some type of predictable pattern. Simon's description and advice had been spot on. Deep down, under that thick leather exterior was a sensitive, warmhearted man. On the outside, especially at first, was a man who preferred to work and keep to himself. She couldn't help but think of Walter Matthau's character in *The Bad News Bears*, sans the ever-present beer can. Actually, she had more than twenty years of dealing with someone like Charles because he was essentially a slightly gruffer version of her father. The fact that she had grown up a Yankee fan and had been to the stadium numerous times to watch games with her father was a plus in working with Charles.

A season ticket holder for almost a quarter century, Charles had seen the very tail end of "The Mick's" career, as a boy, and had watched them struggle through the early seventies, reach the top again during the Reggie and Billy Martin period and then fall off again for almost twenty years before Derek Jeter, Mariano Rivera, Paul O'Neil and the rest of the new-look Yankees started winning titles in bunches. Fortunately for Mackenzie, she had been there for the down years as well as the newfound success. Charles was quick to dismiss the "bandwagon brokers" who found it stylish to buy front row seats for a ridiculous price earned by speculating with other people's money, and wear Yankee caps with their Armani suits. "Hell, they don't even show up for a lot of games, and if they do, they come late and leave early," he was quick to point out.

But more than anything, he was a dedicated restorer. He handled the jewel encrusted twelfth century cross with the tenderness of a father with his child. The cross itself was not particularly large, fifteen feet high and ten feet across, however, every inch of the gold plated cross was encrusted with precious and semi-precious jewels, as well as a piece of the "true cross," held in place in a golden wire webbing. It wasn't uncommon to find pieces of the true cross embedded in such a relic. In fact, the term *reliquary* meant that the artifact contained a relic, whether that be the bone of a saint or a piece of the true cross. In theory, the "true cross" was the cross upon which Jesus himself was crucified. As Charles pointed out, proving that it was actually the true cross was far from a scientific endeavor.

"Imagine, if you will," he said, as they peered under the large round magnifying glass at the grayish brown piece of wood that he held with tweezers, "communication between villages in the Middle Ages was slow and subject as much to rumor as fact. If you were an enterprising purveyor of religious artifacts, you could sell the same saint's finger about a hundred times before anyone started questioning its veracity. Then, even if you did start questioning whether what you had purchased was the real thing or not, the salesman would have been long gone, perhaps even in another country."

Mackenzie piped in. "And if you had just paid dearly for what you thought was a relic, then you were certainly not going to admit that you had been duped and were now holding onto some dead guy's finger."

"Exactly," agreed Charles. "Based on what I've read and seen over the years, if you just do some simple extrapolation, then there are probably enough pieces of the 'true cross' floating around the world to do a pretty good job framing Notre Dame Cathedral."

They both laughed at that image. Charles set the piece of wood into a small plastic box for safe keeping until he was ready to reattach it to the cross. He turned off the light from the magnifying glass and turned to Mackenzie.

"But, you know, whether this is actually a piece of the true cross or not isn't as important as believing that it is. Faith is important. It guides people. It gives them something to aspire to. I'm a fact based person and a realist, but I don't underestimate the power and value of faith. If you believed that this little piece of wood somehow made this beautiful cross even more powerful and that helped you believe that you were part of something greater than yourself, then perhaps you would push yourself to achieve something greater than you thought was possible."

She wasn't sure what prompted her, but for some reason she was suddenly interested in learning more about Charles. "Charles," said Mackenzie, "why did you become a restorer?"

Charles sat down on the round swivel stool next to the worktable and motioned to Mackenzie to sit on the adjacent stool. He folded his large hands into his lap and began speaking.

"Many years before you were born, I was an altar boy in our local Catholic church, Immaculate Conception. I was captivated by all of it, the ceremony, the robes, everything. I used to serve at the 7 a.m. mass three days a week. I'd ride my bike there before school, even in the winter when it was pitch dark, and there was snow and slush on the road. There was something special about it because I got to go behind the scenes, where normal people couldn't go. I remember putting on my cassock with the other altar boys and watching the priest prepare the wine and the hosts and put on his cassock and alb. Then we came out and everyone stood. It was like being on stage. Of course the priest was the main character, but we served our roles as well. Without a doubt, at that point in time I thought I was going to grow up and become a priest."

Mackenzie noticed that he had an interesting habit of switching his hands every thirty seconds or so. He started with his right over his left, then switched to left over right, and so forth. She imagined that he could have cracked walnuts in those massive yet gentle hands, had he wanted to.

"But I remember one Easter we were preparing for mass and someone dropped one of the special chalices that we only brought out for high mass, for special occasions like Christmas, Easter, communions, and stuff like that that. Well, I don't remember who actually dropped it, but this beautiful chalice that had been with the church for decades fell on the marble floor and cracked in five places. I remember everyone just staring at this golden cracked cup that lay on the floor and was just ruined. You could have heard wax dripping from the candles. It was like all the air was sucked right out of the entire church. I remember instinctively kneeling down on the ground and picking up the chalice. Everyone else still hadn't moved. I held the chalice in my hands and asked the priest if it was all right if I tried to fix it. I don't remember exactly what he said, but he looked at me warmly and said that yes, I could, but it wasn't likely that anything could be done."

Mackenzie listened intently. She couldn't even imagine how to begin repairing a cracked metal chalice, especially as a young boy, with no formal training. "What did you do?" was all that she could think to ask.

"Looking back, I'm sure that I didn't do a very good job of it. Certainly not to the standard of what we would now call professional restoration. But I took it back to my dad's workshop in the basement. I carefully hammered out the dents and I soldered the cracks. Then I heated the gold coating with a torch he had and started polishing the warm gold covering as best I could to even out and cover the solder marks. I got it to look pretty good, I have to admit.

"The day before Easter Mass, I brought the chalice to the priest and asked him what he thought. He held it up to the light and turned it around and looked closely from all angles." Charles mimicked the priest as he turned his head to and fro looking up at the imaginary chalice he was holding in his enormous hands.

"He set the chalice down and turned to me, and I'll never forget what he said. 'Charles, this is the closest thing that I've personally seen to a miracle. The Lord has worked his wonders through you to restore this chalice. We will use this for Easter Mass. Thank you for what you have done. You have made the church proud.'"

Charles leaned back a bit and let out a warm, full laugh. "I'm not sure how much of a miracle it was, but I know, as a ten-year-old boy, I had never felt more important. It was then that I knew that I had a gift for fixing things. Not just everyday things, but sacred objects. Crosses, chalices, patens, ciborium, statues and things like that. That was my calling. I didn't know what a restorer was at that point, but I knew I wanted to do something where I could help bring back the beauty of objects that had been damaged."

For a moment Mackenzie forgot where she was. In front of her was this bear of a man with the tenderest of hearts who had ultimately found his true calling. He was an artist, a true artist in his own right, and he had found his niche in the world. Tears welled up in her eyes while she listened to Charles's story and she turned away and dabbed her eyes with her sleeves. She turned back to Charles with red cheeks and puffy eyes. "It sounds like you made the right career choice," she choked out.

"Yeah, I think so," Charles nodded calmly, his big hands resting on his knees. "This is all I've ever wanted to do."

How lucky he is, thought Mackenzie. *So few people get to live out their dreams.* She wondered what it was that she had always longed to do.

❧ Chapter 13 ❧

Anthony knelt in one of the small side chapels inside the spaciousness of St. Patrick's cathedral. He loved the gothic grandeur of St. Patrick's. It reminded him of the awe-inspiring European cathedrals he remembered from his youth. While he enjoyed the coziness of smaller churches, there was something that drew him to the majesty of these architectural wonders. During Sunday mass it was easy to get lost in the enormous congregation. For someone who did not like drawing attention to himself, it was perfect.

He liked these quiet moments. He often came to St. Patrick's early in the morning right when it opened to the public. There were a few early risers who had come to worship quietly, pray for loved ones or just to spend some moments in contemplation before starting their day.

He felt comforted by his relationship with the Catholic Church. It had always been there for him, through good times and bad, a steady beacon on a distant shore that provided solace on stormy seas. He was not devoutly religious, but he did go to mass every week. For him there was something very soothing about the rituals and traditions of the church. He was not always pleased with the church, nor did he agree with all of its teachings—like most believers in most faiths, he took the teachings that applied most to his life and made them his own and tried to live by them. To him the church was very much like a parent with an alcohol problem. It could break your heart, disappoint and embarrass you, but most of the time you felt loved and were proud to be a part of it.

For all its shortcomings, the church was something very familiar to him. As the world changed around him there was always one touchstone, a place whose edifices and rituals remained essentially unchanged since he was a boy, and that was the Catholic Church. For all its warts, it was his church, and he still felt a kinship, a sense of belonging.

He lit a votive candle and knelt in front of the altar deep in thought. No matter where he was in the world, he had lit a candle on March 4th for as long as he could remember. It was a day that made him reflect and think back longingly of happier times, but also to reminisce over his greatest mistakes.

Regret is an insidious emotion, he thought. It lies dormant for years, never coming to the surface, and then one memory, a dream, a single event would awaken the sleeping monster and rekindle the flame of remorse inside him. Once relit, that flame built upon itself, a self-sustaining, perpetual occupier of his thoughts and emotions. He knew that everyone had regrets. Things that we wish we could go back and do over in a different way. But those deeds were long gone. Maybe that was the problem with regret, he thought. He could not change the past, nor could he forget his missteps. They were part of who he was.

Anthony recalled what it was like to be truly in love. He still remembered how his only true love looked when she slept, how her hair smelled and what it felt like to hold her closely in his arms. He had never loved anyone so completely before or since. Their life together ended all too suddenly, leaving him with a void he had never been able to fill. But the vast majority of his memories with her were of the happiest times of his life. The excruciating pain of her loss was worth enduring to have shared his life, even a small part of it, with her. He looked at the flickering flame of the candle and imagined her here with him, kneeling beside him like they had done countless times in church. He longed to hear her voice one more time, to kiss her soft lips and to see her eyes light up like stars on a summer night when he made her laugh. He reflected quietly on her memory and on his life. He wondered if he was happy with the life he had chosen. Was this what he was meant to do? Did he regret the choices he made? Was it time to make a change, to head down a different path, not knowing where it might lead? Did he have the courage to do it? He was not sure. He had asked himself these questions many times over the past several years and there were still no clear answers. Or maybe there were and he was not willing to hear them. He prayed for not only forgiveness for his mistakes but also for clarity and strength to choose the right path moving forward.

❧ Chapter 14 ❧

Mackenzie was carefully recording the current state of her most recent project with Anthony. Daddi's 1334 *Madonna and Child Enthroned with Angels and Saints*, a tempera on wood painting in a beautifully carved steepled wooden frame. The Ufizzi in Florence sent it the previous week for Anthony to work on even though they had a team of restorers who could have handled the project locally. Mackenzie was chronicling every aspect of the painting, using the grid approach that Anthony preferred. It was slow, painstaking work, but it was the type of focused, detailed, and clearly delineated task that she relished.

As the name implied, the central characters of the painting were Mary with the baby Jesus, seated on a large altar chair in the center of the painting. On either side of them were four female angels, two with brown robes and red albs, and another four with bluish green robes and matching capes. In the very front of the painting at Mary's feet stood Peter and Paul. As was common of such paintings in the fourteenth century, Mary and the baby Jesus were almost twice the size of the other characters. This was both to demonstrate their importance as well as an early attempt to denote perspective and depth, more than a century before Brunelleschi laid out the standards for perspective that are still used today.

Mackenzie had chronicled and photographed, both in standard and UV light, a little over two thirds of the painting. She was focused now on the upper right hand corner of the painting and the two angels with the brown robes. The first angel had her hands held together in prayer with the tips of her fingers directly below her chin at her neckline. The second angel had her hands crossed in front of her with her hands gently pressed against her left and right chest. As Mackenzie focused the magnifying glass in more closely, she noticed something that caught her attention, mostly because it was odd.

She hadn't noticed it under normal magnification, but now it was very clear. The right hand of this second angel, which rested over her heart, was clearly out of proportion. More specifically, the little finger was abnormally long, almost as long as the index finger. It was hard to see the fingers of the other hand clearly, partly because of the way that it was positioned and also because of the fading that had occurred over time, but it looked as if the fingers on that hand were normal.

Pre-Renaissance painters weren't known for their keen attention to detail when it came to fingers and proportion, but this still seemed odd to her. She went back and looked at all of the other hands in the painting, a total of twenty five hands, because three hands were hidden, either underneath robes or behind the altar seat, and while some of them were difficult to make out, they all seemed to be relatively consistent. In no case other than the upper right angel's right hand was the little finger significantly longer than what one would expect it to be. Clearly, it was never as long as the index finger, except for this one angel. She made a note of this peculiarity in her log and continued her analysis of the painting.

It took her another full week to finalize her analysis and cataloging. She and Anthony sat next to each other at the worktable and reviewed her analysis. There were a number of areas that showed significant deterioration and would require restoration. Her ultraviolet photos demonstrated that most of these areas were actually places where the painting had been restored previously, most likely in the nineteenth century, although supporting documentation was inconclusive about the exact time or who the restorer might have been. It was clear, however, that these areas had been painted over. Under the UV light, the more recent paint showed up slightly darker than the original. Anthony speculated that they would likely find that these areas had been painted in oil on top of the original tempera base and the difference in the materials was creating the problem.

They made it to the last section of the documentation when Mackenzie pointed out the odd finger she had found.

"This is really strange. I couldn't replicate it anywhere else in the painting. Look at this angel's little finger on her right hand. It's so long that it seems like it was a mistake."

"Did you look to see if it had been touched up by the restorer?" asked Anthony while he looked at the finger using a magnifying glass.

"Yes, there's no indication that this particular area was altered at all. There's no damage to either of those two angels and all the paint looks original. I just don't know why he'd make this finger so much longer. It didn't catch my eye at first, and when you look at the painting from a distance you wouldn't even notice it, but now I can't take my eyes away from it. Have you ever seen anything like this in Daddi's paintings before?"

Anthony continued looking through the magnifying glass at that area of the painting for a moment and then pulled away. He arched his back and pulled both hands through his hair, resting with his fingers intertwined behind his head.

"No, I cannot really say that I have. At least I do not remember seeing it before. It must have meant something to him, but I am not sure what that might have been."

"Should we try to fix it?" asked Mackenzie. "I have to admit that it's sort of driving me nuts."

Anthony placed the palms of both hands on the workbench and looked at Mackenzie.

"Remember what we do here: we restore, we do not improve. Neither of us knows why he made one finger longer than normal, but I have to assume that he did it for a reason. It is not our place to second-guess the intentions of the artist. You will just have to get used to her long finger." His tone was terse and it caught Mackenzie slightly by surprise. He paused, as if shaking off a memory, and then continued in a gentler voice. "Now, we need to start putting together a plan of attack for fixing this thing. You want to give it a shot and then go over it with me?"

Anthony had always designed the restoration plan, the specific steps and sequences they would use to repair the damaged artwork. This was the first time that he had asked her to give it a try. In fact, outside of some very simple projects, she had never put together a plan of her own. But she wasn't going to turn down this opportunity.

"I'd love to," she said. "I'll have something for you to review in two days."

"Sounds good. Looking forward to seeing it. Now, if there is nothing else, I think I am going to call it a day. Given that there will not be anything to review for two days, I am going to take the opportunity to stay home tomorrow and catch up on some things."

Mackenzie wished him well and started mapping out her ideas on the restoration plan. She was excited about the opportunity to design her own restoration plan. At the same time, she couldn't help but think about how Anthony had responded to her bringing up the lady's finger. He certainly hadn't wanted to spend much time talking about it. Something about it didn't sit well with him. Maybe he was just losing patience with her constant focus on trivial details. In any case, he trusted her to put together a plan, and that was exactly what she was going to do.

❧ Chapter 15 ❧

Anthony sat in his studio, which was large enough to serve as a master bedroom in most houses. Light filtered in from the windows. The teal green walls were covered with paintings of varying styles and schools, mostly late pre-Renaissance through high Renaissance, and mostly Italian. It was an amazing collection of works that would easily fill an entire display room at the Met. On the hardwood floor were stacks of completed paintings in elaborate carved wood and gilded frames. They were stacked five to eight deep in places. There were still more completed canvases simply laid out in stacks on the floor, two and three feet high.

Anthony sat in front of a blank canvas on an easel with his hands lightly clasped under his chin in a contemplative pose. He had taken the next two days off from the Cloisters while Mackenzie worked on her plan for the Daddi they were restoring.

She' is a sharp girl, he thought. How many people had seen those paintings over the past five hundred years and never noticed anything unusual with the finger length of any of the characters? It was never mentioned in any of the art textbooks, the gallery histories that followed the paintings, or even in any of the previous restoration notes. He couldn't help but smile when she mentioned the finger. It caught him off guard and he hadn't known what to say. Sometimes painters do things for reasons that are theirs and theirs alone. That was the truth. Every time he saw those paintings, he noticed the long finger on the beautiful woman. It was the first thing that caught his eye, the first place he looked. But how could he explain that to her? She wouldn't understand. No one would. Painters have their reasons and sometimes those reasons get buried with the painter. Sometimes they don't.

He focused his attention on the blank canvas in front of him, much like a writer stares at the blank page. Unlimited possibilities exist with a blank canvas. No decisions have been made, no colors chosen, no figures outlined. Nothing to limit the potential of what the painting would ultimately become. But blank canvases were also frightening. They had their own polarity that pushed outward and made it hard to even get started with the first brushstrokes. Much as the blank page taunts every writer, so too did the canvas. But his task today wasn't to come up with a new painting. That was always a tedious challenge that could take weeks or even months. No, this was much less stressful. He would be making a copy, a reproduction of an original work, which was in many ways just as much of a challenge as painting an original, but without the up front drama of deciding what and how to paint. That was already decided and had been perfected by the original artist. His challenge now was which artist and which painting to choose.

He had painted reproductions of masterworks from dozens of different artists, many of which could easily be mistaken for originals. But making a true reproduction required extensive research and meticulous attention to detail. If you wanted to pass a reproduction off as an original, you had to match the age of the canvas, which often involved paying for worthless old paintings and then carefully cleaning them to get back to a fresh canvas. Then you needed to prepare it with the same materials and techniques that the original artist would have used. It required choosing pigments that were used at the time of the original work. Making a true reproduction was a painstaking and tedious process, one that Anthony did not feel like undertaking at the moment.

On the other hand, just making a simple copy was straightforward and relatively stress-free. Mostly he did it because he loved the paintings themselves and the style and skill of the artist. Others he painted because they were challenges. Velázquez was always difficult for him to paint. The incredibly clean, almost invisible brushstrokes were hard to replicate. His *Portrait of Pope Innocent X* was one of Anthony's personal favorites. Velázquez captured the cold, ruthless ambition of the pope while also showing the frailty and fear of an old man. Trying to master Velázquez's technique and bringing out the luster from the pope's scarlet silk robes always confounded him. No matter how many times he painted it, and over the years he had made over a dozen reproductions, he was never satisfied with the sheen of the robe contrasted with the almost featherlike delicacy of the white linen vestments he wore underneath.

When Anthony was at a loss for what to paint, he tended to come back to his favorites, Italian painters of the early and mid-Renaissance. Giorgione, Bellini and Botticelli were some of the artists with whom he felt the most comfort and familiarity.

After some thought and reflection he decided on his next work, *Portrait of Giovanna Tornabuoni* by Domenico Ghirlandaio. He had always been impressed with Ghirlandaio's use of colors. While he had painted in the late fifteenth century, some of his work would foreshadow artists such as Vermeer almost two hundred years later. Anthony chose this painting not only because it depicted a young, beautiful Florentine noblewoman, but also because it had an error of tragedy to it. The subject herself was gorgeous, dressed in precious clothing with flawless skin and a calm, yet regal countenance. For all of her elegance, wealth and beauty, though, this woman had died in childbirth less than a year after this painting was completed. Her beautiful eyes, looking off into the distance, could not have foreseen what lay ahead. It was exactly this combination of beauty and sadness that appealed to him.

He leafed through one of the many large art books in his collection until he found the appropriate painting and set that up on a small easel beside the canvas. He thought he should be able to get pretty far with two full days ahead and began preparing his palette. Making a solid reproduction was the type of artistic challenge that he relished. It also gave him a feel for the artist himself, the way he used light and color, how he made his brushstrokes. That knowledge and experience would be useful, should he decide to paint other works in the style of this artist.

∾ Chapter 16 ∾

Mackenzie came to work early that morning to get prepped for the restoration that she and Anthony were about to begin. The rainy spring was over and the warmth of the New York summer was just beginning. Days were long and the sun rose early, which made it easy for her to wake up at the break of dawn, have a quick breakfast with her father, who inevitably was up no matter how early she rose, and then head to the Cloisters before the traffic started to get heavy.

Earlier in the week the Cloisters had received Filippo Lippi's *Madonna and Child Enthroned with Two Angels* from the Met. After working almost a full year at the Cloisters, she realized that it wasn't uncommon for the Met to send paintings to the Cloisters for restoration. The Met had such a large collection of artwork that they needed to rotate their collections from time to time. That provided the Cloisters with an ideal opportunity to take care of major or minor restorations as needed. For the Cloisters, it was a nice opportunity to add another piece to their displays, even if it was only for a year or two.

Mackenzie had prepared a three-ring binder as well as a digital copy on her hard drive containing all of the research and technical analysis that she had completed over the past four days. She skimmed through the binder again to refresh herself on any key points that Anthony might ask her about when he got started on the painting. She hated to be caught off guard or appear unprepared. Ever since she was little, it was something that drove her to study harder, work later, and focus on details. Fortunately, and because of her due diligence, her fears rarely materialized.

The painting itself was tempera and gold on wood, painted in 1437, and was approximately 4 x 2 feet. Lippi, more commonly known as Fra Lippi, was a highly regarded Florentine painter in the late pre-Renaissance period, patronized by the Medici and the king of Naples, among other notables. Raised as an unwanted child in a Carmelite friary, he took his vows as a friar in 1421. Not to be confused with more devout priest-artists such as Fra Angelico, Fra Lippi actually renounced his vows and left the priesthood after his affair with a nun, Lucrezia Buti, left him with a son, Filippino, and a daughter, Alessandra.

After finishing their initial review, as was their custom, Anthony had written down a series of pigments for Mackenzie to grind, including the quantity and size of the grind for each. They had completed four paintings together and by this point Mackenzie was used to the routine. It would take her at least a couple of days, sometimes even a week to acquire the pigments and grind them to the specifications that Anthony wanted before he would actually begin painting. Fortunately for her, Anthony used the same pigments over again and even the grind was almost identical for each application. In some cases she didn't even need to grind new pigment because she had enough left over from the previous restoration.

One of her favorite parts of the restoration process was to sit and watch Anthony paint. At first she feared that he would feel self-conscious with her sitting next to him as he worked, but he told her he didn't mind at all and that he was used to painting with other people around, whether they be other painters, restorers, or technicians. Sometimes he was very quiet and focused when he painted while at other times he was open and talkative. He was always receptive to her questions and answered them thoughtfully, going into as much detail as Mackenzie could absorb.

As they sat together to start the touch up work on the Fra Lippi, he laid out his thin wooden palette, which looked like it was about a hundred years old. The dried, ground pigments were all laid out in a row on a small table next to them along with a glass bowl filled with a mixture of egg yolk and water that Mackenzie had prepared that morning. He never mixed more of the pigment with the egg yolk mixture than he could use in small batches, usually just enough to last him about fifteen minutes. Otherwise, he told her, it would start to dry and the consistency of the tempera paint would become too thick and difficult to control, or worse, it would crack. He always kept five sable hair brushes with him, ranging from pinpoint spotters to broad flats. When he began mixing paint, lead white was first, which he put in the center of the palette, and then he would add ultramarine blue, verdigris green, red cinnabar, lampblack, and yellow ochre in a semicircle around the white.

Once the primary colors were set on the palette, he mixed the shades that he wanted with the pigments getting lighter as they got closer to the white center. There was a simplicity that belied its elegance. With this humble palette, he was able to paint a full range of colors. Mackenzie kept her notepad open and took notes on every step. She also took pictures of the palette and all of the pigments and tempera paints with her iPhone. She smiled to herself because after doing this for the fourth time, she knew exactly how the palette would look. Anthony worked smoothly and quickly with no extra movements. It took him less than two minutes to go from a completely barren palette to one alive with what was almost an infinite range of colors and shades.

She knew from her own experience as a painter that every artist had their own personal palette that they painted from. Some tended to be on the brighter side than others, Van Gogh's versus Rembrandt's for instance, but there were certain color schemes that seemed to fit each person and that was reflected in the palette of colors and hues that they worked from. The fact that Anthony had his own palette of colors wasn't unusual at all. It struck her as odd, though, that he would use that exact color scheme in working on four different painters, especially when those artists were separated from each other by a span of up to three hundred years.

"Anthony, do you mind if I ask you a question?" she asked somewhat sheepishly.

"I would be a bit surprised if you did not," he replied without shifting his attention from his painting.

"You know that I'm a little bit obsessive when it comes to keeping notes and tracking stuff, right?"

"Yes, which is a very good quality for a restorer, by the way."

"Well, I've noticed that you seem to use the exact same palette of colors no matter what painting or artist you're working on."

He brushed his nose with back of his right hand without breaking his focus on the painting. "Hmm, I never really thought of it that way, but you are probably right. It is just the palette that I am most familiar with so it makes it a lot easier to work from." He continued painting, focusing on folds in the Madonna's robes that had clearly faded over time.

"But I've seen you work on four very distinct artists. Isn't it hard to match their color scheme with one palette?"

He turned to look at her with what seemed to be a quizzical stare. "Do you think that we were off in any of the shades or colors we used in the four paintings compared to what was used in the originals?"

"No, I definitely didn't mean to imply that," she stumbled, hoping that she hadn't inadvertently offended him. "The color schemes were identical to what the original artist used. The restorations turned out marvelously." She paused. "But I guess that's sort of what's confusing me. I can't imagine that the same palette would work on a Cezanne as well as a Rembrandt. Vermeer definitely had a different color scheme than say Picasso or Giorgione. What if you were restoring a Rembrandt? Wouldn't you have to change up your palette to significantly darken the hues and bring more auburns, burnt sienna, or Van Dyke brown into the painting?"

Anthony had turned to continue painting quietly while she explained herself. He was quiet and focused, going from palette to painting and back with the occasional nod to show that he was listening. For what seemed to Mackenzie like an hour but was probably closer to a minute, he remained silent.

He set his brush down momentarily, grabbed a smelly, turpentine soaked cloth and wiped his hands and then the wooden handle of the brush. Clutching the rag he turned to her and responded thoughtfully, calmly. To her, he actually seemed intrigued by the question itself.

"I have never really thought of that, but maybe that is one reason why I do not restore Rembrandts, Vermeers, or Cézannes. My area of specialty is pre-Renaissance Italian paintings. The color palette of those artists tends to match my natural palette. I guess I have always set up my palette this way. It is probably like different styles of cooking. I bet if you walked into the pantry of five different chefs from Tuscany, you would find an amazingly similar set of basic ingredients. You would probably find the same thing if you looked at Chinese, Indian, French and Mexican chefs as well. There would be a lot of overlap within a given cuisine. But you would expect that an Indian chef would have a very different set of basic ingredients from which to use than his Italian or French counterparts. It just seems that the palette I work from matches up nicely with the color schemes of those Italian artists I work on."

He shrugged his shoulders to emphasize that this was just the way it was, and then turned back to the painting. He set the cloth down and then proceeded to mix some more pigments with the egg mixture, adding them to his palette.

"I have never tried to restore an impressionist painting. I would not be comfortable doing it. Those artists saw color and used paints and textures very differently than I do. We all have our comfort zones, so to speak, and mine tends to fall somewhere in Italy between 1220 and 1480. Outside of that, I would imagine that both my palette and my technique would need to change. I am not sure I would be able to adapt." He paused and then laughed. "Fortunately for me, there are very few people who focus on this time period, so I have never had to look very hard for work. Somehow, it keeps me busy."

Mackenzie was glad to hear him laugh. She tended to ask a lot of questions. Her dad always called her Curious George. He actually bought a Curious George stuffed monkey for her on her eighth birthday, which she still had. Sometimes she felt that she asked too many questions and was afraid that people might take it the wrong way. Like she was prying. She wasn't, at least it didn't seem so to her. It was just hard for her to let things go once she got them in her head. She leaned forward on her stool with her hands on her thighs.

"Okay, that makes sense. I guess you're right in terms of general color schemes for artists from similar regions and general time frames."

He continued painting quietly before responding. "Remember that technology moved a lot slower back then than it does now. Artists apprenticed under other artists and they tended to use the same colors and techniques that had been handed down from one teacher to another. The number of pigments available was also significantly less than what you find today. You can go online and find fifty shades of blue already ground, mixed and ready to use. Back then you had about three, and for some colors, maybe just one. Artists had to learn to build their color palettes from those basic colors, which ultimately limited to some extent the colors you see in their paintings."

"That makes a lot of sense," she admitted. "Okay, I'm going to stop bugging you and let you concentrate on your work."

"Your questions are good ones. You are not bugging me. Besides, it helps pass the time. Touching up the Madonna's robes can get a bit tiresome."

While it did make sense to her that artists in a particular era would use similar color schemes, it still seemed odd that he could accurately match the work of four separate artists across a time span longer than the history of the United States, with the exact same palette of colors. Her observation did seem to catch him by surprise, though. It seemed like he needed to give it a lot more thought than he usually did in answering her questions. Maybe, like he said, it was something that he never really thought of before.

❧ Chapter 17 ❧
Florence, Italy, April, 1437

Bored with life, childish, and impossible to please was how Fra. Lippi summed up Donatella Alessi's nature. In some ways he felt sorry for her, but realized that there were many more deserving individuals who deserved pity than spoiled young women who had been given everything, expected all of it, and appreciated none of it. Donatella served as the model for the Madonna in his latest painting, which was now finished, as was, fortunately, his association with her.

Her husband, Giuseppe, had paid for the entire painting himself, which now sat in the *Chiesa di San Lorenzo*, the Medici's home church.

Lippi remembered the day, almost a year ago, that Giuseppe came to his studio to petition the work. Decked out in elaborate silk robes with diamond and gold rings almost falling off his fingers in an ostentatious show of wealth, Giuseppe was just the type of client who Lippi seemed to attract as of late. Rich, ambitious and willing to do anything to curry favor from the church and, perhaps more importantly, the Medici. Lippi had recently taken it as a personal challenge to see how ridiculous a price he could ask such distastefully successful individuals for his services. He listened carefully to what Alessi wanted and then matter-of-factly gave him a price that was five times what he normally thought was reasonable. Up to this point, four times the reasonable amount had been his record, so this would be a personal best. He poured a glass of wine for his guest and one for himself, eased back in his chair, and waited for Giuseppe's response.

Of course, as a shrewd businessman, Alessi tried to negotiate a better price and countered with a price that was half of what Lippi had offered. Lippi listened to his rationale, which he had to admit was quite sound. But at this point in his career, as the premier painter in Florence, and even more importantly, as the favorite artist of Cosimo de' Medici, he didn't have to negotiate on price. He had come to realize that indifference, fame and talent were powerful chips in the negotiating process. He crossed his palms casually, looking distractedly at the calluses that the paintbrush had worn over time on his fingers. He nonchalantly told Alessi that he understood his position, and his counter-offer was reasonable. He smiled graciously and offered the names of several artists who he thought could do a wonderful job for that price, and possibly even less. He would be happy to make a personal introduction if Signori Alessi liked.

He watched with guilty pleasure as Giuseppe stammered and backtracked his way into agreeing to Lippi's original asking price. They always did, thought Lippi. The one thing Alessi insisted upon was that his young wife, Donatella, serve as the model for the Madonna. The words "young wife" never failed to catch Lippi's attention. He replied casually that he would make the final determination as to her suitability, but that he was open to using Donatella if that was Signori Alessi's wish. He, of course, would need to meet with her in person to make such a determination.

Lippi often wondered if it was all those years spent in forced celibacy at the hands of the Dominicans that drove him to chase women as voraciously now that he wasn't associated with the monastery. It certainly had something to do with it. Whether it was caused by pent-up frustration or an act of defiance, he wasn't sure. Probably a bit of both. Whatever it was, he had to admit that he was not only drawn to and enticed by attractive women, but he was actually quite good at seducing them as well. The feigned indifference, his talent with the brush, his fame and tight connections with the Medici, as well as his boyishly handsome good looks tended to melt even the iciest fortresses. He smiled inwardly when Alessi made his request, which was actually a way for Alessi to save face in the negotiating process. Little did he know that it was also a prime opportunity for Lippi to seduce his wife, assuming, of course, that she met his standards.

Their first meeting took place in his studio in Giuseppe's presence. Donatella had been raised by a wealthy Florentine family. As such, she was aloof, bored and spoiled. She pouted like a young child when she didn't get her way and she obviously knew how to control Giuseppe, who was fifteen years her senior and not particularly handsome. Lippi, however, was a master at his craft. While she pretended to be above all of this, he knew that every woman in Florence would give her eyeteeth to have him paint them as the Madonna in one of his masterpieces, especially one that would hang in the Medici's church.

Eyeteeth, however, were not on Lippi's shopping list. He approached his work with a detached professional demeanor, focusing only on the task at hand. He positioned and repositioned her in various poses, made her look up, down, left, and right. He took notes and made the occasional stray comment without giving away anything. At the end of the session he relayed his observations to them in an almost clinical manner. He went over her bone structure, the slope of her nose, the size of her forehead, her long arms and large hands. There were many flaws that made her less than an ideal model. He paused for effect as he detected a look of panic in both Donatella and Giuseppe, at which point he knew that he had her. He broke the tension by saying that despite all of those imperfections, there was something captivating, perhaps even magical about her eyes. The sadness, the distant stare was mesmerizing. He could transform those beautiful eyes into something that people would talk about for hundreds of years.

Like a master puppeteer, he played them both to perfection. Giuseppe shook his hand profusely and kissed him on both cheeks, expressing his admiration and gratitude with tears of joy, and relief. He nodded casually to Donatella, who looked at him like she had probably never looked at another man before. She was his, and they both knew it, without having to say a single word. He told Giuseppe that he would need to work extensively with Donatella on her posing to come up with just the right look. You just can't rush these things, he explained, which of course Giuseppe agreed to without hesitation. Lippi realized that Giuseppe probably welcomed the opportunity to keep Donatella occupied with something that would engage her so that she didn't spend all day moping about the house complaining.

Over the next six months Donatella came to his studio three times a week. Much of the time was spent talking, sipping wine and eating savory cakes. Some of the time was spent posing and trying on various outfits, hand chosen by Lippi and paid for by Giuseppe. And, of course, some of the time was spent making love, whether in his studio or in the attached bedroom, which he found to be much more comfortable. She willingly gave herself to him, whenever and wherever he pleased. She was young, beautiful in a classical way, and eager to please the great artist who had stolen her heart.

Lippi, of course, enjoyed his time with her, just as he enjoyed his time with countless other beautiful women of the city. Florence, Siena, and all of the surrounding countryside provided an endless stream of fresh produce for him to sample. His primary constraint in terms of his carnal conquests was time, because at this stage of his career neither money nor beautiful women were in short supply. But over the course of their eight-month relationship, he saw Donatella for the spoiled child that she really was. Worse yet, she was cold hearted and conniving as well. She spoke ill of her husband, her parents, and almost everyone she knew. Lippi himself was bored with her and thought that perhaps she was bored with him as well. He really didn't care.

He finished the painting, which turned out to be one of his greatest masterpieces; *Madonna and Child Enthroned with Two Angels*. He gave his Madonna the vacant, far-off stare that reflected Donatella's shallow nature, albeit in an alluring and slightly mischievous way. Upon completion, the painting was unveiled in an elaborate ceremony paid for by Signori Alessi and attended by elite of Florence, including the Medici. It was hard for him to tell whether Donatella liked his depiction of her or not. He didn't care one way or another because he was convinced that she was incapable of liking anything anyway. With the painting completed, so too was their relationship. While she asked him if she could see him again, he advised her that it was better to move forward, to focus her attention on her husband who obviously loved her.

Such was his life at this point. Painting, seducing beautiful women, and carousing with the rich and famous of the world's greatest city, was all that he had wanted and he took full advantage of it.

∾ Chapter 18 ∾

It was quiet. Everyone had left for the evening, the last of them making their way out a little more than an hour earlier. Mackenzie was in the bowels of the Cloisters by herself. She enjoyed the quiet. She always had. There were a number of loose ends she wanted to wrap up on her newest restoration project. This was the second Lippi she had worked on in the past two months. She loved his style, his choice of colors and the way that the key players in his paintings seemed to be looking right at you, like they knew you were looking at them. While there were more celebrated artists from that period, she somehow felt a personal connection with Lippi.

This painting was actually in good shape. There were just a couple of minor touch ups that needed to be made to bring it back to its original glory. Not bad for a painting that had been around for more than five hundred years. She was almost finished with her review and documentation of the piece. She wanted to wrap it up that evening if at all possible so they could begin the restoration process in the next couple of days. This particular piece, *Madonna and Child with Stories from the Life of St. Anne,* was scheduled to be back at the Met in two weeks, so there was some urgency to getting things finished quickly. By this point she had worked with Anthony for just over a year and he had confidence in her ability to accurately and completely document an entire painting as well as lay out an initial plan for the restoration process. She relished his trust in her.

As she made her way through the painting, making comments regarding various components, she paused. She moved the magnifying glass closer to focus on something she hadn't seen before. The foreground of the painting was dominated by a young, beautiful, sad looking Madonna with a cherubic baby Jesus on her lap. In the background were eight women performing various functions, such as carrying baskets and attending to a woman, Mary's mother Anne, seated in bed with the young Mary at her birth. That wasn't unusual at all; in fact, it was quite common in paintings of that genre. What struck her about this one was the hand of one of the women, the young maiden at the far left hand side of the painting. More specifically, the little finger on the maiden's right hand, which was long. The woman was only a minor figure in the painting and was largely obscured by another woman in front of her. She seemed to fade into the background of the wall, her hand and fingers an almost insignificant detail. You could barely make it out unless you specifically looked for it. Mackenzie wondered why Lippi would go out of his way to make one of her fingers so long.

She felt an eerie tingle down the back of her neck. She had seen the exact same thing less than six months ago when they were working on the Bernardo Daddi restoration. Unable to focus on the Lippi painting anymore, she pulled up her notes on Daddi's *Madonna and Child Enthroned with Angels and Saints*. It didn't take her long to find her description of the woman's finger in that painting. It was the same little finger on her right hand. She pulled up the enlarged picture she had taken of the woman and zoomed onto her finger. Comparing the image on her screen and the painting in front of her, there was a striking resemblance. Not just the hand and the finger, but the two women looked incredibly similar; same hair color and length. It was hard to make out her eye color, but both women had dark eyes. They both had gentle, attractive faces as well, especially when compared to the other women in the painting, even the Virgin herself.

She and Anthony had recently finished another Lippi painting, *Madonna and Child Enthroned with Two Angels*. She didn't recall seeing anything unusual in that painting. She pulled it up on her screen and also pulled out her notes on the painting. There were only four figures in that painting, the Madonna and the baby Jesus, and two angels in the background. Only the fingers on Mary's right hand were visible in the painting. The little finger was indeed the shortest of all fingers, like it should be.

She then pulled up an online directory of all known Lippi paintings. There were eighty-six distinct paintings, including frescos and triptychs. Of those there were twenty-seven where a woman other than the Virgin Mary appeared. She was able to identify one woman with a long pinkie finger in ten of those twenty-seven. All of them were on the woman's right hand. She made magnified copies of each of these women and printed off color prints for each painting. Her heart was racing at this point. This was beyond strange.

She immediately pulled up the database on Bernardo Daddi. There were forty-two Daddi paintings in the database. Many others, she knew, were frescoes on walls in Florence and throughout Italy that had deteriorated badly over the years and were almost now un-restorable. Of the paintings she reviewed, the woman with the long finger appeared in three of them, including the *Annunciation* that they had restored earlier. Like she had with the Lippi paintings, she zoomed in on the woman and her finger and then printed out a high quality copy of it.

Time passed without her even knowing. When she glanced at the clock on the wall it was almost ten. She'd been looking through these paintings for over three hours. Mackenzie organized the stack of color prints she had made and put them into a protective pouch and then into her leather portfolio bag. It just didn't make sense. Why would this woman with the long finger keep turning up in Lippi's paintings and also in some of Daddi's, two painters separated by almost sixty years? Could this just be some strange coincidence?

Although she hadn't finished her documentation, she couldn't concentrate on her work anymore that evening. Besides, being all alone in the basement of a fourteenth century building at night, even if it was in a twenty-first century room, started to feel a lot spookier than it had before she had found the woman with the finger. She packed up her stuff, covered the painting with a protective cloth, and made her way to her car. As she drove home she wondered what Anthony would say about the fingers. Would he laugh at her? Was she being silly? Maybe sleeping on it and approaching it in the morning would help her get some clarity. She sure hoped so.

❧ Chapter 19 ❧

"Is that all you're going to eat, Kenz?" asked her father as she wolfed down a slice of toast slathered with apple butter. She sipped coffee out of her insulated travel mug as she got ready to head out the door.

"Yeah, I wanted to get an early start this morning," replied Mackenzie while she chewed.

"Well, that's not really enough to get you through till lunch," he said as he skimmed the sports section. "I can scramble you up a couple of eggs in two minutes flat. Wanna time me?"

She laughed. "No, Dad, I'm fine. I'll get something at lunch." She reached over to the fruit bowl on the kitchen counter and grabbed a banana. "This should be all I need."

"All right," grumbled her father. "If you pass out at work and knock over a Rembrandt, don't blame me."

"Dad, there are actually people who fast for several days without passing out. Besides, Rembrandt was post-Renaissance."

"Mm," he grunted without looking up from the paper. "By the way, did you feed Othello yet?"

"Yes, I fed *Octavius* when I got up." She opened the door and stepped out to her car. "I'll call you when I'm leaving. Shouldn't be late."

"Sounds good. Drive safe."

After sleeping on her discovery of the unusual fingers, Mackenzie decided not to say anything at this point and instead finished up her analysis and documentation of the painting so they could get started on the restoration. She wanted to get to work with plenty of time before Anthony showed up so that she'd have everything ready.

She put in a solid two hours before anyone else showed up and was almost finished with the documentation of the entire painting when something else caught her eye. In the lower right hand corner of the painting was the artist's signature. That wasn't unusual because the previous Lippi she worked on had a signature in the same place. Many painters, even up through the nineteenth century, did not sign their works. It was more of a personal preference among artists. Lippi was one of the artists from that period who did sign his paintings.

His signature was both small and relatively simple. The only thing that might be considered odd about it was the way he dotted his *i*'s. From her experience, as well as the way she signed her own name, most people with *i*'s in their names finished them with either a simple dot over the *i*, or would make a forward leaning slash, like an apostrophe. That was mainly because while you wrote your name you were moving from left to right, and the slash was easier to make leaning forward, towards the right. In Lippi's case, however, his *i*'s were finished with backwards slashes. Mackenzie tried writing her own name as well as Lippi's. Without thinking of it she made forward-leaning slashes. When she tried to make backwards-leaning slashes, she found it to required a great deal of effort. She really had to force herself to write it that way. She could understand if Lippi signed his name leaning backwards, the way some people and especially a disproportionate number of left-handers did. But Lippi signed his name leaning to the right. He must have consciously thought about making the backwards slashes.

While the backwards slashes themselves weren't particularly odd, they were, at least from her experience, rare. What struck her as odd was that she had seen the exact same thing before, a little over four months ago. Bernardo Daddi finished his *i* the exact same way.

She printed out pictures of the two hands as well as the signatures from the two Lippi's and the Daddi and laid them on the work surface in front of Anthony, who was at the moment skimming through one of the latest volumes of the *Journal of Restoration Science*.

"Anthony, I don't want to interrupt you, but I'd like you to take a look at these."

He set down the journal and then glanced at the five photos without saying anything. For a very brief instant she noticed him purse his lips slightly and the lines around his eyes tightened. He turned to Mackenzie. "So, what do we have here?"

"I'm not sure," she replied hesitantly. "I just thought it was odd the way these two artists dot the *i*'s in their signatures, and even stranger than that is that they both have paintings with a woman with an unusually long little finger. It's the same finger on the same hand in both of these paintings. Take a look."

Anthony moved the mounted magnifying glass closer so that he could focus on each of the paintings. He moved slowly from one painting to the next, carefully comparing each one. Finally he pushed the magnifying glass aside and looked at Mackenzie.

"I am not really sure what this means either. My guess is that it is just a coincidence. You seem to have stumbled upon some idiosyncrasies from two different artists. I am sure there are a lot of things like this that go unnoticed all the time. The main reason they go unnoticed is because they do not really mean anything."

"But don't you think it's odd?" Mackenzie interjected.

"I think a lot of things are odd," replied Anthony, sounding slightly bored with the conversation. "That does not mean that I spend a lot of time thinking about them, especially when I have other, more important things to work on."

He seemed to be a bit edgy. He never really got angry or raised his voice but she noticed that his tone was more clipped and direct. She didn't say anything while he continued.

"Mackenzie, while I applaud your attention to detail and what appears to be a real gift for seeing connections between disparate things, we need to get this painting finished in two weeks and we do not even have a finalized restoration plan."

"But, I—"

"I know. It is odd. It is a strange coincidence, I agree with you. What I am saying to you is that we have an important job to get done here and we do not have much time to do it. What you have found is interesting, but it is not helping us move this restoration process forward and that is what I am most interested in at the moment. When we get this done, then you are free to look for women with long fingers and backwards leaning *i*-'s to your heart's content. Right now, I want you to focus on finalizing the documentation and getting me a restoration plan."

She knew he was right. This wasn't helping them with their restoration and that was the most important thing at this point. She felt like a silly schoolgirl wasting her time passing notes to her friends. She also hadn't heard him talk so directly to her since her first week or so on the job and hoped she hadn't angered him.

"Anthony, you're right," she said apologetically. "I'll get this finished today and have an initial plan as well as all the documentation in your hands by the end of the day. I guess I just got intrigued by this and it distracted me more than it should have."

"Mackenzie," said Anthony in a much more soothing tone, "there are many interesting and wonderful things in the world that deserve our attention. Unfortunately, we only have time to pay attention to a fraction of them. I am looking forward to getting started on this. It is in pretty good shape right now, but with a little work she will be almost as good as she was when Lippi finished her."

That was more like the Anthony she knew. He was task-focused without question, but he was also patient, calm and reserved. She was relieved to hear him say this.

"Yeah, I agree." She went back to work on the restoration plan that she had started earlier. It still needed work, and he was right, they didn't have time to focus on obscure details at this point.

❧ Chapter 20 ❧

Mackenzie's father made his way downstairs only to find that his daughter was already up and had the dining room table covered with pictures of old paintings. Her head was buried in her work as she made notes on a pad of paper. Octavius was curled up in a padded chair in the corner of the room. Neither of them heard him come down.

"Now this is a first," he said as he stood at the table. "For the life of me I can't remember when you've ever beat me out of bed. What are ya workin' on?"

Mackenzie looked up from her note pad, surprised but not startled.

"Hey Dad, good morning." She stretched her arms and back as she sat upright in the chair. "I've got something that's been bugging me and I just can't put it down."

Joe couldn't help but laugh. Every detective in the world knew that feeling. The loose end, the missing puzzle piece, what psychologists called lack of closure. It's what kept them going, the juice that drove them to work until the crime was solved, the last tile that completed the mosaic. Mackenzie was definitely his daughter, he thought. She had always been like this, even as a little girl. She not only liked putting together puzzles, she liked making them. When she was eleven, she had a Jackson Pollack painting matted onto cardboard and then meticulously cut it into a three-hundred-piece puzzle with some stencils she made and an exacto knife. She spent the next two days putting it together. He tried to work on it with her, but it was so abstract that he found it impossible. Even when it was completely finished it looked to him like a garbled mess of spilled paint. She told him it was considered one of the twentieth century's greatest paintings. Wherever she got her appreciation and understanding of art, it certainly wasn't from him. He liked paintings that actually looked like something. Edward Hopper was as abstract as he was willing to go. Beyond that, it was like some smart ass kid was playing a joke on everyone and waiting for the hidden camera to appear so they could laugh at all the idiots who thought this crap was actually art.

Mackenzie's mother hadn't been particularly artistic either, but her father had been. Grandpa Enis was a decent sketch artist back in his day. Of course, he'd done it as a hobby instead of trying to earn a living at it. Mackenzie had been only twelve when Grandpa Enis passed, but the two of them had formed a strong bond. He'd seen her talent from an early age. Heck, everyone saw her talent. She had been the best painter in every school she went to right up to college, and one of the best there as well.

Mackenzie and Grandpa Enis used to sit together at the dining room table, the same one she was sitting at now, and draw or paint for hours at a time, just the two of them. He had encouraged her from a very young age to draw, to paint and to sketch everything that interested her. He would tell her what he liked about her sketches and paintings and point out where she could have improved them. He'd be firm and objective, but gentle and nurturing at the same time.

Grandpa Enis had been a good man. Joe had always respected him. Like much of his generation, he grew up during the depression and then went to serve his country in WWII. He saw some bad stuff over there, but he never talked about it. Killing a man wasn't something to brag about or to take lightly, he had once said when Joe first joined the police force. And it never left you, no matter how long you lived.

Joe himself knew that to be the case as well. He had spent four years as a marine in Vietnam during the late sixties. It helped prepare him to become a police officer. While he didn't regret anything he did there, the pointless loss of life he saw was something that still haunted his dreams.

Joe looked down at the table. "What's goin' on?"

"I don't know really, but something just doesn't seem right with two of the artists we've been working on."

While he didn't know anything about art, he sure as hell knew about solving problems. It's what he dedicated his entire life to doing.

"Let me get a cup of coffee and then we'll see if a retired cop can bring any insights into your conundrum."

When he returned, she explained what she had found, showing him the various long fingered women from the paintings as well as the similarities in the two signatures. Joe listened attentively, reflexively took some notes on a piece of paper ,and occasionally asked clarifying questions. After finishing up, Joe sat back in his chair and absentmindedly rubbed his chin in silence.

While he was pondering it all, she added, "I'm not sure if any of this means anything or whether I'm getting myself worked up over nothing. The worst part is that I think my curiosity just got the best of me and I made a fool of myself in front of one of the senior restorers."

Her father leaned forward, put his hands flat on the table and said, "I've had my share of feeling like an idiot, and sometimes it was well deserved, but lot of times it wasn't. Would this senior restorer be this Anthony guy you've been talking about, the superstar from Italy?"

Mackenzie blushed. "Yes, one and the same."

"Did you show these irregularities to him?"

"Yes, well, some of them, not all. I didn't really have time to lay out a good solid case because I'm still not sure what I've found. I told him about the ladies with the long finger and also about how it was odd that Daddi and Lippi wrote their *i*'s in almost the exact same manner."

"And what did he say?" asked her father, gently stroking his unshaved chin.

"He told me that I needed to focus on getting the restoration plan completed because we have a tight deadline, which is very true."

"Anything else?"

"He said that there were a lot of odd things that he'd encountered over the years, but that he hadn't focused a lot of his time on them because they didn't have anything to do with restoring paintings."

"Did you detect any defensiveness in his response?"

"No, well, maybe a bit at first," she admitted reluctantly. "But mostly I got the feeling that I was wasting his time and potentially putting the project in jeopardy."

Joe grunted. "What do you know about this Anthony guy?"

"Nothing really, only that in the words of my boss, 'Anthony Bataglia is a true artist.' When he finishes a restoration, even when the original was terribly damaged, it's impossible to know that it was ever touched by anyone except the artist himself."

Her father nodded. "What did you say his last name was?"

"Bataglia, Anthony Bataglia," replied Mackenzie.

† † †

Later that afternoon, while Mackenzie was at her yoga class, Joe called a number that he hadn't called in over a year.

"Detective Angstrom, how can I help?" came the reply on the other end.

"Yes, Detective Angstrom, this is Joe Ferrara. I hope I'm not interrupting you from catching bad guys."

"Holy shit! How the hell are you, Joe? It's great to hear your voice!"

"It's good to hear your voice as well, Chris. You keepin' the city safe?"

"As you know, the beauty of New York is that there is always plenty of work to keep us detectives busy. Good for job security. But at the moment, it's a pretty quiet day. No decapitated bodies washing up at the port or anything like that. I imagine you didn't call to ask me about my case load or what an asshole the captain is, so what can I do for you?"

"No, you're right about that. I already know the captain's an asshole. He was ever since he was walking the beat, and I imagine a good while before that." They both laughed. "I'm trying to find out something about a guy that works as a restorer over at the Cloisters. There's something odd about the guy, but I don't know what it is."

"What are you thinking? Forger? Art thief?"

"No idea, probably just a reach. But something about him raised my antenna and I've learned that it's a good idea to pay attention to your antenna.'

"Amen to that," agreed Chris.

"I hate to ask, but do you think you could dig around a bit and find out anything you can about him? I know you're busy, but if you've got any time on your hands, I'd really appreciate it."

"Whatever I can do for the esteemed chief detective Ferrara," replied the man with a laugh. "Seriously, I'll see what I can do. What's the guy's name?"

"His name is Anthony Bataglia. He currently works as a restorer at the Cloisters. Supposedly, he also worked at the Ufizzi in Florence, but I have my doubts."

99

"Sounds like my ex-partner isn't able to completely give up the job after all. Give me a week or so and I'll see what I can find out. You think he might be mobbed up?"

"At this point, I'd just like to learn a bit more about him."

"Okay. I'll let you know. Take care."

"Thanks, Chris. I really appreciate it," he said again.

Joe hung up the phone, sat back in his chair, and wondered what it was that bothered him about Anthony Bataglia. Maybe he was just being an overprotective father. That was certainly part of it, he had to admit. But there was something that bugged him. Mackenzie wasn't sharing everything with him. Was she falling for this guy? Whatever it was, Joe was going to find out as much as he could about him. He took a sip of his coffee and looked out the window. Sometimes he wished he was a bit more trusting of his fellow man. It was a trait he had admired in his wife. But thirty years on the force had jaded him. He was always looking for the viper in the weeds, because the ones you didn't suspect were the ones that bit you.

❧ Chapter 21 ❧

Anthony left the Cloisters at 6 p.m. It was a warm summer evening and it would be light for at least two more hours. The Hudson, densely lined with verdant green trees on both sides, glistened as it flowed slowly on its way to the Atlantic. Birds chirped loudly in the trees and visitors left the Cloisters and walked south through the park. Anthony loved warm summer nights. They reminded him of growing up in Italy and walking in the Tuscan countryside alongside rows of cypresses that gently swayed in the breeze and orchards heavy with olives, apricots and chestnuts. It would take him almost forty-five minutes to walk to his apartment, but to be outside, walking through the great park, along the mighty Hudson, was something he relished.

There was very little traffic in this northwest corner of Manhattan. It was actually hard to imagine that it was still part of one of the most densely populated cities on earth. The soft breeze that blew in his face from the south brought fragrant smells of honeysuckle and gardenia. He passed a few people, who had probably stopped to visit the Cloisters, or maybe just to see how far north Central Park actually went, but other than that he was by himself. It was probably as alone as you could get and still technically be in Manhattan.

As he made his way farther south, the number of people increased exponentially. Summer was the time for softball leagues and soccer games. Musicians played together in ad hoc groups. Lovers walked hand-in-hand, meandering along the myriad trails, stopping along the many bridges to look onto the ponds. The large art deco apartments on Central Park West marked the western boundary of the park. He left the park, walked under the stone underpass, and made his way to the entrance of his building. The doorman stood watch, dressed in a crisp blue suit with gold stitching around his sleeves and at the edges of his collar, matched by two gold buttons in front. If you didn't know better, you might mistake him for an officer in the U.S. navy.

"Welcome back, Mr. Bataglia. Beautiful evening."

"Hi, Jack. It certainly is. I think that God made the winters so cold here so we could enjoy the summer that much more."

"I don't disagree with you there, sir," replied the doorman.

Anthony entered the grey stone building and made his way to the elevators.

The doors opened on the twentieth floor. Anthony walked out of the elevator and down the hall to his apartment, entered the electronic code, and opened the door. The room was filled with natural light coming in from the floor-to-ceiling windows that overlooked Central Park. The reclaimed hickory hardwood flooring that ran through most of the four-bedroom suite gave a rustic feel to the otherwise modern interior. He loved the way the knots and imperfections in the honey and auburn streaked wood looked. There were hand woven Turkish and Persian carpets on top of the wood floor in the various rooms to help add color and, of course, warmth in the winter.

After he showered and changed into well-worn jeans and a simple black tee-shirt, he went over to the bar and poured himself a glass of single barrel bourbon on ice. Pappy Van Winkle was what he had been enjoying for the past year. Originally he had thought the name to be idiotic, but the bourbon itself was smoky, sweet and sour, and very smooth. He thought it was a play on the Washington Irving classic but it turned out that the Van Winkle family really made bourbon, in very small quantities, and Pappy was the patriarch of the family who had started the movement. Only in America would the name of a fine liquor bear a name that made you think of a toothless old coot sipping a ceramic jug on his front porch while he played the banjo. While he loved single malt scotch, he also enjoyed other finely crafted beverages from around the world. He had recently been introduced to single barrel bourbons by Tommy Rowles, the bartender at Bemelmans Bar. He had to admit that despite his initial trepidation, these were every bit as sophisticated as his beloved single malts, fine cognacs and Armagnacs, as well as some of the gentler grappas from his native country.

He turned on the stereo, which started playing Chet Baker's smooth jazz trumpet from the sixties. He thought of the young Chet Baker, handsome and talented. Though he did not play as well as Miles—no one really did— his vocals stood easily on their own. He could have made it just as a singer. It seemed like in the early 1960s, the world was his for the taking. Tragically, like many artists in the mid part of the twentieth century, these extremely talented individuals fell victim to the temptation of heroin and other drugs. Anthony felt a pang of despair and sadness for those who wasted away their lives and talent and left this world far too soon.

He sipped his bourbon and listened to the jazz in the background. The light from the park was softening as it grew towards dusk. Colors faded to shades of steel blue and vanilla white. The sun was already behind his building and the shadows seemed taller than the trees. The lights of the apartments on the east side of the park came alive as their occupants returned home.

He opened up his MacBook Air on the leather-topped Thomas Moser desk. He went to Ancestry.com and logged into his account. It already contained a number of well-mapped genealogies that he had researched. He started a new search. This time he typed in Mackenzie Ferrara and followed the tree as far as he could.

∼ Chapter 22 ∼

It was well after six on a Tuesday evening. Most of the other restorers had packed up and left for the day, including Anthony, who left at lunchtime to take care of some errands. There was sort of a lull in the action with very few active restorations taking place. Mackenzie was wrapping up some documentation paperwork and was also trying to dig up whatever she could find in the art history archives about a woman with an abnormally long pinkie finger. So far she was having no luck. She might reach out to some of her old professors at NYU to see if they could point her in the right direction.

Simon stopped by her workstation carrying a leather folio. Mackenzie thought that Simon always looked like he had just stepped off of a GQ photo shoot, even though he was at the end of a full workday. His lightweight linen suit looked like it had been freshly pressed, and he kept his tie fully knotted and tight at the neck, even after normal work hours.

"Hello Mackenzie, looks like you're one of the last ones here, as usual. Anything important?" he asked her cheerfully.

She pushed herself away from the computer and swiveled her chair to face him.

"Not really. Just tying up some loose ends. Sometimes when I'm working I forget what time it is and then next thing you know I look around and I'm the only one here."

"Psychologists call those flow states. You become so absorbed in what you're doing, time and the rest of the world seem to flow past. You're fortunate; very few people experience those states on a regular basis. They are some of the highest level of intellectual engagement humans can achieve." Simon set his folio onto the work surface and unwrapped the leather tie that held it together. When he opened it, there were several old-looking papers as well as an official looking document.

"I'm sorry to break your flow for something so mundane. Lately I find myself less in flow states and more in the much less absorbing state of dotting *i*'s and crossing *t*'s." He pulled out the top document and turned it over where there were several signature lines, some of which had been filled in already. "I need you to sign off on the restoration you and Anthony did for the Daddi, which, by the way, turned out spectacularly. Somehow I must have missed you when I originally was finalizing this. Anthony has already signed, so all I need is your John Hancock and this will be official and wrapped up."

"Of course, I'm sorry if I was away when you originally got it signed. I hope it hasn't created any inconvenience," said Mackenzie.

"Nonsense," replied Simon, waving his hand,. "We have rights to the Daddi for another two years, so it will be hanging proudly here at the Cloisters for some time. We just needed to get the paperwork put to bed so that everything would be in order."

Mackenzie felt relieved. The last thing she wanted was to be seen as a bottleneck. She had always prided herself on her work ethic and punctuality. She wasn't sure when Simon had the paperwork signed by Anthony because she didn't remember missing more than a few days in the past year. In the previous restorations she had worked on, she had been the first one to sign, and it was Anthony or one of the other lead restorers that Simon had to chase down. She preferred it that way. She took the beautiful black enameled Mont Blanc pen that Simon handed her and prepared to sign her name to the document. When she looked at the signature directly above where she was supposed to sign, she felt her heart stop beating. She had an immediate, uncontrollable urge to vomit right then and there.

"Mackenzie, are you alright?" Simon asked, placing his hand on her shoulder trying to steady her.

She took several deep breaths, trying to regain her composure. She could not have been more shocked if she had seen her mother's ghost appear right in front of her. On the signature line directly above her was Anthony's signature. It was the first time she had actually seen it. The *i* in Bataglia was dotted with a backward slash. It was identical to the signatures she had seen for both Daddi and Lippi. Thoughts swirled in her head. How was this possible? What did it mean? Had Anthony painted, and then signed for these paintings as Daddi and Lippi? If he had, that would make him a forger. Was he a forger? Could it be possible?

Simon shook her shoulder gently, trying to get her attention.

"Mackenzie, is everything alright? You look like you've seen a ghost."

She looked up at Simon. She had actually forgotten that he was there. In her mind she was somewhere, not here, not anywhere. Lost in an abyss of confusion, dissolution, and anger.

"I'm sorry, Simon," she responded trying to put on a smile. "I don't know what came over me. I'm fine now."

"Are you sure?" Simon still looked concerned. "We don't have to do this now. Would you prefer to go lie down somewhere? There's a couch in my office, you could rest there."

She shook her head and smiled. "No, I'm fine. It was just a temporary thing. I got a bit lightheaded. It was probably because I had been looking down for so long and then looked up and the blood rushed out of my head. I feel fine now." She picked up the pen, which she had dropped on the workstation. She carefully signed her name on the line above her printed name.

Then, without thinking, she had an idea.

"Simon, would it be okay if I took a photo of this with my iPhone? I've never seen my signature on a document with Anthony's and I'd like to have one to put in my scrapbook." Without waiting for Simon to respond, she fished in her bag and took out her phone.

Simon hesitated a bit—it was a strange request. "Well, um, yes. I guess there isn't a problem with that," he stammered.

She carefully pointed her camera at the signatures, focusing on Anthony's.

"Thank you so much," she said, smiling after clicking off two shots. "I know it must sound goofy, but I like these types of things. I'm very nostalgic. I guess I've always been that way, but especially since I lost my mom."

"Yes, yes, of course," recovered Simon, putting the documents in the folder and tying the leather binding. "It's important to capture important moments in your life."

"Thank you, Simon. I'm sorry I gave you a scare. Not sure what happened, but I'm fine now." She packed up her work, put some of it into her drawer, locked it, and then put the rest in her shoulder bag. "It's probably just my body telling me that I have to get home and get something to eat."

"I think you're probably right. Good night, Mackenzie, I'll see you tomorrow." Simon made his way back to his office.

Mackenzie headed out the door shortly thereafter, eager to get home. On her way to her car she called her father and told him that she'd be coming home soon and that she had something important to share with him.

❧ Chapter 23 ❧

J oe's phone rang. It was Detective Angstrom calling.

"Hi Chris, what's the word on the street?"

"The operative word would be 'weird.' I've got some interesting news about your man Bataglia, if you've got a minute."

"Hell, Chris, I'm retired. That's pretty much all I've got is a whole bunch of minutes sewn together into a huge, boring quilt. I'm sitting down, and have a pen and pad in front of me. What did you find?"

"Well, nothing illegal, no buried bodies but definitely some interesting stuff. This guy is definitely not your average Joe Blow. Anyhow, from what I was able to find out, which admittedly wasn't much, Mr. Bataglia lives in The Beresford, in a luxury condo on Central Park West. Now there are a couple of interesting things about that. The first is that I found out that he lives on the twentieth floor in a four-bedroom apartment; you and I would call it a suite. I don't have a firm price, but based on some comparable properties, we're looking at $11 to $15 million for a place like that. Not too shabby for a restorer at the Cloisters. Maybe we should have thought of that instead of joining the force," Chris added with a laugh.

"Funny. I'm pretty sure that most restorers aren't paying for $15 million condos," responded Joe. "If they are, I need to up Mackenzie's share of the rent."

"I hear ya. Here's the weird thing. According to city records, this condo is owned by the Di Bernardi Family Trust. And get this, it was purchased with cash in 1929, the year the building opened. They were one of the original owners. So it looks like Mr. Bataglia must be some type of trust baby. I'd never heard of the Di Bernardi Foundation, which is based in Italy, so I reached out to some guys we know on the Italian police department. We did some joint stuff with them a couple of years ago related to heroin trafficking and money laundering between the New York and Italian mafia, remember that?"

"Like it was yesterday. In fact, it could be yesterday because my guess is that it's still happening today," replied Joe somewhat cynically.

"Unfortunately, you're pretty much right about that," replied Chris. "So if you're done complaining about why we still can't stop drugs from getting into the country, here's what I did find out about the Di Bernardi Family Trust. If you weren't sitting down before, make sure you're sitting down for this. It's really odd. This Di Bernardi Trust is old, and I'm not talking New World old, I'm talking Middle Ages old. It's one of the oldest trusts that exists in Italy—and probably the world. It was established in the mid-sixteenth century, 1568 to be exact, by a man named Giordano Di Bernardi. It's based in Lucca, which is about an hour west of Florence, and it owns a number of properties, including the apartment in New York, a pretty sizable estate outside of Florence, which seems to generate money from olives, wine grapes, chestnuts, and sheep's milk cheese, and an apartment in Florence. It pays out some money to charities every year, mostly ones related to schools of art, and has a pretty sizable art collection that it loans out to galleries around the world. But beyond that no one knows much about it. It pretty much operates below the radar. Files tax returns, etc. It does keep money in Swiss bank accounts, but it doesn't pay tax on any interest because, well, because it's sitting in Swiss bank accounts."

"Wow, I didn't even know there were trusts in the sixteenth century," blurted out Joe, becoming even more amazed and confused about what he was finding out about Anthony.

"Yeah, actually neither did I," admitted Chris. "I did a little bit of research and found out that they go back to about the twelfth or thirteenth century in England. Basically, it was a way to protect the property of the wealthy landowners who went off to fight in the Crusades. Before that, they'd go off, and just in case they were to die, they deeded their property to a relative with the basic understanding that they should take care of their heirs or, hopefully, turn it back over to them when they returned. As things go, sometimes those relatives liked the property a bit too much and decided to keep it for themselves, whether the original lord of the manor returned or not. It created a lot of headaches. And so where issues of money are involved, lawmakers stepped in and personal trust laws were developed."

"Fascinating," admitted Joe. He always thought that Chris would have made an excellent historian. As it was, he did make an excellent detective.

"From a legal standpoint creating a trust only requires three things. You need 'intention,' in other words, a clear intent to create a trust. In this case it would seem that Giordano Di Bernardo demonstrated clear intent. You need 'subject matter,' or defining the property subject to the trust. Because trusts can last for generations, it can be pretty open. So, for instance, the trust could include all money, property, stocks, etc., that currently exist as well as any future investments made by the trustees based on the intent of the trust itself. So if you had a million dollars in 1900 and you decided to invest in General Electric, Standard Oil and buy up some choice property in Manhattan, then by say 1950, that million would probably have grown twenty to fifty-fold. All of those assets, as well as anything else the trust bought, such as artwork, etc., would be included in the trust. And finally, the third thing you need is an 'object,' which is more commonly referred to as a 'beneficiary.' In other words, the person or persons who benefit from the assets of the trust and how those assets are paid out."

"Makes sense so far. So am I to assume that Anthony Bataglia is a beneficiary of the Di Bernardi Trust?"

"Bingo. Trusts are very private entities. They don't need to report much of anything unless they want to. Specific terms of the trust itself are not public, like they are in wills. But one thing that they need to do is file a tax return and that's where you can find out all sorts of things about their holdings, beneficiaries, etc.

"From what I was able to find out, Anthony is the sole beneficiary of the Di Bernardi trust, and has been for a long time, maybe fifty years. And this is no small trust. This is pretty substantial. If you look at its reported liquid assets, cash, stocks, gold, etc., then it's in excess of $75 million. If you add in the value of the artwork, it's probably ten to twenty times that amount— tough to estimate but based on some of the paintings it has, some Michelangelos, Botticellis, Dürers, Van Goghs, Monets, Vermeers, and dozens more that I didn't remember. I'm no art historian, but it's a pretty serious list, even from a novice's standpoint. Some of these are on loan to the Ufizzi, the Louvre, the Prado, the Met, and the Hermitage. It pretty much loans most of these out for free and takes a tax break for the value of the loan. Sort of a nice strategy when you think about it. It doesn't cost the museums anything and allows the trust to deduct tens of millions in taxes every year, which probably completely covers any taxes owed on its investments.

"Just from a casual accounting, I would estimate that the Di Bernardi Trust holds in excess of a billion dollars in assets. It's definitely no mom-and-pop operation."

"Wow," exclaimed Joe sitting back and his chair, his mind in a haze. "Is there anything else we can find out about the trust and Anthony in particular?"

"Well, I was able to get the name and address of the trustees of the trust. Like I said, it's based in Lucca, Italy. I'll email you the contact information, as well as everything I've received from the Italian police. I think that's all I've got. Hopefully this helps you out a bit."

"Chris, I really appreciate all of your help. I know this isn't part of your caseload and I'm sure you're up to your neck with that as it is. I don't really know what I'm looking for, but it just seems like a lot of things don't add up," admitted Joe. "This guy is starting to concern me."

"Happy to help out. I owe you a lot more than this for all you did for me when I was making my way up in the department. If you do find something, let me know. I'm curious myself."

"Thanks, Chris. I'll let you know what I find. Take care."

Joe hung up the phone and leaned back in the kitchen chair and slowly stroked his chin. So not only did Anthony live in a multi-million dollar luxury condo in Central Park West, but he was the primary beneficiary of a billion dollar trust that owned hundreds of millions in priceless paintings. Besides that, he had been the beneficiary of the trust for over fifty years, and yet Mackenzie was convinced that he was in his thirties. Maybe Mackenzie was just really bad at estimating ages.

He'd have to find out more. They should know more about the signatures that Mackenzie had provided him in a day or two. He'd sent them off to a friend at police headquarters for analysis. He wasn't sure what they would turn up, but at this point his sixth sense told him there was definitely something odd going on at the Cloisters. Given that his daughter worked there, he wasn't going to let this kettle whistle for very long.

Chapter 24

Mackenzie sat in a small diner in midtown Manhattan with a tall glass of iced tea on the table and her cell phone to her ear. On the other end, the line rang several times before someone answered.

"Hello."

"Signor Frantinelli, this is Mackenzie Ferrara from the Cloisters in New York." She wasn't sure if this was a good idea, but after weighing the risks, as well as the crazy per minute charges she would be accruing, she decided that it was worth a try.

"Ah, yes, Ms. Ferrara. I'm glad we could connect," said the man in flawless English highlighted with a distinct Italian accent.

"Thank you for responding to my email and setting up a time to talk."

"No problem. What would you like to know about Signor Bataglia?"

"What can you tell me about him?"

"Well, from what I know, Signor Bataglia started working here at the Ufizzi in 1973. Like many restorers, he came to help after the flood of 1966. There were so many restorers who volunteered their time to help us with the damage that had been done to so many of our paintings."

"1973? That's more than forty years ago. Are you sure we're talking about the same person? Might there be another Anthony Bataglia who worked at the Ufizzi? Maybe his father?" asked Mackenzie skeptically.

"No," said the man without hesitation, "there was only one Anthony Bataglia that worked for the Ufizzi. I know him well. He was one of the best, if not the best restorer we ever had. His work is amazing, a true artist."

"How long did he work at the Ufizzi?" probed Mackenzie, still trying to make sense of the situation.

"Let me see, hmm," he paused while he thought. "Yes, he worked here until about 2003 when he retired. But after several years he asked for a recommendation to volunteer his time to the Cloisters in New York. I asked him if he still wouldn't rather work here at the Ufizzi, in fact, I actually begged him to come back. But he preferred to go to New York, so of course I wrote him a wonderful letter of introduction."

"Just out of curiosity, how old would you say that Mr. Bataglia is?

"Well, I have to admit that Signor Bataglia is blessed with a very young face and the body of a runner. Angelic, we would say here, even though I'm sure that sounds overly feminine to American ears. He looks much younger than his age. I would say that he is in his early sixties, perhaps, maybe older, but that's only because I know how long he worked with us. Is there a problem with Signor Bataglia, Ms. Ferrara?"

"No, no, none whatsoever," she stammered, not wanting to set off an alarm. "We're planning on doing a profile on some of the restorers here at the Cloisters and I wanted to get some more background information on him for the article. Please don't mention anything to him. I want to surprise him with the information I've gathered, sort of a 'this is your life' type of thing. I'll send you a copy of the article if it ever comes out. Thank you very much for your time, Signor Frantinelli. If I can ever be of service to you, please do not hesitate to contact me."

"Thank you Ms. Ferrara. It is my pleasure. If you find yourself in Florence, please let me know. Ciao."

"Ciao," replied Mackenzie.

She hung up the phone and finished writing a few notes on her yellow legal pad. How could this be? Anthony looked like he was in his early to mid-thirties. From what she'd just heard, Anthony would have to be in his mid to late-sixties. Could it be possible that she was that far off in her estimate of his age? That didn't seem possible. Mick Jagger might be in good shape for a man in his late sixties, but no one would mistake him for a thirty-year-old. Something didn't make sense. In fact, a lot of things didn't make sense.

† † †

Joe returned home from a long walk around the local park. He got bored sitting around the house all day, but wasn't particularly interested in going to the gym. As far as he was concerned, long walks on warm summer days were pretty much all the exercise anyone needed. As he opened the fridge and grabbed a cold can of Budweiser, his cell phone rang. He didn't recognize the number, although he knew it came from a New York City area code.

"Hi, this is Joe," he answered.

"Hello, detective Ferrara. This is Tom Lawrence, down at forensics."

"Yes, Tom, thank you for getting back to me." He took a seat and got out a pad of paper. Octavius jumped up on the kitchen table and started walking back and forth, rubbing his head and torso against Joe's arms.

"Detective Llewellyn asked me to run some analyses for you on some signatures you provided in digital files. I was the document examiner assigned to analyze them."

"Thanks, Tom. I'm sorry to have troubled you with this."

"No problem at all. Of course, as you know it's more difficult to compare signatures when we don't have samples of the ink or the paper they were made on. These were particularly challenging because some of them came from what appear to be old paintings. They were very faded. I had to enhance them as much as possible without distorting them."

As a detective, Joe found forensic analysts to be indispensable and annoying at the same time. They always felt it necessary to explain in excruciating detail everything they had done as part of their analysis. At the end of the day, all Joe wanted to know was what the results were and how confident they were in their findings. But they were doing him the favor so he didn't push. He sipped his Bud and let Tom explain his craft.

"I ran comparative analyses on four distinct signatures. The results suggest that it's very likely that these four signatures were all made by the same person. As you know, we likely wouldn't be able to prove it in court, but I would feel confident supplying my findings to a prosecutor to use as corroborating evidence."

Joe nodded. "So what you're telling me is that you are confident that the same person made all four signatures."

"Yes, sir. Based on my analysis, the odds that the signatures for Berlinghieri, Lippi, Daddi and Bataglia were made by the same individual are over 95 percent. That would meet the scientific standard in terms of this type of evidence. Would you like me to email you my findings?"

"Yes, absolutely. Thank you again, Tom, I really appreciate it."

"You're very welcome, sir. It's my pleasure."

After providing Tom with his email address, Joe sipped his beer and absentmindedly stroked Octavius's side while the cat gently purred and stretched his arms in front of his head, opening and closing his paws, grasping at air, "making biscuits" as Joe's grandma used to call it. Four signatures all matching the same person suggested to him that the same person had painted or at least signed all of the paintings. Why would someone sign paintings they didn't paint? That didn't make sense. The fact that the other three artists had been dead for over five hundred years led him to believe that he was dealing with things he was much more familiar with than pre-Renaissance art, namely forgery and fraud.

∾ Chapter 25 ∾

Mackenzie could barely concentrate on her work that day. The image of the backwards-dotted *i* had stuck in her head from the moment she saw it sitting there on the signature page. Fortunately, it was a slow day. She asked Simon if she could leave at noon and he didn't object. After all, she put in so many extra hours most of the time that he pretty much gave her carte blanche with regard to her schedule. She called her father from the parking lot and headed home for an early weekend. He had actually asked her at breakfast if she thought she might be able to get home early that evening. Perhaps he had something in mind as well.

When she walked into the kitchen, her father called to her from the dining room. It looked like a strategy planning center, a war room. Her father had a large white board on a folding stand set up in front of the table, the chairs pushed against the wall. The table was covered with various documents, including the copies of the paintings Mackenzie had made, pictures of the signatures she had taken and a number of other official looking documents that she wasn't familiar with. *What does he know?* She hadn't even told him about the signature and yet he had all of this pulled together. He must know something that she didn't. She wasn't sure whether she was excited or scared. Probably a bit of both.

"Hey, Kenz, glad you could make it home early. Thought we'd go through what we know so far, and believe me, there's a lot to go through. I just brewed a pot of coffee so if you want some, help yourself."

She scanned the room. "Dad, where did you get the white board?"

He smiled proudly. "Bought it down at that new office supply store. Always liked having these at work, but never thought I'd need one at home. They come in handy for laying out your thoughts, especially when there are a lot of moving parts and you're working with someone else."

She still wasn't sure what all of this meant, but she was happy to see that she wouldn't have to work it all out on her own. "Sounds like you've learned more since we last talked. I've got some news to share as well. It's kind of strange." She set down her bag and took out her note pad and put it on the table along with the other bits of information.

"Well, let's get a cup of coffee and start making our way through this. I have to admit that this is one of the strangest cases I've ever worked on, and I've worked on a bunch of weird ones." Her father made his way to the kitchen and poured a cup of coffee for both himself and Mackenzie. They both took it black.

She hadn't seen her father like this in over a year, maybe more than that. He'd been putzing around the house ever since he retired, trying to find ways to stay busy. She'd actually never seen her father in the heat of battle. He usually kept that side of himself at the office. She could see that the admiral was back at the helm and he liked the way that the smooth, worn handle of the ship's wheel felt in his calloused hands.

"Dad, it's not really a case. There hasn't been any crime committed, at least to my knowledge," Mackenzie protested, somewhat half-heartedly.

"Listen," her father responded, "where there's smoke, there's fire, and there's a hell of a lot of smoke billowing out of the place you work, and most of it seems to be coming from this Anthony Bataglia character. I'll bet you dollars to doughnuts that we've got something here that goes way beyond just some strange coincidences."

Mackenzie sat down in one of the chairs facing the white board and sipped her coffee. Even in the summer, she and her father always drank hot coffee. Never seemed out of place to either one of them. She imagined that he built up his coffee drinking habit working twelve-hour days as a detective.

"I hate to think that Anthony is involved in anything illegal. He just doesn't seem to be that type of person."

"Well, let's not jump to any conclusions one way or another," her father cautioned. "The way to proceed here is to lay out everything we know and then start putting the pieces together."

He proceeded to share with her what he had learned about Anthony and the di Bernardi Foundation. He also presented her with the results of the forensic analysis, which he had printed out. For her part, she shared what she had gathered about Anthony's role at the Ufizzi, specifically the timeframe that would make him at least sixty years old, which seemed impossible.

"I've got something else to share with you. I just finished pulling it together this morning." Her father sat down and sipped his coffee while Mackenzie went to the white board and started making notes while she talked.

"Over the past two weeks I pulled every piece of information I could find on any restoration where Anthony was the lead restorer. He is nothing if not prolific. Now, depending on the severity of the damage to the original work of art, a good restorer can work on maybe four to five restorations a year. Some restorations take six months. Some are completed in less than a month, although those are rare." She paused, "Over the past seventeen years, Anthony was the lead restorer on 112 works of art. That is an enormous body of work, especially for someone in his mid-thirties. If we assume that he's thirty-five years old, that would mean that he's been doing almost seven a year since he was eighteen! That's unheard of!"

Her father listened intently, scribbling some notes on a pad of paper in front of him.

"Isn't it unusual for someone to be able to do restorations at such an early age?" he asked.

"Oh, absolutely," she responded. "At least in the U.S., before anyone would let you work on the restoration of a major work of art, especially as the lead restorer, you would have had to complete a masters in fine arts and have about two years working as an assistant restorer. If you do the math, that means that most people would start working as lead restorers in their mid-to-late twenties, assuming everything went smoothly." She paused. "Clearly, Anthony was flagged at an early age as an impresario, like a fourteen-year-old chess grand master. But it's extremely rare. My guess is that there are more teenage chess grand masters in the world than teenage lead art restorers. Maybe it's different in Italy. Up until very recently the Europeans focused more on apprenticeships than on formal education, but that doesn't mean they become lead restorers any faster.

"112 restorations over a seventeen year period is a lot. But what's really strange is that all of them cover only eight artists: Berlinghiero Berlinghieri,

Bonaventura Berlinghieri, Marco Berlinghieri, Giotto di Bondone, Bernar-do Daddi, Taddeo Gaddi, Fra. Lippi and Filippino Lippi. Now, I know that he specializes in Italian Renaissance artists, but still, it's a bit odd that you work on almost seven restorations a year for almost twenty years and you've only touched the work of eight artists. I casually asked some of the other restorers at the Cloisters how many artists they had worked on and most of them couldn't even give me a number. Most sort of shrugged and said, 'a couple dozen or so, maybe more.'

"So, just for giggles, I looked a couple of them up. Here's what I found: Charles van Arden has been restoring art, mostly reliquary pieces, some manuscripts, etc., for over twenty-five years. During that time he has worked on over ninety-four pieces, or about four a year, and has worked on art from over eighty-three different artists. He's only worked on the same artists more than once four times, in twenty-five years!

"Ariadne Estrada has been restoring art for fifteen years and has been a senior or lead restorer for just over ten. During that time period, she was lead restorer on thirty-six artworks, or slightly less than four per year. She also does a lot of authentication work so that number might be a bit of an underestimate of her capacity. She has worked with twenty-eight different artists during that time and has worked on artwork by the same artist more than once four times.

"Now that may be strange, but at the same time it may just be that he prefers to specialize in works that range between the twelfth and fifteenth centuries in Italy, and mostly in and around Florence. I'm not sure."

She set down her marker and continued. "The other thing is that I haven't been able to find out anything about his training. When I asked him about it, he's been very evasive, or, more appropriately, vague. He usually says something like, '*Oh, I picked it up here and there. Learned by watching,*' or something to that effect."

"Did you ever ask him who he watched?" asked her father.

"Once, during lunch, I asked him that. He shrugged it off with, '*There were many people who helped me out early on. Too many to name, really.*' Then he redirected the conversation to some aspect of our restoration, like, '*Let's take another look at how our paint has set. I'm afraid we may have added more than we needed. More than the artist had intended originally. I'm concerned that we may see some cracking.'"* She smiled to herself as she remembered that interaction.

"At first I had been really concerned and looked hard for flaws. I never found them. His technique is flawless. He never used too much or too little of anything. I pretty much realized it was his way of saying that he didn't want to talk about something. I didn't think anything of it at the time. After all, we all have things we'd rather not talk about. Now I'm not sure if there might be something more to it."

"I think there is a lot more to it," agreed her father. "But it's probably a good idea not to push him too hard, at least not directly." He paused, took a sip of coffee, and then stood up and took the marker from Mackenzie and started writing on the white board. Octavius methodically made his way in from the kitchen, paused briefly as he looked up at Mackenzie and gave a "meow" before jumping onto one of the padded chairs against the wall. He proceeded to clean himself, sitting with one back leg straight in the air.

"Okay, let's summarize the key things that we know so far," Joe said.

"First, let's start with the inconsistencies of his real age. From what you've said, he looks like he's in his early to mid-thirties. But we have direct evidence from the guy at the Ufizzi that he, or at least someone named Anthony Bataglia, worked there starting in 1973. That was thirty-six years ago. If you assume that he started working there when he was eighteen, which would be very young, as you said, then he would be about fifty-four. You said that the director thought that he would be about sixty or so now, which would fit with the timeline. So no matter how you slice it, we have a man who looks at least thirty years younger than he should. That should be red flag number one." He took out a red marker and wrote *AGE DOESN'T MATCH* in red letters in the top left corner of the white board, and circled it.

"The second piece of information has to do with the di Bernardi Foundation. If my sources are correct, and I have no reason to doubt them, Anthony Bataglia is the sole beneficiary of a foundation that was started in the Middle Ages, is headquartered in Lucca, Italy, and is worth upwards of a billion dollars. Most of the wealth of that foundation is based in its extensive art collection, which it loans out to museums around the world and reaps millions of dollars in tax breaks. It also owns the luxury apartment he currently lives in, which is estimated to be worth about $15 million. It was bought in 1929, the year the building opened, with cash." He wrote, *DI BERNARDI FOUNDATION* to the right of his first entry and circled it.

"I think that what you just told me about his restorations is significant as well. I'm not really interested in how prolific he is, but I am intrigued about the limited focus of his restorations, especially when we consider what we know about the signatures." He wrote *FOCUSED RESTORATIONS* to the right of his previous entry. "What were the names of the artists you mentioned?" Mackenzie relayed the names of the eight artists that Anthony focused on while her father wrote them down under his heading.

"Now, for the final piece of information, which as far as I'm concerned, is the most significant." He wrote, *SIGNATURE MATCHES* on the top right hand side of the board, and circled it. He then drew lines from that circle to the names of Berlinghiero Berlinghieri, Bernardo Daddi, and Fra. Lippi.

"Do you think you could get samples of signatures from these other artists? I could have them run it against what we already have," he asked.

"Sure," she responded. "I can try at least. Some of them may not have signed their work but I know for a fact that Giotto and Filippino Lippi signed most of theirs."

"Good, the digital photos you took last time seemed to work." He paused, setting down his marker and returned to his seat while they both stared at the board.

"Dad, you have any thoughts about how all of this connects together?"

"I've got an idea, but I'd like to hear your thoughts. I'm pretty sure you're thinking the same thing I am, although you might not feel comfortable with it."

He was right about that, she thought. She didn't want to think anything negative about Anthony; in fact, she was actually attracted to him, which made it that much worse. But her dad had always taught her to let the facts speak for themselves and at the moment they were singing a pretty grim funeral dirge.

"Well," she started, "I don't know how all of these things interrelate, but I'm willing to bet that the Anthony Bataglia currently working at the Cloisters is not who we think he is. In addition, it would seem that we might have a very successful forger on our hands. I don't know how the whole di Bernardi Foundation plays into this, but it could be just a front for getting these forgeries placed in galleries around the world. These pieces are extremely valuable and there aren't many people who would know a good fake from the original. But is that all there is to it? He's an art forger with a very focused repertoire."

"From what you've told me, that might be enough. After all, millions of dollars in tax breaks, as well as potential sales of forged artwork is a great way to not only make a lot of money, but also to launder a lot of profits, all couched nicely in an obscure private trust that has operated below the radar for several centuries and keeps most of its money in Swiss bank accounts. It has all the makings of a very sophisticated operation, something that goes far beyond Mr. Bataglia. What if some of the money that flows through the di Bernardi Foundation isn't particularly 'clean,' if you know what I mean. People doing bad things need a way to make their money seem legitimate. Running it through a five-hundred-year-old trust that donates millions in charitable loans of priceless artwork isn't a bad cover."

Mackenzie sat back in her chair, thinking. She looked over at Octavius, who had finished his cleaning routine and was curled up, deep into a late afternoon nap. *How could this be?* she wondered. *Anthony seems so genuine, so real. Was it all just an act? Is he really a master forger impersonating the real Anthony Bataglia?* If that was the case, what happened to the real Anthony Bataglia? Had he been murdered and replaced with a counterfeit who knew how to paint well and carry on the act? It was hard for her to take in all at once. After several moments of silence, she spoke.

"Dad, I need to find out more about Anthony. I'm having a hard time coming to grips with this."

"I agree. We don't have anything that would hold up in a court of law, and we don't know of any laws that have been broken. But before you go digging too deep, just remember that if this Mr. Bataglia you're working with is a forger, he's not going to respond positively to you poking your nose around. And if he is part of a larger operation, those people may take it upon themselves to make sure that their investments are secured, whether that requires violence or not." He paused and looked directly at Mackenzie. "I guess what I'm saying is be careful."

"I will. Don't worry. I've been taught by the best." She forced a smile, because at this point she was scared.

"Famous last words," grunted her father. Quickly changing the subject, he stood up and started towards the kitchen. "I don't know about you, but I'm getting hungry. I was going to grill up some Italian sausages with peppers and onions. Sound good?"

"Yeah, Dad, it sounds great." One thing she learned from her father over the years was that no matter how hard a case got, it was important to eat and, if possible, eat well.

❧ Chapter 26 ❧

Mackenzie sat in the cab on her way to meet Anthony, trying to calm her nerves. Earlier that afternoon he had asked her if she would like to join him for drinks and some music at his favorite bar later that evening. It caught her by surprise but was certainly not an unwelcome invitation. This would be a great opportunity to try to get a bit more out of him, hopefully when his guard was down. There were a lot of unanswered questions that she and her father had unearthed. Most of what they knew didn't paint a particularly rosy portrait of the man going by the name of Anthony Bataglia.

She wondered why he had reached out to her. They had been working on a number of restorations together over the past several months, so maybe he thought it would be a nice idea to get together outside of work and just relax. That seemed innocent enough. But she couldn't help but wonder if there was something behind this seemingly harmless offer? She had told her father about the invitation and he said that she should go, but be on guard. He was convinced that this man, Anthony Bataglia, or whoever he was, was connected to something much bigger and probably criminal in nature. While she wasn't sure what Anthony was all about, she couldn't help but be attracted to the man. In other circumstances this would have been an ideal first date. But she would have to temper her excitement at this point and instead focus on learning as much as she could. She hoped she could do it without raising any suspicions on his part.

Her taxi pulled up in front of the Carlyle Hotel on 76th street and Madison Avenue, one block east of Central Park. Anthony was standing outside the hotel casually talking to the doorman. He had left work early and changed from jeans into a light summer weight tan suit with a blue crew neck silk tee-shirt underneath and dark brown loafers.

"Sorry I'm late," said Mackenzie as she met him.

"Not a problem. You are not late at all," replied Anthony.

They made their way into the hotel and walked through the lobby to Bemelmans Bar in the back. Even though it was the early evening and it was still very bright outside, the bar was almost two thirds of the way full and dark inside. According to Anthony it was always dark in Bemelmans. That was part of the charm. They found a table in the corner. Chris Gillespie was well into his first set. His warm baritone and rich piano playing had just started into Billie Holiday's melancholy classic "But Beautiful."

"Love is funny or it's sad… or it's quiet or it's mad…"

"This is great!" said Mackenzie as she settled back against the leather booth and looked around the bar.

"Yes, this is one of my favorite places to come. I love listening to Chris sing the old standards. His piano playing is probably even better than his voice, but he has a great voice," Anthony said.

A waiter in a crisp white dinner jacket and black tie came to their small table and set down a plate of potato chips and mixed nuts and looked at Anthony.

"Good evening, Mr. Bataglia. It's good to see you."

"Same here, Kevin."

"Can I get you something to drink?" asked Kevin.

Mackenzie looked at the drink menu and ordered a pomegranate cosmopolitan. Anthony ordered a sixteen-year-old Lagavulin on the rocks.

Mackenzie leaned towards Anthony and said, "I've been in New York for a while and I've never even heard of this place."

"What makes great cities special are these types of places," replied Anthony. "This place actually is not that much of a hole in the wall. The Café Carlyle on the second floor is one of the premiere venues for great music. Woody Allen performs here almost every week with his New Orleans jazz band. Bobby Short played there for more than twenty years."

Mackenzie looked at him and smiled. "You mean the director, Woody Allen? I didn't know he played in a jazz band. I have to admit that I have no idea who Bobby Short is."

"Was, actually. He passed away a few years ago. He was married to Gloria Vanderbilt, but the reason he was famous was that he was a phenomenal singer and piano player, much like Chris Gillespie. I used to come here and listen to him sing Cole Porter and Gershwin classics. It was wonderful. He brought a gentle energy to songs that could make you laugh and cry at the same time."

Their drinks arrived and Mackenzie took a sip of hers.

"This place seems pretty old."

"Well, I guess it is. It really depends what you mean by old, but this is one of the classic hotels of New York. It was one of the most famous hotels after World War II. JFK used to have a couple of suites here and rumor has it that he knew of some underground tunnels that connected to the subway that he used to bring in some 'acquaintances,' including Marilyn Monroe." He gave her a knowing smile.

"It certainly has the feel of a bar from the thirties or forties."

"I thought you would like it," nodded Anthony as he took a slow sip of his scotch.

Chris Gillespie started into "How About You?"

"*I like New York in June, how about you? I like a Gershwin tune, how about you?*"

They both sat back and just listened to the lyrics and piano playing emanate through the bar. Mackenzie looked around at the wallpaper, which were paintings from the Madeline series of children's books, written and illustrated by Ludwig Bemelmans, who used to be a resident of the Carlyle Hotel. She thought that they looked like a mix between Dr. Seuss and Winnie the Pooh.

"It seems like you come here a lot," said Mackenzie.

"I guess I do. I live relatively close, so it is convenient for me. I find it a good way to relax after a day of looking at paintings," responded Anthony.

"Must be nice! Central Park East isn't the shabbiest of neighborhoods, you know. I didn't know that painting restoration was such a lucrative profession." She played dumb, knowing full well where he lived.

Anthony looked at his scotch for a moment and then calmly responded, looking at her with soft but penetrating eyes.

"I have been fortunate with money. I have not had to think about it for a long time. But I actually live on the west side. Still, it is a nice walk across the park. Even in the winter it takes me less than twenty minutes, door-to-door. It is actually just a five minute cab ride depending on traffic, but if the weather is agreeable, I prefer to walk."

Mackenzie noticed his shyness in talking about money, and made a mental note of it. She had met a lot of kids from old rich families while she was in undergrad at Bryn Mawr. Most of them dressed like Bohemians in tattered jeans and smoked clove cigarettes. You'd never know that they came from families who had been rich for generations. Some were definitely snobby elitists but she found most of the really rich kids never talked about money or dressed any differently than anyone else. It was as if their money in some way alienated them from everyone else and they were trying to fit in. If your family is worth $50 million, you don't have to tell people that you're rich. But she suspected there was more to his reticence than just being raised with wealth. If what her father learned about the di Bernardi Foundation was true, then Anthony was worth close to a billion. That seemed hard to even imagine looking at him here.

"Now that you know where I live, what about you?" asked Anthony with a smile that broke the momentary silence.

"Me? I used to live in the East Village, near Washington Square," replied Mackenzie. "But after grad school I moved in with my dad in the Bronx to save some money."

"What does your father do?" asked Anthony innocently.

"Well," paused Mackenzie, not sure whether she should make something up, but in the end decided against it. "He used to be a detective but he retired about a year ago. So now he pretty much just paces around the house, looking for things to keep him busy."

Anthony nodded without showing any reaction one way or another. "And what about your mother, if I might ask?"

"My mom was a pharmacist, but she passed away three years ago."

"I am sorry to hear that. It must have been very difficult for you and your father," replied Anthony, his eyes gentle with concern.

"Yeah, it caught us all by surprise. My dad took it especially hard, although he's one of those tough old guys who has a hard time showing his feelings."

"I apologize if I brought up bad memories. I should not ask such personal questions. Please forgive me."

"You don't have to apologize at all." She smiled and changed the subject, "Anyhow, I'm really glad that you asked me here."

"I am glad you were able to join me," he replied with a warm smile. "It gets lonely coming to places like this on your own, even if the music is great." He nibbled on one of the potato chips from the tray on the table that always seemed to refill itself when it got close to empty. "Besides, you can help me stop eating so many of these potato chips. On my own I go through about four refills and call it a dinner. Not the most balanced of meals." He laughed, looking into her eyes.

"Well, they have mixed nuts as well, you know," she said, smiling playfully. "That should help balance out your diet." She nodded at him. "You certainly don't look like someone who has to worry about his weight, or, for that matter, someone who spends his time eating potato chips all night."

He nodded. "I did not say that I eat potato chips for dinner every night." They both laughed and listened to the music.

When the song finished, he continued their conversation. "Did you enjoy living in the East Village while you were in school? It is very artsy, is it not?"

"I know, it's sort of a cliché, right? Art major living in the Village. But when I first came to New York, I thought that Greenwich Village was *the* place to live. It was all I ever thought about New York. You know, struggling artists and musicians sitting around in coffee shops, smoking cigarettes and talking about the gallery show of some up and coming artist, or going to a hole-in-the-wall club to listen to a new band. It's a pretty funky place. I really liked it."

"So it was everything you thought it would be?"

"Probably not, but in hindsight that's not such a bad thing. It turned out to be a lot better than I imagined," continued Mackenzie as she finished her drink. "There are definitely a lot of artsy people, but mostly it's just interesting people who aren't necessarily artsy, or Bohemians or anything that out of the norm. Most of them are just cool. They aren't stuffy and they're very open-minded and intelligent. They like art, but they're not caught up in the latest show or the 'it' artist of the moment. I've met some of the most interesting people in my life just hanging out on the outside patio of a tiny little restaurant, sipping a glass of white wine on a hot summer day and just watching people go by."

"Sounds like you found exactly what you were looking for. Would you care for another drink?"

"I'd love one. This was the best Cosmo I ever had, seriously."

"Tommy Rowles has been the bartender here for almost fifty years and is pretty famous for his cocktails. Are you the adventurous type?" he asked playfully.

"Well, that depends. I once had a hot chili infused martini and I thought I would die. So I guess you could say that I'm cautiously adventurous," she said, laughing.

"Cautiously adventurous. A pretty good approach to life in general, really."

Anthony made eye contact with Kevin, who was near the bar and came right over to the table.

"Yes, Mr. Bataglia. Can I get you and your guest something?"

"Kevin, my friend, Mackenzie, here is cautiously adventurous. She enjoyed the pomegranate Cosmo and would like to branch out and put herself in Tommy's hands. I myself will have another Lagavulin."

Kevin picked up their empty glasses and smiled at Mackenzie.

"Miss, I am glad that at least one of you is cautiously adventurous," he said leaning closer to Mackenzie. "We have to stock extra bottles of Lagavulin because Mr. Bataglia here never ventures beyond its cozy confines. Gracious and generous, yes. Adventurous, no."

"When you have tasted perfection, Kevin, everything else is a mere imitation," laughed Anthony.

"Well said, Mr. Bataglia," Kevin added a playful bow. "Miss, I will be back with something that I think you will love." With that, Kevin walked towards the bar with their empty glasses.

"Wow, you really do come here a lot, don't you?"

"We all have our weaknesses," said Anthony.

Chris Gillespie started into their version of Dave Brubeck's classic,

"Take Five."

"You said you come here by yourself a lot. Do you always come here alone?" Mackenzie asked, not sure if she wanted to hear the answer. What if this was his place to bring all his dates? She was probably one in a long string of women that he brought here. *He's a wealthy, talented, handsome European man in his thirties with an apartment on Central Park West. Wouldn't be too hard for him to find a date, oh, maybe anytime he wanted,* thought Mackenzie.

"Sad to say, but yes, I usually come here by myself. I find it to be very relaxing."

Good answer! thought Mackenzie. If he was lying, he was at least pretty good at it, which raised just as many concerns as it alleviated. But she didn't think he was lying, at least not about this. She felt that he did probably spend a great deal of time alone. He certainly wasn't the most outgoing person she had ever met. At the Cloisters he pretty much kept to himself and focused on his work. That was really one of the things that she found most attractive about him. She tried to remind herself of why she was here. It was hard. Even though the evidence seemed to be screaming out that he was a forger, perhaps involved in an international fine arts scam of some type, he was still very charming. Was his charm part of his way of throwing her off his trail, of disarming her? If it was, she had to admit that it was working. She tried to remember what her father had told her many times. Intelligent sociopaths, like John Gotti, are by far the most dangerous individuals in the world. They are charming, charismatic, and know exactly which buttons to push. It's hard not to be captivated by them.

"How long have you lived in New York?" asked Mackenzie. "Dr. Davidson said that you were here on loan from the Ufizzi for several years."

"Yes, my initial term is only for four years, but I have some flexibility should I want to stay longer. I have been here for a little less than three years now."

"You seem to have settled in well." According to her father, the apartment he lived in was purchased in 1929. She wondered if he himself had only lived there for a few years or if that was just part of the story. Maybe the *real* Anthony Bataglia had lived there for a much longer period of time but this person, whoever he was, had only recently assumed Anthony's identity.

"You speak English flawlessly. You must have learned to speak when you were in Italy."

"Yes, I picked up English at an early age," he agreed. "In Europe it is important to speak multiple languages, and English is the second language for most people."

"I also noticed that you don't use contractions. Is that on purpose?" She had always found that strange, but had grown accustomed to his unusual way of speaking.

Anthony smiled. "I had a very strict teacher when I was learning English who would not let us use contractions. She felt that it was too informal and made people sound uneducated. She was British and did not look favorably on how her native tongue was being bastardized. It was probably her own personal crusade to save the queen's tongue." He took a sip from his glass. "Old habits die hard. Whenever I try to use a contraction, it seems very awkward for me. I guess I stopped noticing years ago. Do you find it odd?"

She finished munching a potato chip and took a sip of water. "No, I didn't mean it that way at all. It's unusual, but I wouldn't say that it's odd. I think there is an old-world elegance to it. I've just never heard anyone speak so eloquently without using contractions. I wouldn't make it five minutes if you paid me a hundred dollars."

Kevin returned to their table with their drinks. He set Mackenzie's drink in front of her. It was light pink with sparkling bubbles.

"Miss, Tommy sends over a Passion Royale for you to consider. It uses a passion fruit infused vodka, lime juice, and champagne."

He set Anthony's scotch in front of him.

"Mr. Bataglia, Tommy sends over his regards. He says that this is a newly opened bottle for you to consider," smiled Kevin.

Mackenzie took a sip and let the liquid fill her mouth and then gently roll down her throat. It was mildly sweet with a hint of lime. The champagne made it bubble and tickle as it went down.

"This is wonderful! Please tell Tommy that I am not disappointed," Mackenzie said holding up her glass.

"Wonderful," said Kevin as he set down a new bowl of nuts and potato chips, "I will pass that along to Mr. Rowles."

"How do you like New York compared to Florence? I'm sure they are quite different."

Anthony took a slow sip of his scotch.

"New York is much better designed for handling millions of people. There are a lot of people, but there is also a lot of space for them to spread out."

"What about the winters? Florence doesn't get as cold as New York, does it?"

"No, I have to admit that the first winter I was here was a bit rough. I do not remember feeling that biting cold wind in all my life. But it makes the inside of a warm house or bar that much more inviting."

"I've always lived in the Northeast, so those types of winters are all that I really know. I definitely enjoy the change of seasons, and Christmas time in New York is hard to beat," said Mackenzie as she snuggled back in the leather couch and held her drink with both hands.

They both turned and listened while Chris made his effortless progression from jazz to Bach and back to jazz in finishing Brubeck's classic.

After the three hour session finished and they had worked their way through several trays of potato chips and a few more drinks, Mackenzie steeled her nerves and decided now was as good a time as ever.

"Anthony," she said with as much confidence as she could muster, trying to talk above the flutter of butterflies she felt in her stomach. "I hope you won't find this too forward or inappropriate in any way, but I would love to see your apartment. I've never been inside any buildings on Central Park West, let alone an apartment. Does yours have a view of the park?" *What a dumb question!* She took a sip of water, trying to keep her hand from trembling.

Anthony sat back in the cushioned seat and thought. Then he smiled and said, "Yes, why not. Tomorrow is a day off, and it is still quite early, so it would be my pleasure." He stood up and offered her a hand to stand up as well, which she gladly took.

Okay, she thought, as they walked out the door, *so far so good. Now, let's see if I can pull this off.*

❧ Chapter 27 ❧

As Anthony mentioned, it was about a twenty-minute walk from The Carlyle to his apartment building. They carried on superficial chitchat on the way. Mackenzie was too nervous to come up with anything remotely intelligent or interesting to say. She had a tendency to just chatter incessantly when she was nervous, so she forced herself to be quiet. The doorman was there to greet them.

"Beautiful evening, Mr. Bataglia." He opened the doors for them, nodding to Mackenzie as well.

"Yes, indeed it is Jack. Thank God it has cooled down a bit. Thank you." They walked through the plush hallway to the elevators. They rode up to the twentieth floor and arrived at the door of his apartment. "This is the place," he said punching in the combination on the electronic keypad. "I did not know that I would have company, so I cannot guarantee that the apartment is in any shape for entertaining." He pushed open the door and they made their way inside.

He took off his shoes and calmly gestured to her. "The New York winters are terrible on my rugs, so I make it a habit to never wear shoes inside, even in summer. I hope you do not mind."

"Not at all. Makes a lot of sense. I did the same thing in my apartment in college. My dad says the dirt builds character in the carpet so I got out of the habit of taking them off when I moved back in."

Stunning! That was the first word that came to her head as she entered the apartment. It was not only spotless but everything, the wall sconces, the wood paneling, the floor and the carpets, were immaculate. If someone had told her to design the perfect Central Park apartment she couldn't have done better than this, and would have been hard pressed to even come close.

Would you like a glass of wine, or perhaps something a bit stronger?"

he asked as he led her down the hallway. He paused in front of an in-wall Eurocave wine refrigerator with a sleek black glass front. The refrigerator sat beside a small recessed bar.

"A glass of wine would be great." *Keep a clear head. You can't afford to get drunk while you're in his apartment. You're here for a reason.* She could almost hear her father talking to her, telling her to stay focused on the task at hand.

"I'm thinking that an Argentinean Malbec would be nice." He pulled a bottle from the refrigerator and expertly opened it with the ease of a sommelier.

"I don't think I've ever had Malbec before," she replied, watching him work. She was happy to see that the wine was from a previously unopened bottle. *At least I won't be drugged on my first glass.* "But as you have already discerned, I'm open minded," she added.

"Yes, I remember. Cautiously adventurous." He poured them each a large, crystal glass. "Cheers. I hope you like it."

She took a sip. It was round and rich and very flavorful.

"Mm, this is nice, thank you."

"You are very welcome. It is so much nicer not to have to drink alone." He led them deeper into the apartment. "Come, let me show you around a bit."

They made their way into an enormous room with floor-to-ceiling windows that looked out on Central Park and the lights of 51st street. What really caught her eye, however, was not the view, but the paintings on the wall. The three walls that were not filled with windows were covered with some of the most amazing paintings imaginable. It was like walking into a gallery room at the Met, or better yet, the Uffizi. She couldn't speak. She consciously focused on not dropping her wine glass, which she grabbed with two hands because both of them were trembling. She realized that she must have been standing there with her mouth wide open, but there was nothing she could do about it.

There were paintings that she knew must have been from Italy in the fourteenth through sixteenth centuries. The styles were unmistakable. But she wasn't familiar with any of them. She would have likely placed some of them as Giottos, Gaddis, Bellinis, Giorgiones, some Daddis, a Tintoretto, at least two Veronese, and even a Lippi. There were also clearly some that looked to be the work of Raphael, although again, she wasn't familiar with these particular works. She counted fourteen paintings across the three walls. All of them were masterpieces and likely to be worth a fortune. If they were really originals of the artists she thought, then this collection would be worth tens of millions. This confirmed what her father told her about the di Bernardi Foundation's holdings. She wasn't, however, sure what this meant about Anthony. If he was a forger or a thief, or whatever he was, why had he agreed to take her to his apartment with all of these masterpieces staring out so brazenly from the walls? He obviously wasn't afraid of her seeing all of this. But why?

She wasn't sure how long she had been staring, spinning in a small circle trying not to pass out.

"These paintings are amazing!" she finally exclaimed. "This is an incredible private collection."

"Thank you," responded Anthony calmly as he sipped his wine. "As you know, I have an affinity for art, and these are some of my favorites. Please, have a seat and I'll put on some music."

She needed to take a break of some type. There were too many emotions swirling in her head right now to even attempt conversation. She needed time to regroup.

"Do you mind if I use your restroom?"

"Of course not," he said while he was fiddling with a flat paneled music system in the wall. "Just down that hallway, first door on your right."

"Thanks, be right back." She took her purse and made her way down the hallway. She felt her breath coming back to her. Some light jazz came on through speakers that were flush mounted in the ceiling, probably throughout the entire apartment, she thought. The bathroom door was open and she was about to step in when she saw that there was another room just down from the bathroom on the other side of the hallway with its door slightly ajar. She silently crept her way down the hallway hoping that he couldn't see her from the living room.

Upon reaching the door, she cautiously stuck her head inside and looked around. The lights of the room were out, but there was still enough light from the city to see inside. It was an art studio, a large one. There was a painting sitting on an easel that clearly looked like a Vermeer, but only partially painted. Her heart was racing. She almost fainted as she looked around. All four walls of this room were covered in what looked to be priceless artwork. Beyond that there were stacks of paintings, at least ten-deep against two of the walls. She noticed that one of the paintings in the stack was the exact same Vermeer that was sitting on the easel, except this one was finished. It was spectacular. She would swear that it was an original. *There's no doubt,* she thought. *He's a forger!*

For the second time in less than five minutes, she couldn't breathe. She tried to calm herself. Somehow she made her way to the bathroom, ran some cold water in the sink and splashed it onto her face. She looked at herself in the mirror and tried to get her composure back. *I've got to get out of here, now!* She flushed the toilet without ever using it, reached into her purse, and grabbed hold of the small pepper spray canister she carried with her. One thing about having a cop for a father was that you didn't get caught off guard very often. She took a deep breath and made her way back down the hallway and into the living room.

Anthony was sitting on the large tan leather couch sipping his wine and looking out over the park. He smiled at her when she appeared.

"It is not much, but I found a little soppressata and some aged Parmegiano for us to nibble on, just in case the potato chips and nuts were not enough." He motioned to a hand painted ceramic tray on the living room table.

"Anthony, I'm terribly sorry, but I have to leave." She tried not to sound panicked but didn't slow down as she made her way back to the entrance.

He stood up from the couch, surprised.

"Is everything all right?"

She tried to remain calm. "Yes, I feel weak-headed. I may have caught something. I need to get home." She grabbed her shoes and started to put them on.

Anthony caught up to her and put a hand on her shoulder as she bent down to put on her shoes. She stiffened, holding onto the small can in the palm of her right hand, ready to strike if necessary.

"Are you sure you would not prefer to lie down on the couch for a few minutes? I can get you some water." He sounded genuinely concerned.

"No, I'll be all right." She stood and looked at him, forcing a smile. "I probably had too much to drink and I think I'm coming down with a cold. I'll be fine. I just need to get home."

"Okay, let me walk you down," he said reaching for his shoes.

"No, I don't want to trouble you. I feel terrible for ruining your evening."

"You did not ruin my evening at all. I had a wonderful time. I just feel bad that you are not feeling better. At least let me call down and have Jack get you a cab."

She opened the door and was already halfway-out when she looked back.

"Thank you. That would be great." She paused. "Anthony, thank you for inviting me tonight, I enjoyed it." She made her way into the hallway and headed to the elevator.

"Me too," he waved and watched her until the doors closed.

Once in the elevator, she finally felt that she could take a deep breath. Her mind was rushing. Had she really seen what she thought she saw? Those were clearly reproductions of famous paintings, and most of them were excellent. She was confused and sad at the same time. She had feelings for Anthony, feelings that went beyond a casual relationship, and she sensed that he had feelings for her as well. All of that was now out of the question.

Jack greeted her at the door, where there was already a taxi waiting. He opened the car door for her, smiled and wished her a nice evening. She told the taxi driver her address and then sank back into her seat. In spite of herself, she started to cry.

❧ Chapter 28 ❧

Daddi, along with Giotto, two of his apprentices, and several guards had spent the previous four days traveling on muddy roads, and sleeping in strange beds, on their way to Assisi. The morning air in Assisi was warm and fresh. Daddi woke early and was excited to finally see the object of their quest, Giotto's famous frescoes of the life of Saint Francis. After a generous breakfast he, along with Giotto and the other artists, Gaddi, Buonarroti, and Orcagna, made their way to the upper basilica of San Francesco. It was truly a spectacular building that was even more impressive up close than it was from a distance. The outside was made with pinkish white stones that had been quarried from Monte Subasio.

With Giotto as their guide, the group filed into the upper portion of the church, which, according to Giotto, was the most complete and spectacular of the two parts of the basilica. Daddi immediately felt a sense of familiarity surround him upon entering the church as the sweet, pungent smell of frankincense perfumed the air around him. Compared with the brightness of the early morning, it was darker and cooler in the church. It took a minute for his eyes to adjust to the dramatic change. He closed them and took in the atmosphere of the great open space.

A single, long nave with a beautifully ornate vaulted ceiling ran through the upper basilica. Filtered light entered through tall stained glass windows along both sides of the nave. With the smoke from the candles and the lingering remnants of the incense used in the early morning mass, the sun's light came through in long, distinct rays of muted color. It reminded him of watching the sun peek through dense clouds over the Arno River in Florence just before sunset. He could almost count the individual rays of silver and yellow light.

The nave of the upper basilica was long and spacious. The vaulted ceilings were bordered with patterns of crosses and leaves. Eight vaulted bays ran the length of the nave, four on each side. Each bay was divided into an upper and lower section. The upper portion of each bay contained a stained glass window surrounded on each side by two frescoes depicting a total of thirty-two scenes from the Old and New Testament. Daddi and the rest of the group ambled slowly with heads raised, taking in each of the different scenes.

Giotto suggested that they make a complete pass of the entire upper basilica before focusing in on any one area so as to get a feel for how the paintings fit into the whole. That made a lot of sense, from Daddi's perspective. Many of the older churches in Florence were comparatively sparse in their interiors with only a handful of focal paintings. Here he saw that the entirety of the interior was itself a work of art.

After they made one complete walkthrough, which took the better part of an hour, they returned to the front and focused on the lower portion of each bay. Below the richly decorated dado that separated the upper and lower portions of the bay were three frescoes, side-by-side, which depicted the life of Saint Francis of Assisi. These frescoes, twenty-eight in total, including two in the east galleries beside the entrance and two on the entrance wall, had been painted by Giotto himself between fifteen and twenty years ago.

For Daddi, the frescoes themselves were stunning. They were clear, simple depictions of the Saint in vivid colors, without additional gilding or iconographic influence that characterized most paintings from that time period. The faces of the people in the scenes were detailed and lifelike. Unlike most of the works that had come before, it these were three-dimensional individuals talking, watching the Saint, engaged in their daily activities. Even the scenery in the background, the buildings, churches and balconies appeared true to life and appropriately proportioned.

Daddi knew how proud Giotto was of these works because he often talked of them. He could see the fatherly pride that shone in Giotto's eyes as he looked upon these works, which had occupied a good part of his early life as a painter. He had to grudgingly admit that Giotto was a better artist than he. Even paintings that Giotto had made twenty years earlier looked more realistic and lifelike than Daddi's most recent works painted the previous month. He was more impressed than he was envious, but nonetheless, his slow burning competitive pilot light never really went out.

Daddi looked around at the assembled group. All of them had painted and studied with Giotto. He had influenced and guided each and every one of them. Still, it was hard not to be taken aback by the sheer beauty, detail, and realism of these scenes. Without knowing anything about the Saint, one was able to understand his life and truly feel what he was like and why he was canonized so quickly after his death. These were not ornate depictions of an otherworldly being that was too far from this world to touch. This was the life of a man who had given up his wealth and life to serve God, his fellow man and the animals around him. Daddi could see the mixed look of admiration, awe and frustration in each of their eyes. They all knew they were in the presence of a greatness that was beyond their reach.

"How was it that you were able to paint such masterful frescoes almost twenty years ago?" asked Daddi. Daddi knew that Giotto relished his role as unquestioned master. But he also knew that he was not shy in sharing his approach, his technique and his knowledge with any who were interested.

As Daddi expected, Giotto obliged without hesitation.

"You have to understand that there were many artists working in the basilica at that time. I knew some of them but many were from as far away as Rome as well as other parts of Tuscany. I was not sure myself how best to make these paintings. I contemplated using mosaics or painting onto wood panels and affixing them to the walls. But there was an artist here at the time named Pietro Cavallini who was truly revolutionary in his use of this new technique. He had painted other frescoes in the convent of Santa Cecilia and the church of Santa Maria in Rome around 1290. I was, of course, much younger at the time and captivated by his description of this approach. He had already finished a fresco on the life of Isaac and was working on another when I first met him. Let's take a look at them." Giotto led the group over to the two frescoes, *Isaac Blesses Jacob* and *Esau in Front of Isaac*, in the middle register of the third bay.

"You can see that these are the works of a true master and definitely influenced me in many ways. There was more realism to them than anything I had painted up until that time. Cavallini was a gracious teacher and showed me how to utilize the fresco technique that I had never seen before. Once I watched him and he explained the logic of the process, it seemed so straight-forward. He told me that he actually came upon the technique out of neces-sity. He had been commissioned with a number of projects in Rome, where he had planned on using traditional mosaics. However, he did not have the time to complete all of his projects using that technique and experimented with just painting on the fresh plaster versus applying the tiles. He said that he was able to cut almost half the time and that he liked the result even bet-ter than what he would have been able to achieve with a mosaic. I think you would all agree that the fresco approach is superior."

Daddi and the others voiced their agreement en masse. There was really no comparison between the two approaches. Most of the younger men had actually never even completed a mosaic because that approach was largely being overtaken by the faster and less expensive fresco technique. Daddi had completed a number of mosaics, but doubted that he would ever do one again now that this technique was available.

Giotto continued, happy to be holding court for his loyal subjects. "I spent almost six years working on these frescoes. At the time they were by far my greatest accomplishment, both personally and professionally. I learned more about painting and about myself, what I was capable of achieving as well as my limitations, than in any other works that I have done before or since. I also learned how to delegate to my assistants," Giotto said, laughing.

"Of course my brush touched every one of the frescoes, and the design concept and color scheme were all mine. But when all is said and done, by the time these were finished, I had a team of six competent artists working with me and I was quite adept at teaching others how to follow my lead and do the actual painting. You gentlemen, of all people, should know my skills in delegating. I bet that I actually only painted about thirty percent of these." He looked around with a conspiratorial smirk. "But do not tell anyone." The group laughed, albeit somewhat uncomfortably, with Giotto.

Daddi thought that no one remembered the names of the other six art-ists who painted almost all of these beautiful frescoes. He also knew that Giotto, while gracious in sharing his knowledge and technique, wasn't as generous in sharing his fame. Daddi never heard Giotto mention the names of those six artists and imagined that he never would. It was Giotto and

Giotto alone who took credit and received the adulation, and the lion's share of the wealth. These were Giotto's frescoes, after all.

He wondered what Gaddi and the others thought about their master. How much of Giotto's works had they already painted for him, or would in the future? Like it or not, he couldn't deny that Giotto knew what he was doing. In fact, there was a certain genius to it, which up until this point Daddi had failed to see. Giotto certainly had no problem taking credit and reaping the spoils of his success, whether it was fully earned or not. There was obviously a reason why Giotto was one of the most successful and prolific painters in all of Italy. It was becoming much clearer to Daddi. Being a true artist was one thing. Being a famous and wealthy artist was something entirely different. He had long tried to master the former. He vowed then and there to pursue the latter with abandon.

Chapter 29

Whether Mackenzie liked it or not, most mornings started early. Octavius didn't sleep well in the summer and usually woke Mackenzie up at 5:30 a.m. because he was hungry or hot or both. Either way, he had developed a skill for efficiently knocking things off her nightstand one by one until she got up. This morning was no different, although today especially was one in which Mackenzie dreaded the idea of getting out of bed. She wadded up a pair of socks lying by the bed and threw it at Octavius. That gained her about five minutes of respite. As she pulled the covers over her head, trying to squeeze out a few more minutes of rest, he returned and began anew his dismantling of her alarm clock, books, earrings, and reading lamp.

Cats are one of man's greatest companions, smart, loving and playful, thought Mackenzie. But they live on their own schedules and have their own agendas. She had learned through experience that when they want to get up and eat, it's best to just give in and feed them. Otherwise they will taunt you for your stubbornness or for holding onto the misguided illusion that you can impose discipline on their mercurial ways. She realized that her efforts at escaping the day were in vain. Whether she wanted to or not, she had to get out of bed, if for no other reason than to feed the cat.

Mackenzie had returned to her house the previous night, clearly shaken by what she had seen at Anthony's apartment. She was confused, frightened, angry, and, more than anything, hurt. How could he have led her on? She had trusted him, looked up to him, admired him, and even found herself growing increasingly attracted to him. She felt like a fool who had just come to the realization that she had been played by a world-class con man. Her father had been up when she came home, but she hadn't wanted to talk about it with him or anyone at that moment. She went to bed and tried not to cry herself to sleep. She had not been entirely successful.

As she headed downstairs, her father was already up, reading the paper on the front porch. When the weather was good, he spent a good deal of time sitting on the two-seat glider or one of the rocking chairs. She'd asked him why he hadn't enclosed the porch like some of their neighbors in order to enjoy it during the winter as well. "Haven't gotten around to it yet," was his usual reply.

After she fed Octavius the canned food delicacy that he had so persistently demanded, she walked out on the porch with a cup of coffee, sat down on the glider, and began to gently rock on its smooth track back and forth. For some reason Octavius didn't pester her father about food, at least when Mackenzie was home. He saved his personal brand of torture for her, which, in a strange way, she found charming.

"Hi, Dad. You're up early."

"Yep," he said, his nose stuck in the paper, which he held open with both hands. "Old habits are hard to break, I guess." Without looking up, he asked her, "You feeling better this morning? You were pretty shaken up last night."

She held her coffee mug in both hands and blew on it to cool the black coffee slightly.

"Yeah, I feel better than I did last night, but I don't feel great one way or the other."

Without looking away from the paper he asked, "Want to talk about it or do you want to wait a bit?"

"Let me finish this coffee first and then I'll tell you what I found."

He folded the paper and set it down on the side of his rocker. "Sounds good to me," he said, standing up. "I'm going to get another cup myself anyway."

After he returned from the kitchen with a fresh cup of coffee and the rest of the pot, he refilled Mackenzie's cup and then set the half filled carafe down on the small side table.

He sat quietly and listened as she explained her evening with Anthony, from their time at Bemelmans bar to his apartment and what she had found in his studio. He listened attentively without interrupting. She sat with her feet up on the glider's cushion and her arms wrapped around her knees.

When she finished, her cheeks were flushed and her eyes heavy with tears that she tried desperately to hold back.

"I feel like such an idiot for trusting him as long as I did. No matter what you told me, I didn't want it to be true. Despite what we found, deep down I just couldn't let myself believe that Anthony, or whoever he is, was doing anything wrong," she said, holding her knees even tighter. It was hard for her to even voice these words without tears welling in her eyes.

Her father waited patiently as she slowly rocked back and forth. Finally he broke the silence.

"I know how you feel. I've been in the same position many times myself." He poured her another cup of coffee and then poured himself one as well. "I don't want you to stop trusting people, Mackenzie. It's something that happens to us cops over time and it's a terrible way to go through life, whether it's justified or not. Most people are who they say they are, and sometimes when they're not, it's for no other reason than they're trying to hide something that they don't want to know about themselves. The other thing to know is that if you're dealing with a true master criminal or psychopath or whatever you want to call them, you probably have no chance anyway. They'll fool everyone, even the cops. They're the toughest ones to catch, but if you're lucky they eventually screw up and that's when you get 'em." He paused before continuing. "I'm not sure what Anthony Bataglia's gig is, but it's clear that there's something more than what appears on the surface. He's not just some restorer from Italy that happens to work at the Cloisters. There's a lot more to it than that."

He reached to his side and pulled up a plastic Ziploc bag that was lying underneath his folded newspaper. He held it up and then passed it over to her.

"Found this little ditty stuck in the front porch this morning."

She grabbed the plastic bag in the top corner with her thumb and index finger, holding it out in front of her. In the bag was a short dagger with a six-inch stainless steel blade and a black wooden handle. There was also a rectangular index card, impaled halfway up the shaft of the blade. On the card in bright red lettering were the words, "LEAVE IT ALONE!"

She looked at it for a minute, not sure what to say, and then handed it back to her father.

"Jesus, Dad, that's a pretty scary message! Do you think it came from Anthony?"

"Well, I'm not sure," replied her father, setting the bag on the side table. "My guess is that it's not from Mayor Bloomberg. Whether it's from Anthony or not, it's definitely from someone telling us that they don't like us poking around in their business. It's also a pretty real threat because they are showing us that they know where we live and that they can make it to our front doorstep without us knowing. I'm going to send it down to get some prints off it, but my guess is that whoever did this is smart enough not to leave any. But you never know. Always good to check."

She couldn't believe that Anthony would resort to this type of threat. Then again, she wasn't sure about anything anymore, at least as it related to the man known as Anthony Bataglia.

"I don't know about you, but getting daggers stuck in my front porch tends to make me hungry," said her father trying to break the tension. "I'm going to brew another pot and then cook us up a decent breakfast. We can talk about our next steps after that."

Chapter 30

On Saturday evening, Mackenzie called Anthony and asked if he would be able to meet her for breakfast at a small diner on 55th. When he asked what it was about, she told him that she couldn't tell him over the phone but that she wanted to talk with him before Monday. After a long discussion with her father over the pros and cons of various approaches, Mackenzie finally insisted that she would meet him one-on-one and tell him what she had found. In fact, she would show him what she and her father had found, and ask him to explain himself. Though her father wanted to question Anthony with her, he had acquiesced at the end. All the same, he'd insisted that they meet in a public place and that he would also be there, just not at the same table. If Anthony was indeed involved in an international forgery, art fraud and money laundering organization, then he may very well be dangerous, or at the very least his partners would be. The dagger with the blood red message helped him win his argument. He would just be there for insurance.

Mackenzie was sitting in a booth against the wall with a fresh cup of black coffee on the table when Anthony walked in the door, two minutes before their agreed upon meeting time of 8 a.m. *He's punctual, you have to give him that,* she thought. Her father was sitting in one of the round, swivel seats with the red vinyl covers that had been the hallmark of diners since the 1920s. Like many of his fellow breakfast-goers, he read the newspaper and drank coffee.

Anthony's face lit up when he saw her and came to the table. "Good morning Mackenzie, I was glad you called because you certainly left in such a hurry the other night. I was hoping that it was not something I said." He paused and then looked at the seat across from her. "May I?"

"Of course," she forced herself to smile. "I was the one who invited you here. Thanks for coming on such short notice."

A waitress passed with a pot of coffee and asked if Anthony wanted a cup, which he did.

"I'm sorry I left so suddenly the other night," she hesitated. "I really enjoyed listening to music at the bar. But," she paused trying to decide what to say, "I, ah, I guess I became very disoriented all of a sudden."

Anthony looked at her. "I hope everything is fine now."

"Better, yes, but I don't know if everything is fine." *This is awkward*, she thought. There's no use playing around at this point. She and her father had agreed that the best approach would be to overwhelm him with the evidence they had and then let him respond. They would learn a lot from his response.

"Before we order breakfast, there are some things I need to share with you. I'd like you to listen to all that I have to say before you respond. It will be easier that way. After that you can ask as many questions as you like, or just tell me to go to hell and walk out. It's up to you."

"Wow," responded Anthony, sitting back in the booth, folding his hands under his chin, as if in silent prayer. "You certainly know how to start off a breakfast meeting with a bang." He smiled. "I promise not to interrupt, that is until you tell me that it is all right to do so."

She started by explaining what they had found about the di Bernardi Foundation, that it had assets of close to a billion dollars, most of which was in artwork and that Anthony was the sole benefactor. She explained that his signature and that of Daddi, Lippi and Berlinghieri were found to be close enough under forensic analysis to be considered evidence in court, and that, in all likelihood, they had been signed by the same person. She mentioned how she found it strange that he used the exact same palette of colors no matter which artist he was working on. She told him that they had talked with the director at the Ufizzi and he told them that Anthony Bataglia had started working as a restorer thirty-six years ago and that his best estimate was that he should be well into his sixties by now. She said that she wasn't sure what was going on with the women with the elongated finger but she was sure there was something that tied it all together and connected Anthony to those paintings. Finally, she told him why she had left his apartment so quickly the other night. That she had seen the multiple copies of the various artists in his studio. She spoke for almost fifteen minutes with little more than a pause to sip her coffee. When she was done, she laid her hands flat on the table and looked at him.

"That's what we've found. Do you have any questions?"

Anthony had remained relatively impassive during her presentation of the evidence. He had nodded at times, not necessarily in agreement, but in acknowledgement that he understood what she was saying. He rubbed his chin with the palm of his hand with a thoughtful expression as he assimilated all that she had said.

"I think that I only have one question at this point. When you say 'we,' who are you referring to?"

"I mentioned to you that my father was a lead detective and had recently retired. He's been helping me work through all of this, with some support from friends on the police force."

"I see. That makes sense," he nodded. "I am not sure if I have any questions. You have pieced together an amazing amount of information. I applaud your diligence and intuition. What does it all mean?" He looked at her inquisitively.

She had hoped that he would just admit to it, own up like they did on detective shows like *Murder She Wrote* when the suspect knows they've been caught. It was wishful thinking, she knew.

"Unfortunately, I'm left with the conclusion that you are someone who has taken the name of a respected art restorer named Anthony Bataglia, that you are working with an international art ring that is defrauding museums around the world out of millions of dollars each year, and ultimately, that you are a forger." There, she said it, as much as it pained her. "Finally," she added, "I believe that you know that we've been getting close to the truth and that you or someone from your organization tried to scare us yesterday morning with a not so subtle warning."

"Oh my," exclaimed Anthony with surprise. "I have no idea what you are referring to in terms of a warning. I certainly would never threaten anyone, especially you. But with regard to the other things you have mentioned, I can understand why you would come to that conclusion. It is very reasonable and logical given the information that you have presented. If I was in your shoes, I would think the same thing." He paused, clasping his hands in front of his face, and gently bouncing his fists against his lips while he thought.

"There is no easy answer to what you have presented. In fact, the truth is even more convoluted and disturbing than the conclusion you have so eloquently arrived at."

"If you're not a forger, then how do you explain all of this?" asked Mackenzie, clearly exasperated.

"I am not ready to explain anything at this point. But I can assure you that I am not a forger, nor am I working with any international art forgery ring. On that, I give you my word," he said in earnest.

"I'd like to believe you, but words are cheap and the facts are what they are. You're going to have to do more than that to convince me." Her anger at being deceived by him in the first place was coming to the surface.

Anthony thought for a moment without responding and then replied calmly, "I am not sure how I can completely prove to you that I am not a forger. But what we *can* do is authenticate the paintings that we have restored so far, as well as some that I have in my personal collection. You could use Ariadne for the job. I will personally pay for her authentication fee as long as you coordinate it. I will have no contact or interaction with her at all and everything she shares will go directly to you. That way you can at least feel comfortable that the paintings we have been working on are originals. I am not sure if I can come up with a better solution. Does that work for you?"

Mackenzie now was the one forced to think. She sat for a minute mulling over his solution. It seemed quite reasonable. It wouldn't completely exonerate him, but it would go a long way. She wished she could consult her father, but at the moment that wasn't possible. All the same, she didn't have to give him an answer right now. She could buy herself some time and run the proposal past her father.

"It sounds like a good approach. Give me tonight to think about it and then I'll let you know my thoughts tomorrow at work." *There*, she thought, *the best of both worlds*. Like her father said, if Anthony really was a master criminal, he would be one step ahead of her anyway. Putting both of their heads together should at least reduce the risk of getting taken. That said, this step still wouldn't explain the roomful of paintings she had found at his house that were clearly reproductions of original masterworks, nor would it provide an answer to the women with the long pinkie finger or the similarities in the signature. She would cover those issues once the authentication results came back.

Anthony nodded. "That sounds fair to me." He rubbed his hands together. "Now, if it is all right with you I would not mind ordering breakfast." He gave her a conspiratorial grin. "It would be nice to expand our eating repertoire beyond potato chips and nuts."

She couldn't help herself and had to smile. "Of course, I'm starving myself. Since I invited you, it's my treat." She decided that until the analysis came back from Ariadne she would treat him as innocent until proven otherwise. It felt better that way.

"In that case I might need to get an extra order of bacon," laughed Anthony.

They made idle conversation for the next thirty minutes, trying to avoid discussing any of the things that she had brought up earlier. It was strained but cordial. It was hard for her not to like him, even if he might be a forger. *After all*, she thought, *Danny Ocean was a very likable thief, especially when George Clooney was playing the role.*

❧ Chapter 31 ❧

After going over Anthony's proposal with her father, Mackenzie told Anthony that she thought that it was a legitimate way of at least determining whether the paintings they had worked on together were forgeries or not. Anthony also agreed to supply four paintings from his personal collection, chosen by him, to be authenticated. He took responsibility and covered the cost of transporting the artwork to the Cloisters, as well as all the fees for Ariadne's services, which, when all was said and done would be upwards of $50,000.

Anthony also handled the communication with Simon, whom he felt had a right to know that they would be using the Cloister's facilities, as well as Ariadne's time, albeit outside of her normal working hours, to authenticate some paintings that he had, as well as to ensure that there were no doubts about the Daddis, Berlinghieris, and Lippis in their collection. Simon offered to cover the fees for the paintings in the Cloister's collection, but Anthony insisted that it was more for his own peace of mind than about any serious concerns about the paintings' authenticity.

While Simon likely found the request odd, he respected Anthony enough to let it go through without any complications. He did insist, however, that the Cloisters would receive an official copy of any authentication for the paintings in their collection conducted by Ariadne, which Anthony agreed to without hesitation. He also told Simon that he would be receiving a FedEx envelope from him in the next day or so. He asked Simon not to open it but to simply hold onto it until the authentication was completed. Once the authentication was complete he asked him to personally deliver the envelope to Mackenzie. Simon agreed to this as well, no matter how odd it must have seemed. Simon had dealt with artists all his life and knew that they were indeed a peculiar breed.

The entire authentication process took almost a full month. Following Anthony's recommendation, Mackenzie asked Ariadne not to share any of her findings until all of them were completed. She also asked for formal documentation of the results for all of the paintings.

Finally, on a day in late September while Mackenzie was working at her station, reviewing documents for a restoration she was going to work on with the Japanese restorer, Takeshi Inada, Ariadne tapped her on the shoulder. Mackenzie turned and saw Ariadne standing there with a thick, three-ring binder in her hand. While she had been anxious to see the results, the weeks had passed and Mackenzie had begun focusing more of her attention on her own work. She hadn't forgotten about the project, but it was not on the top of her mind anymore. She hadn't worked with Anthony on any restorations during the interim and, though the two had exchanged polite greetings, they had not spent any significant amount of time together since Ariadne had started. Now, her excitement and, frankly, her anxiety returned. What if all of the paintings were forgeries? Not only would it mean that the past two years she had spent at the Cloisters would have largely been a complete waste of time, but it would also mean that the man she had trusted and harbored legitimate feelings for was a criminal. In some ways, it was easier not to know the results. But here she was, ready to be faced with the hard, cold facts.

"Hi Mackenzie, I hope I'm not interrupting anything important. I thought you'd like to know that I've finished your project." Ariadne set the binder down on the worktable. "Sorry it took a bit longer than I thought, but there were quite a few paintings and I had to squeeze this in after hours. Nonetheless, it is done."

Mackenzie swiveled in her stool to face Ariadne. "There's no need for you to apologize. If anything, I should be the one apologizing because I know how busy you are. I really appreciate you doing this. I know it was a lot of work."

Ariadne nodded. "Let's hope you're just as happy when you get my bill." She motioned to the binder. "Would you like me to go over the results with you?"

"Of course, that would be great. Do you have the time?"

"Yes, I think that we can go over everything in an hour if that works for you. Then, if you have any questions, you can ask me at your leisure."

"It definitely works for me." Mackenzie pulled another stool over to the table. "If you don't mind, we can go over it right here."

"Works for me," agreed Ariadne.

Over the next hour, Ariadne went through each painting in detail. There were a total of ten paintings, six from the Cloisters collections that had been restored by Anthony and Mackenzie, and four from Anthony's private collection. Ariadne had not been informed beforehand of which paintings belonged to which collection.

Ariadne was able to authenticate and certify nine of the ten paintings, including all of the paintings that Anthony and Mackenzie had restored thus far, which included three Lippis, two Daddis and a Berlinghieri. She was also able to certify three of the four paintings from Anthony's private collection: Edgar Degas's *The Blue Dancers*, Giotto di Bondone's *Joachim's Dream*, and Paolo Veronese's *Apollo and Daphne*. There was only one of the ten paintings that she identified as a clear reproduction, Giovanni Bellini's *Portrait of Doge Leonardo Loredan*, which was originally painted in 1501. The one she had analyzed had been painted within the past five years. It was an excellent reproduction of the original, but it was painted on canvas that was less than eight years old, whereas the original had been painted on a wood panel. In addition, she dated the oil paints used to be between five to ten years old. There was no question that this one was a reproduction of an original.

At the end of the hour, Mackenzie thanked her again for her time and then sat by herself to go through the pages of the report one more time. She had mixed emotions. On the one hand, she was relieved. She wasn't sure what she would have done if the past two years had been spent restoring forgeries. She was also relieved that, at least based on this sample of paintings, there was very little evidence that Anthony was a forger. She was perplexed about the Bellini reproduction, though. Anthony must have known that it was not an original. Why had he submitted it for analysis when it appeared that he had many other originals in his collection? She was also left wondering where to go with all of the other bits of information that had puzzled her and her father. She needed to go over this report with her dad and chart a course for moving forward.

❧ Chapter 32 ❧

Anthony and Mackenzie met for lunch in the enclosed garden of the Cloisters. They sat on a stone bench surrounded by vibrant fall colors. The Japanese maple in the corner wore a stunning bright crimson robe and swayed in the crisp fall air, proudly sunning itself under the clear October sky.

Anthony sipped the sweet, creamy Earl Grey tea that he brought in his thermos and nibbled on the tuna fish sandwich he bought at Pret A Manger earlier that morning. Mackenzie sipped her coffee and ate a salad she brought from home. Earlier in the day Simon had handed Mackenzie the FedEx envelope that Anthony had sent to him a little over a month ago. She brought it with her, along with the binder with Ariadne's report. The envelope was still sealed. They exchanged light chitchat while they ate.

After finishing their lunch, Anthony asked her what Ariadne's analysis had turned up. She explained the findings as Anthony nodded, sipping his tea.

"Based on that, can we conclude that I am not a forger?" he asked her.

"Well," she paused, "I think we can conclude that these particular paintings are not forgeries. Except for the one, which is clearly a reproduction. I was confused as to why you included it as part of the four paintings you submitted. The other three are clearly originals and worth a fortune. Were you aware that the Bellini wasn't an original?"

He laughed. "Before I answer that, please open the FedEx you got from Simon and take a look inside. As you can see on the mailing label, this was sent to him from me before the authentication process began. To my knowledge it has not left his care and has not been opened until right now. That is, unless you opened it already."

"No," replied Mackenzie shaking her head. "Simon mentioned that per

156

your instructions I wasn't supposed to open it without your approval."

Not sure what she would find in the envelope, she ripped open the seal at the top and pulled out a single sheet of handsome fiber paper that one found at the finest stationary stores, which were unfortunately disappearing in the digital age. There was a single paragraph of handwritten text on the page.

Mackenzie, you will find that all of the paintings that we restored are origi-nals. You will also find that three of the four paintings from my collection, De-gas's The Blue Dancers, *Giotto's Joachim's* Dream *and Veronese's* Apollo and Daphne *are originals. Finally, the analysis will show that Bellini's* Portrait of Doge Leonardo Loredan *is not an original. In fact, it was painted about five years ago. I should know. I painted it.*

Anthony

She set the letter down on the envelope and looked up at Anthony.

"If you knew it wasn't an original, why did you pay all that money to have it analyzed?" she asked quizzically.

"Call it playful curiosity. I wanted to make sure that Ariadne's analysis was accurate. Admittedly, it was a pretty low hurdle to jump over given that it was painted on new canvas with new oil paints. But I always thought that I did a nice job on that painting and wanted to see what she would say."

"But what about all of the paintings I saw in your studio? I know that some of them are clearly reproductions because there were two that were only partially finished."

"Of course," he replied without hesitation. "I enjoy painting a great deal and I like to try my hand at painting works by some of the great masters. Some are quite challenging to me. Vermeer, in particular causes me some of my greatest consternation. But it also provides a great sense of achievement when I have painted one well." He paused, looking at the ground. "They are just hobbies, like many things in my life. They bring me peace."

Looking at him now, she saw a quiet, contemplative man who had done her no wrong, and whom she had falsely accused. "Anthony," Mackenzie started, trying to find the right words. "I'm so sorry that I accused you of being a forger. I had no right to do that. You've been so nice to me and I betrayed your kindness by accusing you." Tears welled in her eyes. "I'm sorry."

Anthony looked at the small Japanese maple for a few seconds. It had become his favorite tree in the garden. He then looked back at her.

"I accept your apology," he said quietly. "You clearly dug up a lot of peculiar evidence that pointed in the direction of something strange going on. I can see why you would come to the conclusion that I was a forger. It is a logical deduction based on the evidence you found. At the same time, it was important for me to prove to you that I am not." He paused, "But I understand that does not answer all of your questions, does it? The long finger appearing in multiple paintings, and the commonality of the signatures across those artists, including mine, are hard to reconcile."

He crossed his hands and set them under his chin, placed his elbows onto his knees and leaned slightly towards her.

"What you have found here is quite interesting and quite puzzling as well. Before I tell you my thoughts, what do you think is going on? Now that you know that I am not a forger, do you have an alternative hypothesis?"

Mackenzie thought for a moment and replied, "The only thing that makes sense to me is that Daddi and Lippi belonged to some type of secret society and they used the woman with the long finger and their signatures to pass along some message, or perhaps convey some type of membership or affiliation."

He leaned back and crossed his arms, nodding his head.

"That is actually a very plausible explanation. There were a number of secret societies that existed in pre-Renaissance Europe and continued on through the Renaissance and beyond. The Rosicrucians were one such group. The Illuminati were another. There were Masonic orders active during that time period as well." Anthony paused. "But if that were the case, what type of message were they sending? Any ideas?"

Mackenzie was energized again, having wiped away her tears. She was back to working on solving this puzzle and he was helping her.

"Well, it still could be part of a secret society. Daddi died almost sixty years before Lippi was born. It's possible that the society embedded other symbols in the paintings where the woman with the long finger appeared. I just haven't been able to identify what those other symbols are."

"That makes sense," he agreed. "Have you looked for the lady with the long finger in the works of other artists? If it were a society, you would likely have seen them appearing elsewhere."

"That's exactly what I thought. I scanned through every work of art in the international database from 1300 to 1550, specifically looking for a woman with an unusually long pinkie finger, but I didn't find anything. I kept a log of all of the scans I reviewed. I have it at home. There were over eight hundred individual pieces of art covering nearly a hundred different artists. The woman only appeared in the works of these two artists during about a one hundred and fifty year period that used those symbols." She paused and waved her finger. "What's curious is that while the signature analysis would indicate that Berlinghiero was linked to Daddi and Lippi, the woman with the long finger never appears in his work."

"How do you explain that?" asked Anthony calmly.

"I don't. That's the problem. The secret society hypothesis makes sense, but it's too odd that we wouldn't find similar symbols in the works of other artists of that era. A secret society of two artists, perhaps three, if we include Berlinghiero, none of whom overlapped with each other, doesn't seem very plausible."

"Is there any other hypothesis that you have come up with?" asked Anthony.

She looked down at the ground and then looked at him, slightly blushing.

"There is, but you'll think I'm nuttier than a Snickers bar. I'm actually embarrassed to even suggest it. I think it's impossible, but the only other hypothesis I've come up with is that these were all the same person and they were marking something of importance to them in their paintings."

Anthony smiled. "That is a pretty hard thing to believe, is it not? I mean, like you said, Daddi and Lippi were almost two centuries apart, and if you toss in Berlinghiero, then you are talking about a three hundred year span. That is a pretty old guy, no?"

She laughed. "Exactly, that's why I'm stuck. My one hypothesis seems unlikely because it's just too odd to assume that there were only two and maybe three artists in all of Europe over a three hundred year time period that belonged to this secret society. The other hypothesis I've come up with is totally crazy."

Anthony poured another cup of tea, took a sip and then scratched the back of his head. Then he looked Mackenzie squarely in the eyes and asked, "Do you think it is impossible for a person to live for three hundred years?"

At first Mackenzie thought he was kidding, but he didn't look like he was joking at all. She was clearly caught off guard and had no idea how to respond. *Was it some sort of trap?* If she said that perhaps it was possible, would he laugh at her and say *are you crazy?*, or worse, *are you an idiot?* She knew that it sounded ridiculous, but she also knew there were a lot of strange things in the world that seemed to be utterly impossible and ultimately turned out to be quite mundane.

"Anthony, I don't know what to believe. I can say that I've never heard of anyone living that long except maybe in the Bible or someplace like that. The oldest people I've ever heard of are 110 or thereabouts. But even then, we know that Daddi and Lippi weren't old men when they painted." She grinned. "I'd have to imagine that a 200 to 300-year-old man would look pretty rough."

Anthony laughed. "I would have to agree." He paused, and then he asked her, "Do you think that there is life on other planets?"

"What?" said Mackenzie, not sure what he was asking. "What does extraterrestrial life have to do with what we're talking about?"

"Humor me. Do you think that there is likely to be intelligent life somewhere else in the universe?"

"Well, I was never great at math, but I have watched a couple of science shows and if there are billions of stars and billions of galaxies, then yes, I guess the odds would be in favor of intelligent life somewhere else."

"What about the concept of multiple universes?" continued Anthony.

"What do you mean? Like there's another me somewhere out there in a bizarro world where the other me does everything opposite of the version of me in this one?"

Anthony chuckled. "I am not sure about the bizarro world. But among certain physicists, especially those who study quantum theory, there is a belief that there is no reason, at least none that breaks the laws of quantum theory, why there could not have been multiple Big Bangs. In other words, there could be many universes out there, each developing and evolving independently from each other, but with the same fundamental building blocks, like atoms, and charged particles. I want to know if you believe that to be possible."

"Well, you certainly have a roundabout way of helping me solve my riddle. But, yes, I think it's possible that there are multiple universes. It sounds pretty far out, but two hundred years ago no one would have thought that we could split an atom, or that there even were atoms, or that we'd be flying or landing on the moon, or talking on phones that aren't physically connected."

"I apologize if my questions seem obtuse. That is not my intention. I wanted to know how open you are to thoughts that are considered by most people to be quite extraordinary and impossible."

"Does that mean that I pass the test? Are you going to teach me the ways of the Jedi now, Obi Wan?" Mackenzie asked, laughing.

Anthony laughed as well and then became quite serious. He straddled the bench to face her directly. He leaned forward to where his face was less than a foot from hers and looked her square in the eyes. "Mackenzie, I am willing to share something with you that I have shared with less than a handful of people. It is something incredibly personal. If I tell you, you may laugh at me and think me crazy. That in and of itself would not bother me, and in fact might be the best outcome possible. On the other hand, you may believe me. Either way, I need to know that what I share with you will stay between us. You cannot share it with anyone else, and that includes your father. If you do, then I will have to leave and we will never see each other again. I am being completely serious. I want you to think about whether you want to take on that responsibility."

She looked over his shoulder. A sparrow landed on the statue of St. Francis in the center of the garden. A chill fall breeze blew through the cloistered garden, ruffling the leaves the trees and bushes, including the lone Japanese maple.

Mackenzie looked at Anthony without saying anything, trying to read anything in his expression. There was nothing.

"Wow," she finally exhaled, "you really know how to put together an ultimatum, don't you?"

Anthony broke a slight smile. "I am not trying to be melodramatic. Unfortunately, what I am asking is extremely important and personal to me. You could actually say that it is life and death for me." He paused, most likely imagining the conflict going on in Mackenzie's head at this moment. "Listen, you do not need to make a decision tonight. Think about what I said, and when you are ready, let me know. Now, I need to get back to work. Besides, it is starting to get a bit nippy out here."

⋙ Chapter 33 ⋘

Mackenzie sat in her room that evening and agonized over the decision she found herself faced with. It wasn't that she didn't want to know the answer; it was that she didn't trust herself to keep it a secret. As far back as she could remember, she had never been good at keeping secrets. It wasn't that she was a malicious tattletale, nor did she use secrets as weapons to hold people hostage in some trivial power struggle. She just let things slip because she wasn't what her psychology professors referred to as a "good social monitor." In other words, she pretty much said what she thought without first thinking it through. It was actually one of her endearing qualities. No one would ever accuse her of being manipulative. It just wasn't the way she was wired.

What if this time, even if she tried her hardest, she let slip whatever deep secret Anthony told her? He'd leave and it would be her fault. Maybe it was just as well that she didn't know why there were unexplained symbols in the paintings. Seriously, grand scheme and all, who cared about a woman with a long finger on a couple of 600-year-old paintings anyway? Especially since she wouldn't be able to tell anybody about what they meant even if she knew! What if her father asked her, which of course he would? *"So Mackenzie, what did you find out about those paintings, and the signatures?"* Would she be able to play dumb and pretend that they remained a mystery even though she knew where they came from and what they meant? She seriously doubted her ability to not cave and confess everything she knew. Then it would be too late.

Anthony had essentially made himself into a human Pandora's Box, an irresistible temptation. If he had just said, *"You got me. No idea why the signatures match or why the lady with the long finger keeps appearing,"* she would have been in a much better place. But here she was standing in front of the box, next to the tree of knowledge with apple in hand. Wasn't it destiny? Hadn't Pandora ultimately opened the box and Eve eaten the fruit? Wasn't that the way these parables were supposed to go? Was there any other way? Would there even be a story to tell if Pandora had put the box away and left it forever or if Eve decided there was plenty of other fruit to eat? Of course not; Anthony knew this just as well as she did.

Maybe he ultimately wanted to confide in her, to unload a burden he had held onto for too long. Why not her? Maybe this was some type of romantic game that Italian men played. She didn't know any other *real* Italians or she would have asked them. Most of the Italians in New York were at least three generations removed from Italy at this point. They'd probably laugh at her and say, *Oh yeah, the secret-I-can-only-share-with-you-but-if-you-tell-any-one-then-I-must-leave routine, classic!* Old as Romulus. She sort of doubted that was the case. Anthony was a pretty serious guy in the first place and he seemed to be dead serious about this thing. *But maybe he does want to share it with me,* she thought. Seriously, what in the world could be so important that it had this much baggage attached to it?

Eventually, after endless flip-flopping and second-guessing, she went to bed without having made a final decision. She crawled under the covers, trying not to disturb Octavius, who had already claimed his quadrant of the bed, which inevitably included her half, no matter which half she chose. Sometimes you just have to sleep on it. That's what her dad always told her. It was usually good advice.

⁂ Chapter 34 ⁂

It was a Saturday in late October. At work the previous day, Mackenzie had told Anthony that she could keep his secret. He had asked her to stop by his apartment around 5 p.m. the next day. Mackenzie showed up in the lobby of his apartment building and was greeted again by Jack the doorman and was quickly rung up to Anthony's apartment.

She got out of the elevator and walked to the door of his apartment. She took a deep breath, and then slowly let it out. *This is it*, she thought before ringing the doorbell.

Anthony was dressed in jeans, bare feet and a light yellow sweater. It looked awfully soft, she thought. *I bet it's cashmere, or maybe even alpaca. Whatever it is it sure looks comfortable, and it looks great on him.*

She remembered to take off her shoes. Sitting in the entryway were a pair of violet colored, fuzzy slippers.

"The carpets start getting a bit chilly in the fall. I thought you might prefer these to bare feet," offered Anthony.

She slid on the slippers. They were soft and warm and wonderful. "I must admit that I never had such nice slippers for my guests. I just make them walk around in their socks."

Anthony laughed. "I only offer these slippers to special guests. Everyone else wears socks. In fact, these are yours alone. I picked them up today at Bloomingdales. Would you like a glass of wine?" he asked as they made their way into the apartment.

"Yes, that would be nice," she said following him in. "I really enjoyed the wine we had last time."

He poured two glasses from a Grand Cru Burgundy that he had decanted earlier and handed her a wide bottomed glass with a stiletto stem. "I thought we might try a Burgundy this evening. I have been saving this one

165

for a special occasion." He held out his glass. "Cheers."

She took a sip. It was very different from the deep, powerful Malbec she had tried the last time. This was a very delicate wine with soft flavors of raspberries, cherries and rose petals that filled her mouth with a silky, round texture. It was amazingly complex and yet perfectly balanced. She'd never tasted a wine so refined in her life.

"Oh my god, this is incredible!" she exclaimed.

Anthony nodded. "I am glad you like it. It is one of my favorites."

Even though this was her second time in his apartment, she was still blown away by the stunning view and the paintings that lined the walls. She couldn't get over them.

He saw her staring at the paintings and motioned towards the hallway that led to his study. "If you are interested, I would be happy to show you a few more. I think you caught a glimpse of some the last time you were here," he said with a mischievous grin. "Maybe I can give you a better showing this time."

She gave him an embarrassed look. "If you don't mind. I'd love to see them." She hesitated. "Again, I apologize for what happened last time."

"Do not worry," he said, laughing. "I was just teasing you. I am pretty good at letting the past stay where it belongs." He took her gently by the elbow and led her way towards the study.

The door to the study was open and the light was already on. All four walls were covered with a collection that was perhaps even more spectacular than the living room. There were some Michelangelos, Titians, what looked like Botticellis, and some others that were hard to place but looked Venetian. There were also the stacks of paintings she had seen earlier. She leafed through some of the framed canvases leaning against the wall and through some finished paintings that remained unframed. *There must be hundreds of paintings in here!* she thought.

"Did you paint these or are they originals?" she asked, somewhat out of breath from the sheer volume of artwork in the room.

"Everything on the walls is original, as well as some that are against the walls. I painted a lot of the others that are stacked here, and definitely all of the ones that are just canvases. As I mentioned earlier, it is a hobby. Something I enjoy doing." He paused and then led her out of the study, to the guest bedroom and the master bedroom. The walls of those rooms were stunning as well. The master bedroom was covered in works of late nineteenth century impressionists. There were some Renoirs, Sislers, and Degas as well of a few Monets and at least two Van Goghs. She would swear that these were originals, or the best imitations she had ever seen.

"Are all of these originals as well?" she finally asked.

"Yes, the ones hanging on the walls are," said Anthony nonchalantly. "I have been collecting these for some time, so whenever I have an opportunity to find one that particularly attracts me at a reasonable price, I try to pick it up."

"But if these are all originals, then this collection would be worth hundreds of millions of dollars," said Mackenzie incredulously.

"Probably," said Anthony. "I am not really a collector from the perspective of trying to make a smart investment. I just really love some of these works and admire the artists who painted them. They are sort of like old friends to me that bring back memories, some very good and some painful, but memories nonetheless."

They slowly headed back to the main room. Mackenzie was dizzy and felt that she might pass out. Anthony sensed her discomfort. "Please, sit down," he said, and pointed to the couch.

Mackenzie almost collapsed into the leather couch. Her head was spinning. Anthony had the most impressive private collection of art that she had seen from anyone who was still alive. It was like walking through the Frick Collection, but probably more spectacular.

"Well, you certainly know how to impress."

"I did not invite you here to try to impress you. I hope you do not see this as being crass or anything. I know that you are very appreciative of fine art and I thought you would enjoy some of these paintings."

"Of course," said Mackenzie apologetically. "I didn't mean anything negative. I'm just truly in awe of what I've seen."

"I guess it can be pretty overwhelming the first time you see them," admitted Anthony as he sat down in the matching chair. "Mackenzie, I just want to make sure that we are clear on what we have agreed to. I am not trying to be melodramatic or anything, but this is extremely personal, important, and sensitive to me. I am sharing it because I trust you. You do not have to believe what I am about to tell you, and you may think that I am insane. But I need for you to promise me that you will not share what I tell you with anyone, whether you believe it to be true or not. Are you in agreement?"

Mackenzie nodded. She leaned forward on the couch and looked directly into Anthony's eyes.

"Yes, I've thought a lot about this, and I agree that whatever you share with me will remain between us. I promise."

Anthony nodded. He stood up, walked to the niche in the hallway, and grabbed the decanter. He topped off her glass as well as his.

"We are going to need this, and probably something more before we are done." He sat down on the chair, looked at Mackenzie for a moment and then began.

"What I am going to tell you is quite unbelievable, but it is true. Whether you choose to believe what I say is entirely your decision. I will not take it personally. You may stop me anytime you like, to ask questions, clarify anything you need to or just tell me to stop talking. Having said that, here we go." He took a deep sip of wine and continued. "I will try to go through this in some semblance of order. I have never actually talked about it in this way to anyone before, so excuse me if it appears disjointed. The first thing you will want to know is the story behind the woman that you have so adeptly discovered. The woman with the long pinkie finger was Bernardo Daddi's wife, Angelina. He was deeply in love with her and put her into as many paintings as he could. At one point, it became sort of a game for him. Once he completed a painting he would challenge her to try to locate the woman."

Mackenzie instinctively raised her hand to ask a question.

Anthony nodded. "I think I know what you are going to ask but go ahead."

"That doesn't surprise me and actually makes some sense. But, if she was Daddi's wife, why does she appear in Lippi's work? Daddi died before Lippi was born, so it wasn't as if they were master and student." She was on the edge of the couch at this point. "It also doesn't explain the similarities in the signatures."

"Those are indeed very appropriate questions and observations. The answer to both of them is as straightforward as it is seemingly impossible." He paused, taking in a deep, steady breath. "And, if you are ready, here it is. Berlinghieri, Daddi and Lippi were the same person," he leaned back, took a sip of wine and looked intently at Mackenzie.

"What do you mean the same person?" asked Mackenzie.

"I mean exactly what I said. The reason that Daddi's wife appears in Lippi's work and that their signatures match each other is because they were painted by the same person."

"That would mean that this person would be almost three hundred years old! C'mon, that's impossible."

Anthony nodded in agreement. "I know. It certainly would appear that way. The thing is that *impossibility* is an incredibly malleable concept. Remember when I asked you about the possibility of life on other planets and the possibility of alternate universes? I did that to test your willingness to think outside the normal parameters of what we deem possible.

"Five hundred years ago, it was *impossible* that the earth was not the center of the universe or that man could sail around the world without falling off the edge. Completely *impossible*. Twenty years ago the idea that someone would be able to talk or send a message on a phone the size of a credit card to someone on the other side of the world with neither of them being connected to a physical line was totally *impossible*. There are a lot of things that are completely impossible until they actually happen, and then they are considered completely normal.

"I do not know what is possible and impossible anymore. I can tell you that I have become much more open-minded as I have watched many of the received doctrines we hold onto so dearly fall apart and appear in hindsight to be no more valid than the belief in the four bodily humors or the gods on Olympus. Like I said when we started, I did not expect you to believe me but I also told you that what I am telling you is the truth. Those three artists, spanning almost three hundred years, were the exact same person."

"Okay, are we talking about the transmigration of souls, reincarnation and all that? You know, Daddi is really the reincarnation of Berlinghieri and Lippi is the reincarnation of Daddi? Is that it?"

"No, although I have always been intrigued by the concept of reincarnation. I personally have never observed it, but like I said, I am loath to shun an idea just because I have not experienced it or it does not make sense to me. No, what I am saying is much simpler, although admittedly harder to believe. Berlinghieri never died. He reappeared later as Daddi, and Daddi never died and appeared later as Fra. Lippi."

"But Daddi was a student of Giotto. If what you're saying is true, then Daddi would have been about a hundred years old when he started his apprenticeship. That's a pretty old man to take on as your apprentice. Daddi is described in a number of records as a young man and so is Fra. Lippi. This guy would have been well over two hundred years old when Lippi started painting and there are a lot of written records that describe Lippi's early life as a young man, not a two-hundred-year-old man." Mackenzie couldn't help but be incredulous.

"Have you ever heard of a disease called Progeria? It is also known as Hutchinson-Gifford syndrome? It is a very rare disorder that causes children to age prematurely. Most individuals with this disease rarely live past the age of thirteen, but they look like they are in their sixties or seventies when they are in their early teens."

"Yes, I wasn't sure what it was called, but I'm familiar with it. It's tragic."

"Indeed it is. There is no known treatment or cure. It is a very rare condition, though. There are only about one hundred cases that have been identified in medical history. Then again, they likely did not track it very well until the nineteenth century."

"Okay, but what does Progeria have to do with a three-hundred-year-old painter from the Middle Ages?"

"Think of it this way. If there are certain things that cause someone to age exceptionally quickly, then is it not reasonable to assume that there are also abnormalities, defects, whatever you want to call them, to make someone age very slowly?"

"I guess so, but I've never heard of anyone living past 120, and that's only in this century. It was rare for people to live past sixty in the Middle Ages," responded Mackenzie.

"Very true. But those people who are 120 look old. People are impressed when someone becomes a centenarian, but everyone who reaches one hundred looks the part. Am I right?"

"Yes, that's true. I'm not sure I'm following you."

"It is just this. What if someone did not age normally? What if they grew older in years but they really did not look any older from the outside? What if someone was 150, but only looked twenty? What do you think people would say about that person? More specifically, what do you think people in the twelfth and thirteenth centuries would have said about such a person?"

"You mean that they were in league with the devil or a witch?"

"Exactly!" he exclaimed. "They burned people at the stake for curing people's diseases with medicinal herbs in the twelfth and thirteenth centuries instead of relying on the priests to bleed them to death, pray over them and hope that they get better. You think that they would warmly receive someone who looks like he is twenty but has been around for a hundred years? He would be lucky if all they did was burn him at the stake. Most likely they would have tortured him for days until he confessed his dealings with the devil and then burned him.

"So he does not say anything to anyone. He tries to disguise the fact that he is not aging, or aging very slowly. Then, after a certain number of decades go by and it is unreasonable for him to still be alive, he disappears or stages a funeral, albeit one with no body, or perhaps uses someone else's body. Then, after another twenty or thirty years go by and anyone who may have known him has already passed away, he reemerges as someone else in a different town, or in this case in one of the largest cities in Europe."

Mackenzie listened intently to what Anthony had to say. On the surface, it sounded absurd, but the way he described it, it actually seemed plausible.

"So what you're saying is that if someone really did age that slowly, we wouldn't know about it because he wouldn't go public with it."

"That is precisely what I am saying. Even now, what if you were 300 years old but you looked like you were thirty? If you went to a doctor and explained your situation, they would likely diagnose you as delusional and put you on an aggressive regime of antipsychotics. No one would believe you."

"Anthony, I don't know what to say. On the one hand, this explanation certainly clears up the mystery of the woman with the long finger and the signatures. At the same time, it's pretty hard to comprehend that the same painter could have appeared over a 300 year period."

"You are right. It is hard to comprehend. Like I told you at the beginning, I did not think you would believe me and I do not blame you if you do not." He paused, "Now, there is one final thing that I need to tell you, and this will be the hardest one to believe. I only want you to know that what I am telling you is the truth. But before I tell you, can I ask that you to set your wine glass on the coffee table."

Mackenzie laughed and did as he said. "Sure. This has got to be something good for that type of a setup. I'm all ears."

Anthony stared at her for a moment and without breaking eye contact continued. "The thing you have not mentioned yet, either because you are being polite or perhaps it has slipped your mind, is that my signature also matches those three artists."

Mackenzie stared at him in bewilderment, trying to piece together what he just said. "But," was all she was able to get out before he continued.

"Yes, that person was me. I was Berlinghieri. I was Daddi, and I was Lippi. We are the same person."

❧ Chapter 35 ❧
Lucca, Italy, June 1262

The young priest escorted Berlinghiero through the rectory and knocked on the door to the prior's private study. "Enter," he heard from the other side of the door. The prior's chamber was warm and bright with late afternoon light streaming in from the windows. There was a large bookcase with leather bound volumes of books and manuscripts, most of which were religious texts and illustrated bibles. Some appeared to be secular tomes, most likely Roman or at least copies of Roman texts. Beautiful tapestries depicting biblical stories hung on two of the walls. The prior sat behind a large wooden desk that was surprisingly simple in its structure. While clearly sturdy, with solid columns holding up the large top, there were very few carvings in the wood. The prior sat on a bench behind the desk dressed in a long, scarlet colored silk robe with a neatly braided white belt whose tasseled ends hung almost to the ground. When they entered the room, the prior stood and motioned to the priest.

"Thank you, Father. That should be all for now. Please leave us."

"Yes, Father Prior," responded the priest with a slight bow and then closed the door as he left.

The Prior directed Berlinghiero to a long wooden bench covered with a burgundy colored woven pad. "Thank you for coming on such short notice. Please have a seat."

"When a young priest comes to my house and informs me that the prior of San Frediano wishes to speak with me, I assume that it is worth proceeding with some urgency."

"I apologize if I created any unnecessary anxiety, but I felt that it was important for us to talk."

"Of course. How can I be of service?"

"I am going to say some things that are difficult for me to say, and unquestionably more difficult for you to hear, but please trust that I say them because they are in your best interest."

"Have I done something to offend the church? Or the prior?"

"No, of course not. You have always been a model for others to follow. You and your family have been faithful servants of the church and have graced us with masterpieces that will last well beyond all our lifetimes. Having said that, and forgive the abruptness of this question, but when did your wife pass away?"

Clearly caught by surprise by this question, Berlinghiero bristled slightly. "Excuse me? My wife, Ilaria? She passed away almost twenty-five years ago. Why do you bring that up?"

"And your sons?"

"Father Prior, you know that my sons have all passed away. My youngest, Barone, passed away only this past February. It is beyond me why you bring up these painful things. How can this help me?" protested Berlinghiero.

"Again, I apologize in advance because I know that these questions are painful. As you have said, I know that Barone left us this year. Barone was only five years older than me. His passing has made me realize that my own time here is limited. That is one of the reasons that I felt it was important to talk with you."

"I do not understand, Father Prior."

"Let me be more straightforward. When I was a boy, I already knew of the great Berlinghiero of Lucca. Your work was famous throughout the city and I later learned you were known well beyond Lucca. My predecessor was a man you knew well. When I was a boy and first entered the seminary to study and devote my life to Christ, he was a few years younger than you. And yet, Prior Sebastiano left us more than twenty years ago. He was seventy years old. He was blessed to live a very full life, more than most. I became prior twenty years ago at the age of forty. What I am trying to say, my friend Berlinghiero, is that I am now sixty years old and you were already a father and a well-known artist when I was a young boy. Yet, when I look at you now, you appear to me to be a man of thirty. You look like a man who should have a young family. However, you have outlived your dear wife and all of your sons, who all lived full lives themselves. Still, you look like a young man. How is that possible?"

Berlinghiero squirmed a bit in his seat, shifting his weight uncomfortably. He knew that what the prior was saying was accurate. He himself had asked the same questions. "Father Prior, I do not know how to answer you. I have questioned that myself. I have prayed for answers and received none. I do not seem to age like everyone else. While it is rare for me to look at my image, when I do, I see a young man standing before me. It is as if I have not aged at all during the past sixty years. I have watched the woman I love, the person I fell in love with as a teenager, grow old and pass away in my arms. I have watched my boys grow and become men, become great painters in their own right, start families of their own, and then grow old and pass away. I do not know why I am still here or why I still look young. If you know, I beg of you to share the answer with me."

Without responding, the prior stood up and went over to a wooden cabinet. He withdrew two silver chalices and filled them with wine from a beautifully painted ceramic carafe. He handed one of the chalices to Berlinghiero and nodded for him to drink from it, and then sat down behind the desk. Berlinghiero took a deep sip. The wine was cold as it passed down his throat, but it served to calm him slightly.

The prior took a sip from his chalice, wiped his mouth with a cloth he pulled from the sleeve of his robe, and then continued. "Unfortunately, I do not have an answer to that. I too have thought about this a lot lately. You should know that you and I are not the only ones who have asked these questions. There is a growing concern in the community, and even amongst my priests. How is it that a man can remain so young? It is not *natural*, they insist. As you know, people often seek simple answers to complex problems. If it is not natural, then it is unnatural, and if it is unnatural, then it is the work of the devil. Certainly the church must take some responsibility for introducing them to the dark powers of Satan. I have known you my entire life and know you to be a man of God who has always served his church with honor. But, like I said, not everyone knows you like I do. Most of our congregation, as well as the rest of the inhabitants of this city, is younger than both of us and have not seen what you and your family have provided to the church."

"I apologize for being so obtuse, but I do not know what you are saying."

"What I am saying is this. You must leave Lucca. You must do so soon."

Berlinghiero slammed his hands on the desk and stood up, defiantly. "What? Leave my home? I have lived here my entire life! Where am I to go? What am I to do? Why must I leave the city where I was born, where I have worked and lived and raised a family?"

"I do not know where you should go," responded the prior calmly. He looked at Berlinghiero with sad, knowing eyes. "I do know that the longer you stay here, the more danger you are in. My priests have heard the talk. I have in fact talked with priests who themselves question your longevity. We can pacify the people for only so long. They will ultimately come to take action against what they feel is black magic, or Lucifer's hand. You must sell your house, or leave it to your grandchildren, it does not matter which. Whatever you decide to do, I urge you to do it quickly and then leave Lucca and essentially disappear. Berlinghiero Berlinghieri must become a memory and not be heard of again. You cannot continue forth as you have been. I am truly sorry, but it is because of my affection for you that I tell you this."

"Why, Father Prior? Why has this happened to me? What did I do to bring this curse upon me?" pleaded Berlinghiero, on the verge of tears.

"There are obviously examples in the Bible of men who lived what would be considered the lives of twenty men. Methuselah supposedly lived to be 969 years old. He died seven days before the Great Flood. In fact, according to the book of Genesis, the Lord delayed the Flood seven days to honor the mourning period for Methuselah. His son, Noah, lived to be 950 years old. Even Moses lived to be one hundred and twenty. Obviously, they were not deemed to be in league with the devil. In fact, they were prophets and the chosen men of God. I cannot tell why it is that you have apparently stopped aging. I know that many people would consider it a blessing, but I understand what a burden it is for you. You must reflect on this and hopefully you will come to understand what God has in mind for you." The prior stepped out from behind his desk and took Berlinghiero's hands in his.

"I will do everything in my power to buy you time. I will talk to my priests and help them placate the congregation. But I have to repeat this: you need to leave Lucca soon, the sooner the better. I am not afraid of what I do not understand. That is not something that can be said of most people. You must understand that our congregation is made up of simple peasants and field workers, of shopkeepers, tradesmen, and merchants, some of whom are wealthy, but also illiterate and uneducated. By themselves they are unlikely to do much worse than simply avoiding what scares them. But as a group they become emboldened to destroy the source of their fears. Remember what I say now. It is with the masses and not the individual that you must be concerned.

"Take your belongings, assets, do what you must with your house, but disappear and start a new life. Berlinghiero Berlinghieri must pass from people's memories."

Berlinghiero listened with a quiet resignation. Deep down, he knew that the prior was right. He had himself heard the whispers behind his back. He had watched his entire family pass away before him, not from some untold tragedy but from old age and natural causes. He had lovingly held Ilaria's head in his hand and stroked her gray hair while tears flooded his eyes. He had sat beside each of his three sons when they left the world and comforted his grandchildren, some of whom already looked older than he. Over the past several years he had taken to letting his beard grow longer and limited his interactions with others in the community in an effort to hide his apparent youth.

He was confused and felt hollow. A man should not have to bury his entire family, and suffer their loss. He had been a diligent servant of the church, and a faithful and loving husband and a nurturing, caring father who raised his sons to fulfill their potential, which, ultimately, they each had. Now, through no fault of his own, he was the target of the harshest of accusations, accused of being in league with the devil. He would be forced to leave his beloved Lucca, the only city he had ever known, where he had spent his life carefully building his name, his legacy. He was acclaimed as Berlinghiero of Lucca, the greatest artist of his generation, and now he would have to leave that behind and start life anew.

He lifted his head and looked at the prior. "Father Prior, I thank you for your candor, your wisdom and most importantly, your friendship. As you said, I have known you since you were a boy. I have watched you grow into a man. As much as it pains me, I know that what you have said is in my best interest and ultimately is the only road I can take. I will leave Lucca soon. My house and studio will go to Bonaventura's oldest son, Antonio. I will leave quietly and disappear. Please look after my family."

"I will watch over your family and I will ensure that the name Berling-hiero of Lucca is honored as it should be among the people of Lucca."

"Thank you, Father Prior. I will leave within the week."

"God be with you, my son," said the prior as they walked slowly to the door.

"And with you, Father Prior." He took a last look at the prior's office and headed out the door, into Piazza Frediano. That night, he made his way slowly through the familiar streets that he had known since he was a boy to his house and began preparations for his exit from the city.

⋙ Chapter 36 ⋘

Mackenzie looked at Anthony in stunned silence. She could not speak and had to consciously force herself to breath. She fumbled for her wine glass.

"Do you mind if I have a sip of wine? I think I need one."

Anthony laughed. "Of course, I just did not want you to drop the glass in shock when I broke the news. But it seems like a nice sip of wine would do wonders for you. In fact, might I suggest something a bit stronger?"

"I think anything would help at this point," said Mackenzie after finishing the remainder of her wine in one long gulp.

"I tend to like Ports when the weather gets colder. They are a bit much in the heat of the summer, but they are quite nice on a cold night." He went to a cabinet in the hallway and pulled out a very dusty bottle of 1927 Quinta do Noval vintage port along with two small glasses.

"This one is quite nice. I hope you like it," he said as he poured two glasses and handed one to Mackenzie.

Mackenzie had drunk inexpensive ports before in grad school, which frankly tasted cheap, a small step above cough syrup. This, however, was something completely unexpected.

"Wow, this is fantastic! I've never had anything like this."

"I have been saving this one for a special occasion, and I figure that telling someone that I have been alive for 822 years fits the bill, so to speak."

"Anthony, I—I don't even know what to say. What you are saying is so crazy that it's like I'm in an episode of the *X-Files* and I'm waiting for Scully and Mulder to walk out of the guest bedroom."

"I know. I told you that you probably would not believe me. If I were in your shoes, I would be quite skeptical. I do not know what to say to convince you. In fact, I am not really trying to convince you. It would be easier for me if you just decided I was some crazy guy who thought he was Napoleon and never gave it a second thought. Being considered odd is par for the course for artists. People give us a pretty wide berth. Van Gogh was institutionalized, albeit in San Remy, which is a lovely place to be put away. Picasso used to burn women with cigarettes. The list goes on. So being considered eccentric is not a big deal for me.

"On the other hand, if you truly do believe what I have told you, then I have a lot to be concerned about."

"Why is that?" asked Mackenzie curiously.

"Because if you truly believe what I say, and then break our pact and share it with someone else, there will inevitably be questions. There will be psychiatrists who will want to speak with me, maybe even federal agents who would like to talk with me about back taxes, etc. Compound interest over a couple hundred years could be some serious cash." They both laughed.

"I guess what I am saying is that the worst thing that could happen to me, in all honesty, is for a lot of people to believe that what I am saying is true. I would never be left alone. I would be a freak, little better than the Elephant Man. Being a strange guy who's a little off, living in obscurity, is a lot easier to manage."

"I guess you're right. I never really thought of it that way. Do you mind if I ask you some questions?"

"Of course, I will answer anything you ask." Anthony refilled their glasses with more port.

"Well, for starters, when did you realize that you didn't age like everyone else?"

Anthony paused before responding. "It was probably when I was about fifty, sometime around 1238 or so. I noticed that I looked as young or younger than my son Bonaventura. My wife, Ilaria, was very beautiful, but she looked like a beautiful forty-five-year-old woman and I looked like I was about twenty-five. I had no wrinkles on my face and my skin was very smooth. I did not gain weight like most middle-aged men. Ilaria pointed this out to me on a number of occasions. She was not complaining, per se, it was just that it struck her as odd. Some of her friends had even mentioned it to her. Back then, people were very afraid of things they did not understand, and there were a lot of things they did not understand. If you did not understand it, it was probably magic, and magic meant you were a witch or in league with the devil. Neither of which was particularly good for your longevity.

"I tried to look older. I grew out my beard and let my hair grow long so that you could not see my face as much. I actually came up with a mixture of some pigments that we used along with some ash and other substances and made a cream that would make me look older, or at least a bit dirtier, which made me look older. That helped a bit."

"The art history records show that Berlinghiero died around 1247 at the age of fifty-nine. What happened?"

"Thankfully, record keeping back then was pretty poor. With the help of a wise and compassionate local priest in Lucca, we arranged for Berlinghiero to basically disappear and staged a funeral. I left Lucca and Berlinghiero was buried in a closed casket. Any mystery ended at that point. I was able to sell off much of what I owned to the church, including a number of paintings, and the rest I left to my grandchildren. That left me with enough money to survive for a reasonable period of time."

"So you left Berlinghiero behind and disappeared?"

"Yes, for almost fifty years. I lived in the countryside. I bought a small farm in the hills outside of Siena. I grew beans and barley, raised sheep and lived a quiet life by myself. I lived like that for almost fifty years and then I went to Florence and took on the name Bernardo Daddi."

"You must have been lonely."

Anthony looked down at his glass of port, reflectively. "I have been lonely for most of my life. I have learned to live with it. In fact, it seems quite normal to me to be what most people would call lonely. At that time, though, yes, I was very lonely and very sad. I kept busy farming the land and raising sheep. I painted a little bit just to keep myself occupied, mostly landscapes of my farm. But the thought that I still had grandchildren who were alive and raising families that I would never know was difficult. I did not dare return to Lucca for a long time because I still looked the same as I did when I was there twenty to thirty years earlier. There were many people who knew of Berlinghiero, so it would have been difficult to sneak around undetected. So I just waited until I was sure that anyone who might have known me was already dead. Then I went to Lucca in the guise of a poor farmer and asked around about the Berlinghieri family. My sons had all done quite well as artists and they were well known. They had all passed away long ago and were buried in a graveyard with me, or at least by my casket, and my wife Ilaria. There were probably more than a dozen grandchildren and great grandchildren living in and around Lucca, many of whom had married and taken other names. I knew none of them, nor did they know me.

I went to visit the graves of my family. Even though I had been the one to bury them almost a half century earlier, it still moved me greatly to see their headstones all together. I cried over their graves like a baby. I cried until I had no more tears to cry. It was shortly after that visit that I realized I was ready to start painting again. That is when I moved to Florence, found Giotto, and became an apprentice under him."

After listening to all of this, Mackenzie sat back in her chair and shook her head with both hands, as if trying to clear the cobwebs, or perhaps to make sure that she wasn't dreaming.

"It's just all too much to take in. Seriously, it's like someone just told me that Batman is real. I mean, it's not that I don't believe you or think that you would lie to me, especially with such a strange story, but it's hard to get my head around the whole thing."

"I know," responded Anthony. "Imagine how I felt when I realized I was not aging like everyone else. At the time, back in the thirteenth century, I really thought that maybe I was possessed by the devil. I went to church every day and prayed to God for guidance and to help me understand what was happening. I could not even talk to the priest about it during confession. I had nowhere to turn. It was terrible."

Mackenzie felt awful. She was too busy thinking about how this was affecting her to consider how it must be for Anthony. It was a curse to live forever. At one time or another, everyone dreamed of it, explorers searched for the Fountain of Youth, but in the end it was a Faustian pact.

"Anthony," she said, "this must be incredibly difficult for you. I promise that I will not share your secret with anyone."

"I appreciate that," replied Anthony. "Probably the worst part of all of this is that the friends I make, including you, will all be gone from my life far too soon. Eighty years is a long time to live, but to me eighty years seems more like ten. I have met so many wonderful people with whom I have grown close to, only to watch them pass out of this world. I do not mean to be morbid or melancholy, but the closer you and I become, the more I will mourn your loss."

Mackenzie thought about that for a moment. "But at least I get to hang around this really good looking young guy when I'm old and gray."

He raised his glass to her. "There are always silver linings. It is good to look for them." They both touched glasses and finished the port.

❧ Chapter 37 ❧
Florence, Italy, June 1315

Outside of a cathedral, it was by far the largest building Daddi had ever seen. He was amazed that one family, albeit one of the city's wealthiest, could live in such an enormous house. The newly finished marble walls were expertly cut and set and glistened with the reflected light from hundreds of candles. The smell of roasting meats, rabbits, pigs, ducks and chickens, and breads of all types filled the large room. There had to be at least three hundred people here tonight.

He had been invited to attend a party at the house of one of his largest donors, Giuseppe Speziali, who had recently commissioned several wall paintings for his new house. Daddi wasn't exactly sure what the party was for, but believed it had something to do with the engagement of one of Speziali's daughters.

Everyone at the party was dressed in rich colorful silks and finely woven cotton and sheer linens. Women's long flowing dresses and veils in vibrant colors—reds, blues, yellows and greens—and men in slightly less colorful hats, made the crowd seem like a field of wildflowers in spring. Music floated through the room from somewhere Daddi couldn't immediately locate. The mood was festive and bustling. Dozens of servants moved efficiently through the crowd offering various light treats and silver and gold goblets of wine. Daddi thought that the collection of wine goblets themselves would sell for enough for fifty merchant families to live well for a full year.

Such was the life of the rich, and Speziali was certainly that. The Speziali, along with the Lana and Giudici families, controlled most of the industries and wealth within Florence. The Speziali clan focused on the ever-growing jewelry trade. Not only did they own most of the major gold, silver, copper and precious stone mines throughout Tuscany, they had fleets of ships that sailed regularly from the port at Livorno south to Sicily or north to Marseille and Barcelona to obtain more precious metals and gemstones. They owned the majority of the smelting operations in Florence, as well as the craft shops that turned those fine metals into wine goblets, platters, candleholders, candelabras, and fine jewelry that adorned the wrists, heads, fingers, necks and earlobes of the growing class of wealthy women, royalty and the clergy. Jewel encrusted scepters, golden chalices and Eucharist plates, or paten, were always needed by the myriad of churches and cathedrals that seemed to be popping up every several years in and around Florence and throughout Tuscany. They also owned most of the retail stores that sold the final goods to the populace or to their buyers. They had numerous stores that lined the beautiful gothic bridges that spanned the Arno River like the *Ponte alla Carraia* and *Ponte Vecchio*. And of course, those ships that sailed to Sicily, Genoa, Marseilles and Barcelona to pick up fine metals and jewels also carried with them the fine, finished products which would be sold to merchants in those foreign markets.

Daddi crept his way through the crowd. He really didn't know any of the people here except for Speziali himself, although he was sure they made up Florence's elite. He was hoping to potentially see his old friend Giotto, who had originally introduced him to Speziali in the first place. Giotto was in such demand in Florence that he didn't have time to accommodate Speziali's wishes for eight to ten significant paintings in his new house. Of course, Giotto was no fool. You did not simply say no to a man like Giuseppe Speziali. Instead, Giotto found an elegant solution by convincing Speziali that Daddi was an artist who could better meet his specific needs and that his commitments to the church were such that it would be at least two years before he could begin work on his project.

Like most wealthy and powerful men, Speziali hated to wait almost as much as he hated to be turned down. This created a perfect opportunity for Bernardo Daddi. After all, you couldn't ask for a better sponsor than Giuseppe Speziali. He allowed for greater freedom as an artist than the church, and although he was a shrewd businessman, Giotto had already driven up his price so high that Daddi appeared to be a bargain, even if he was paying three to four times what Daddi could have reasonably commanded at that

185

point in his career. To charge much less, though, would have made Speziali feel as if he was compromising and that was something that he was not willing to do. Daddi, as far as Speziali saw it, which of course was how Giotto had helped him see it, was every bit the painter that Giotto was and it was his good fortune that Daddi was available to paint an entire series of masterworks specifically for him.

A servant approached him with a polished silver and gold goblet of red wine. He took it and continued squeezing his way through the crowd, smiling, offering the obligatory greeting to people he didn't know, but might eventually want to know. He took a sip of the wine. It was smooth and rich, perhaps the finest Chianti he had ever tasted. Round, full, with a velvety finish and no tannic bite that was so common in younger wines. Obviously Speziali was not going to spare any expense to showcase his new home and announce the engagement of his daughter.

Daddi felt that warm, wonderful feeling of comfort and relief that everyone who enters a group of strangers experiences when they finally see someone they know, whether it's a close friend or not. He recognized his old friend and mentor, Giotto, surrounded by almost twenty people listening to his animated stories delivered with a flurry of sweeping arm motions. Giotto was now the most famous artist in all of Florence, and perhaps all of Italy. The elite of Florence flocked to be in the company of the master and listen to what he had to say, and, perhaps more importantly, just to share his aura.

Giotto smiled broadly when he saw Daddi approach.

"My friends," he paused, turning towards Daddi, "we are privileged this evening to be in the presence of one of Florence's finest young artists." The group surrounding Giotto turned to greet Daddi, attention that was at once flattering and intimidating.

"Please welcome Florence's next great painter, Bernardo Daddi," announced Giotto. With an introduction like that the group of people surrounding Giotto almost knocked each other over trying to introduce themselves.

"Signor Daddi, it is my pleasure to make your acquaintance," said an impeccably well-dressed man in his mid forties with a crisp bow and handshake. "My name is Ricardo Fellini."

"The pleasure is mine, Signor Antinori."

This exchange repeated itself a dozen times. Although he was sure that he should have recognized some of the names, they rushed past Daddi in a blur.

"My friend Giotto is much too generous in his praise," protested Daddi humbly, after the initial round of introductions had passed. "I am but a student of the master, trying to catch a glimpse of the light that shines on Tuscany's greatest artist."

"Bernardo," interjected Giotto with obvious delight at his pupil's praise, "you must meet Arnolfo di Cambio, one of the greatest sculptors that Florence has ever produced."

A slight, thin man with green eyes and light brown hair, dressed more plainly than the others, stood by Giotto's side and bowed slightly towards Daddi.

"I have seen your work, Signor Daddi. My friend Giotto does not exaggerate about your skills. You are a master beyond your years."

As an artist, to receive a compliment from a non-artist was wonderful. It made him happy that someone else appreciated his work. To receive such praise from a fellow artist, especially one who is held in such high esteem by a man he idolized, was something completely different. It was a validation of him as a person, of what he had dedicated his life to be. So few see the world the way an artist sees it. The way light caresses the cheek of a beautiful woman, or the way subtle emotions show themselves and then disappear from a stranger's face. Not only to see it but to capture it on a flat wooden plank or a plaster wall, knowing that he was never satisfied with what he had painted.

In his previous life in Lucca, Berlinghiero was the acknowledged master. He was never short of hearing praise from those around him. He had grown immune to it. Bishops, priors and wealthy donors were always offering him effusive exultation. At first he had relished it and then he came to realize that it was that first type of praise, praise by non-artists who liked his paintings, who were moved by them, that meant nothing.

This was different. This was a sculptor, an artist held in the highest esteem, a peer, telling him that he knew of his work and thought that it was, in essence, worthwhile.

Daddi bowed deeply towards di Cambio. "I am humbled by your praise, Signor. Please," said Daddi to the group, "continue with your conversation. I rudely interrupted you."

"Have no fear, my friend," said Giotto. "I was just boring them with a description of a new painting I am working on. Have you seen Speziali yet? He is right over there," he pointed to his right at Signor Speziali surrounded by a swarm of people. "You need to go over there directly and pay your respects," he admonished.

Daddi nodded. "Indeed. I shall return. Please forgive me," he said as he bowed to the group.

He gradually inched his way through the crowd and eventually came to Speziali, who was talking with a group of at least a dozen people that Daddi had never met before.

"Here he is!" exclaimed Speziali the moment he saw Daddi. "This is the man who is going to bring the beauty of Florence into my new home!"

The others surrounding Speziali immediately turned to see whom their host had felt important enough to single out.

"I apologize for interrupting you," said Daddi, feeling like this was becoming his standard greeting at parties. "Thank you very much for inviting me, Signor Speziali. This is the most splendid party I have ever attended."

"I am glad you could make it, Signor Daddi." He turned to the group in front of him, "Please, allow me a minute with the artist."

He placed his arm around Daddi and led him away from the group. "Bernardo, how old are you?"

Daddi paused for a moment, because in actuality this was a surprisingly complex calculation for him. "Thirty-one, Signor."

"Please, call me Giuseppe," said Speziali with a smile. "It is about time that you thought about starting a family, do you not agree?"

Taken somewhat by surprise, Daddi stammered, "Well, I had not really given it much thought."

"Exactly!" proclaimed Speziali. "That is the problem with artists. You are too focused on your art to see what is going on around you. A man of your means should have a family. You are not planning on becoming a monk, are you?"

"No, I have no plans to become a monk."

"That is precisely why you need someone like me to look out for you, my friend," said Speziali with a smile. "I want to introduce you to my niece. Of course, if you find her hideous-looking, then you should run away at once. But I think you might be intrigued. She is a very beautiful girl and she has a bit of the artist in her, from what my sister tells me."

Daddi was completely caught off guard. He was serious when he said that he hadn't thought of a family. He had had a family, a family that he loved dearly. They were all gone now. Their passing had left an empty pit in his heart that he had tried to fill by immersing himself in his work. He had felt dead inside for years after they passed. His family was gone, his home and the beautiful city that he had called home was taken from him. He roamed the Tuscan countryside in a daze for decades before finally settling on a new identity in Florence.

"I am not sure what to say, Giuseppe. I would be pleased to meet your niece when the time is right," he said, trying not to offend this very powerful man who was, at the moment at least, the primary source of his own wealth.

"Well then, you are in luck. She is here tonight. Come, I will introduce the two of you," confided Speziali as he put his arm around Daddi's shoulder and led him to the left and under an enormous archway that led into another room that seemed to be almost as large as the first.

As they made their way through the crowd they were stopped every few feet by guests providing greetings to the host. Speziali was a fine host and a diplomat as well. He had a way of making everyone feel welcome without spending more than thirty seconds with any of them. He greeted all of them by name, asked about their children, their business, and thanked them for coming and then continued his procession forward.

At last they came upon a group of six, four women and two men, talking next to a large, marble column. One of the men facing them stopped his conversation and greeted Speziali with a slight bow and a handshake.

"Giuseppe! We thought that perhaps you would not be able to make it over this far with all these guests."

"Someone told me that this group was drinking all of my finest wine and I wanted to get over here and try some before it was all gone." Everyone in the group laughed.

Speziali, still with his arm around Daddi, said to the group, "I want to introduce you to someone you will be hearing a lot about in the coming years. This is Bernardo Daddi, who will be painting a few soon-to-be masterpieces to grace the walls of my new home. He comes personally recommended by the great Giotto."

The man who first greeted Speziali, held out his hand.

"Greetings to you, Signor Daddi, I am Stephano Castracani, and this is my wife, Giadda." He motioned to the woman standing to his left.

The other man who appeared somewhat younger than Stephano stepped forward to greet them. "Signor Daddi, it is a pleasure to meet you. My name is Gabriel Antinori. This is my wife, Catherine, and my daughters, Gabriella and Angelina," he said, motioning to a tallish woman standing next to him as well as a young, slightly plump woman who was likely in her late teens or perhaps early twenties, and a strikingly beautiful girl who was in her late teens. The younger daughter, Angelina, was stunning. Her name was fitting. She really did appear to be an angel.

Daddi shook Gabriel's hand and bowed low to the entire group. "It is my distinct privilege to make your acquaintance. I had no idea that I would be introduced to such beautiful women this evening."

"An artist and a gentleman," Speziali said, laughing warmly. "Signor Daddi, your talents continue to impress. Catherine is my sister and these lovely girls are my nieces."

"Signor Daddi, my brother is very impressed with your work and speaks very highly of you. Perhaps you would honor us at our home for dinner sometime in the near future."

Daddi tried hard to hold back his excitement over the opportunity to spend more time with the beautiful Angelina.

"It would be my pleasure," he responded trying not to stare at Angelina.

"Catherine," added Speziali, "Signor Daddi is a bachelor and therefore could definitely benefit from some home cooking."

"Then we will need to get together sooner rather than later," said Catherine with a conspiratorial smile to her brother. "We would not want Signor Daddi to waste away and not have the energy to finish your project, Giuseppe."

"If you would excuse us, I have a few more guests that I need to say hello to and I want to show off Signor Daddi to them as well," continued Speziali as he began to lead Daddi away from the group.

As they moved through the crowd, Speziali leaned closer to Daddi. "So, what did you think of my sister's family?"

"They seem to be a lovely family," responded Daddi.

"Well, of course they are. But what I mean is, what do you think of Angelina?" pressed Speziali.

"She is very beautiful, although I obviously do not know anything about her."

"That is exactly what we need to work on. You cannot remain a bachelor all your life. A man needs a family. She is a beautiful girl from a very good family. I have known her for her entire life. She would make you a wonderful wife."

Daddi didn't know what to say. He had not thought about starting another family. He had to admit, though, Angelina was beautiful and he was tired of living alone. Perhaps he had been single long enough. He could also do far worse than having Giuseppe Speziali as part of his family.

"You know, if we do get married, you still do not receive a family discount," quipped Daddi.

"And they call me a tough negotiator!" laughed Speziali. The two continued their way through the crowd.

⸏⸎ Chapter 38 ⸎⸏

It was a beautiful country villa, everything that Daddi had ever wanted and more than Berlinghiero could have dreamed. Daddi had done well; he had commissions with the wealthiest and most famous men of Italy and beyond. With his friend and mentor Giotto now deceased, Daddi had emerged as the premier artist in Florence, which meant that he was one of the premier artists in the known world. His success had afforded him the money to buy something that he had always wanted, a large estate in the beautiful Tuscan countryside.

Rows of vineyards grew thick with dark green leaves and deep, purple grapes that would be picked and turned into wine in the fall. Orchards hung heavy with green olives that would be picked and pressed into fragrant, peppery olive oil. Fluffy, white sheep, most of which would be sheered and whose fine wool would be woven into some of the finest fabric in the world roamed the hillsides. Some of them would ultimately be slaughtered and sold to the markets as lamb and mutton to be consumed by families in the city. Even as a child, more than a hundred years ago, he had loved the Tuscan countryside. Now he had his own piece of it.

The villa had been built thirty years ago by a wealthy merchant, who was a friend and colleague of Speziali. It was Speziali, his old patron, who had told Daddi about this villa and the estate that went with it. Daddi hadn't hesitated to jump at the opportunity. He still kept his house and studio in the city and, much to Angelina's chagrin, spent too many days locked inside it.

Due to his constant focus on fulfilling orders and building his wealth, Daddi had been largely an absentee parent while his daughters, Constanzia and Estancia, were young. They were now grown women, with husbands and children of their own. Even now he still worked many weekends trying to finish up projects with tight deadlines. His work at Speziali's mansion had been a huge hit and word had spread quickly throughout the wealthy merchants and lesser royalty of the city, thanks in large part to Speziali's enthusiastic endorsement. He and his ever-growing team of apprentices had so much work that they had a two-year backlog on orders. His studio turned out an amazing volume of work, some of which was great but most of which, he had to admit, was merely adequate. All of it, though, was extremely profitable. He referred less lucrative work to other artists, many of whom were his or Giotto's former apprentices, who were busy making names for themselves.

He and Angelina sat outside underneath the shade of the delicate purple wisteria, which hung like grapes from the latticed canopy. The gentle flowers swayed in the warm breeze. Angelina sat nestled against Daddi with his arm wrapped over her shoulder. Two glasses of red wine sat on the marble table in front of them along with some cheese and a slab of sausage, both of which came from the farm. He rested his cheek on the top of her head and allowed himself to breathe in the clean, intoxicating smell of her hair. It smelled of lavender and honey, and her. This was heaven, he thought. Life had never been so enjoyable. He wished moments like this could last an eternity, but he knew they wouldn't.

"Bernardo," she purred quietly.

"Yes, my love," he responded softly.

"We should spend more time like this. More time here in the country, where you can relax and spend time with me and your girls and your grandchildren. You are in the city so long and under such stress that it takes you at least a day to relax and start enjoying life."

He thought quietly and let out a very slight murmur. His relationship with Angelina had grown, despite his frequent absence. Angelina grew up in the family of a wealthy merchant and understood that success required sacrifice. But, as she pointed out on numerous occasions, her father always made sure to balance his work with spending time with his family.

"I plan on doing just that, my love," he said after some quiet reflection. "There is just so much work right now that I have to finish and I cannot delegate all of it to my apprentices."

"You know how proud I am of all that you have achieved. Your success has provided us with a very comfortable lifestyle." She continued, still with her head nestled against his chest. "But we could live comfortably on a fraction of what you make. We do not need more money. I am very proud to be married to the famous artist whose name is known throughout the land. But I miss the man that no one else knows. The one who is not afraid to make silly faces for his girls who adore him and crave his attention. You are the husband I always dreamed of since I was a young girl. I just want to have more of you here, with us, rather than pursuing more fame and fortune."

He knew that what she said was true. He felt the same way about Angelina and his daughters. They were by far the most important people in his life. Still, for some reason he was afraid to let his business slip and be overtaken by other artists. After all, people were fickle, especially the rich. He was in favor now, but how long that would last was anyone's guess. He was determined to build up such a strong foundation of wealth and fame, like Giotto had, that he would never have to worry about his family's future or the longevity of his name.

He held her closer and kissed the top of her head. "I will try to slow down and spend more time with you. I know I have not spent as much as I should and I apologize for that."

The next week was his grandson Rocco's, seventh birthday. In keeping with his promise, Daddi took the weekend off to bring his extended family together, to spend time and celebrate. Angelina's parents, who were now in their early seventies, had come to be with their children, grandchildren, and now great grandchildren. His daughters and their husbands came with their children, who ranged in age from two to seven. Angelina's sisters brought their five children along with their husbands.

Angelina worked closely with the cook they kept at the villa to make a memorable meal. Daddi had hand-selected some of the oldest vintages of the spectacular Chianti that his estate produced and that he had insisted upon including as part of the purchase price of the villa and surrounding countryside.

He had not seen Angelina's parents Gabriel and Catherine for several months and the years were clearly catching up to both of them, Gabriel especially. Being with their family was one of the greatest joys in their life and Daddi did what he could to ensure they had experiences like this to share, enjoy and remember.

The children played in the garden and ran through the vineyards. They watched the sheep and fed milk to the little lambs. They played games that only children can invent. The older children served as leaders and mentors to the younger ones. They played, laughed, rolled in the grass, the young ones fell, cried and were consoled by the older ones, and then quickly returned to their games, seemingly forgetting that they had been crying just minutes earlier.

The men stayed close to the villa sipping wine and talking about business and politics. The women, who were all sisters or daughters, worked in the kitchen with the cooks to bring out servings of various antipasti, including some of the cured olives from the estate, along with sausages and cheeses, to enjoy with their husbands. It was a glorious Tuscan summer day. Hot, with a topaz blue sky, a warm breeze, the aromas of grilled meats, dark fruits ripening on the vine and the ever present smell of lush vegetation.

Angelina worked tirelessly. She was the youngest daughter and strove to be respected in her family. She wanted to be the best wife and mother and make her parents proud. Daddi often watched her at such gatherings. She spent her time making sure that the cook knew how she liked her dishes or, more importantly, how her husband liked them. She never rested. Even though they had a small team of servants, she was always watching to make sure that glasses remained full and that no one had to wait too long for something they wanted. Daddi couldn't ask for a better wife to spend his life, or at least this iteration of it, with. He sometimes wondered what Ilaria would think of Angelina, and vice versa. They would clearly be jealous of each other, but in a different environment they would probably like and respect each other. There were so many similarities between the two. They were both youngest daughters and were young when they married. They had both been strong, loving, and caring woman who weren't afraid to share their opinions with their husband, despite being rather quiet and demure when they were

195

with others. Both of them were beautiful. Even as a grandmother, Angelina was young, vibrant and full of life. She was his constant companion.

After a long dinner with various antipasti, freshly made pasta followed by braised lamb, they made a large fire in a pit outside the main house. They sat around the fire as its yellow flames leaped skyward in hypnotic patterns. The men drank *grappa*, the women drank *vin Santo*, and the children ate some of the sweets that had been prepared. They stayed up late into the evening telling stories.

Maria's husband Mario was a particularly good storyteller. He was a silk merchant by trade and traveled frequently to places like Genoa, Naples and even Marseilles and Barcelona. He told stories of the strange people he met and of the dangers of being at sea.

When the fire died down and the evening came to an end, everyone made their way into the house and to the guest rooms. It was a good half-day ride back to Florence, so everyone stayed for the whole evening. The estate was large and spacious and had plenty of room for everyone to sleep comfortably.

Daddi planned on spending more time here in the country. He would often stay here for a week at a time. He was even thinking of making a small workshop in the back where he could paint. His studio was in Florence, as were his apprentices. But, if he planned well, he could bring the correct pigments and dyes and other materials with him when he came and spend a couple of days or even a week painting. He wistfully thought of how he and Angelina would take long walks in the countryside, stop and rest with a bottle of wine and make love on a distant hillside, just as they had done when they were first married. They had been married for twenty-seven years. She was forty-six with two children and four grandchildren, but looked almost ten years younger. In his eyes, she was still the beautiful, intelligent girl that he had married when she was nineteen.

He still looked like he was in his mid-thirties. It was something that people often commented on, much to his discomfort. He would laugh and tell them that it was because he drank only the best wine, and then change the conversation as quickly as possible. He grew a thick beard and used some of his knowledge of pigments to add some grey to his hair and to his beard. But Angelina saw him more clearly than others. He had the lean, tight body of a man in his early thirties, not that of a man in his late fifties. He often caught her looking at him when he was asleep or working on his paintings, when she thought that he couldn't see her. He knew that it must seem strange to her that he did not grow old like everyone else. Daddi was only supposed to be about fifteen years younger than Angelina's father, but he looked as if he could be her father's grandson. Her father had a hard time walking now and became more frail and hunched over every time she saw him. Daddi, on the other hand, looked just the same as he did when they were married. She stopped bringing it up as a topic of discussion because he always gave her the same answer and refused to talk about it more. It was the just the way it was. He was blessed with looking younger than his age and that was all there was to be said.

◦◦ Chapter 39 ◦◦
Florence, Italy, September 1348

Daddi sat cross-legged on the field grass next to the newly dug graves. His farmhouse stood in the distance under an overcast sky. He was alone, again. It had all ended so quickly. The greatest loves of his life were now buried under the cool dirt of the Tuscan countryside, plucked from the world in the prime of their life.

The plague had moved through Florence with devastating speed and ferocity. It had started innocently enough, with the appearance of a bubo or lump, often the size of a small egg, in the groin or armpit area. Once the buboes appeared, they spread quickly to the entire body. Then, black or purple spots would appear on the arms or thighs. These spots were a certain sign of death. Typically it was only a week from the time the first bubo appeared until death ensued.

There were no cures. Doctors were helpless. The clergy preached that it was because of a separation from God, His retribution on the sinners. But many of the clergy themselves fell to the disease. While it hit the poor most severely, the rich and noble families were not immune to its dark fingers.

Constanzia's son, Rocco, was the first to show the telltale signs. He awoke one morning with a swelling in his armpit. The family was still not sure at that time of the severity of the disease and tried to treat him like they would if it was a normal cold or fever. They applied cold compresses and kept him in bed. Angelina went to the house every day to help Constanzia take care of him. It wasn't long until the same symptoms appeared on young Giuseppe, as well as Maria in Estancia's house. Angelina split her time trying to comfort both of them. No one knew how the disease was spread. But these were Angelina's grandchildren. They were her family. She called in the best doctors in Florence and had them tend to the children. The doctors made them apply foul smelling poultices to their chests and drink herbal mixtures they had concocted. It was to no avail. Within ten days of the appearance of the first buboes, Rocco, Maria, and Giuseppe were dead. Daddi saw that they were buried in the church graveyard and that the bishop himself blessed their souls before they passed.

It wasn't long before more of their cousins fell to the disease. Two of Margharita and Christiano's children fell and both of Maria and Mario's children died as well. Soon Mario, who traveled frequently and was exposed to people from many cities and countries, succumbed to the disease.

Less than a month had passed since Rocco had first shown the symptoms of the disease when Daddi decided to move his entire family to his country estate. He invited Margharita and her husband, Christiano, and their young children, Giuliani and Maria, to live with them. He had heard from some of the wealthy families that it was a good strategy to isolate yourself and get away from the big cities. This made sense to him. Although he wasn't sure how the disease was being passed on, it seemed as though it spread quicker in the most densely populated areas.

They hadn't been at the estate for even a week when Constanzia and Marco both showed the first signs of the disease. Angelina worked tirelessly to take care of them, as well as their daughter, Christiana. It was to no avail. Both Constanzia and Marco were gone in little over a week. Daddi buried them on his estate, in a green field under the shade of an old chestnut tree that was his favorite.

It was a very scary time. No one knew what was causing the disease. There was confusion and chaos in the cities and the surrounding countryside. Daddi decided to limit their exposure to the outside world, but it was necessary to get the raw ingredients they needed for food. They had plenty of grapes, wine, olives, and olive oil, and a large herb garden. They had fresh sheep's milk and they could always slaughter a lamb or a sheep for meat. A deep well on the property provided fresh water. But they had no grains for pasta, nor beans for soups and stews. Because they lacked fresh vegetables, Daddi decided to plant a large garden that would provide them with fresh green vegetables like cardoons, fava beans and kale. They went to small markets to obtain their supplies, where they heard terrible stories of how the plague was cutting a wide swath through the city of Florence and the entire countryside. There were stories of similar destruction throughout the entire peninsula, from Sicily and Naples to Pisa, Genoa and Milan. Nowhere was safe. On the road to the market they would pass piles of dead bodies lying by the side of the road, most of which were burned in huge fires. The smell of those fires was something that Daddi would never forget.

Two months had passed since the first outbreak. They lived quietly on the estate, which spread out to almost a thousand acres. Despite Margharita's protests, Christiano felt compelled to go work at his bank for at least a few days a week. After all, he couldn't just live here in the country and do nothing forever. It was about that time that those terrible lumps appeared on Angelina. She was the first to notice them.

Her two sisters, Margharita and Maria, as well as her daughter Estancia, looked after her even though Angelina largely refused to stay in bed. But when the fever took over and the dark spots appeared, they all knew that the end was near. Daddi called the best doctors he knew, as well as priests from Florence to come to the house to see her. He was frantic. He had all the wealth in the world, but it was useless in trying to save the woman he loved more than life itself. The priests said prayers and the doctors recommended the same remedies that hadn't worked for anyone else. Daddi stayed close to her. At night he drank himself to sleep, unable to quiet the ache he felt in his chest. He rarely left her side and barely slept for almost a week. He prayed as well. Not only to save Angelina, but, if Angelina couldn't be saved, then to take his life as well. He was ready to go. He would gladly trade his life for hers. He didn't want to live without Angelina by his side.

He held Angelina as she shook with fever. His heart ached to see her in such distress. He comforted and mopped her forehead with a cool cloth. He cradled her head in his arms and rocked gently back and forth, kissing the matted hair on her head. It took almost two weeks, longer than most, but in the end Angelina fell victim to the disease. On the night before she died, Daddi, crying almost uncontrollably, told her how much he loved her, that he always had, and always would. He held her in his arms and slowly rocked back and forth. He held her hands in his, gently stroking them. She had always been very self-conscious of the long pinkie finger on her right hand and tried to hide it whenever possible. Daddi had told her that was how God had singled her out for him as the love of his life. They had both laughed at that idea, but she had found comfort in it all the same. He always thought that there was some truth to it. Beauty, he told her, was not about perfection.

She was very weak and feverish, but she knew what he was saying and smiled as best she could. She held onto him and whispered to him her thanks for the life they had led. The next morning she was dead.

On a cloudy day with a steady, drizzly rain they buried her next to her children under the chestnut tree. Daddi felt more lost and alone than he had ever felt in his long life. He was angry. Why had this happened? Why had God taken Angelina? Why not take him? He was ready to go. Angelina still had a lot of life to live. Was he cursed to see everyone he loved pass away before his eyes?

A cool breeze blew across the hillside and rustled the leaves in the ancient chestnut tree. Angelina had always loved that tree. His daughters had climbed it when they were young. As a family they had picked the chestnuts in the fall and roasted them over an open fire under the tree while they drank wine and ate the sweet nuts. The tree, he thought, just like himself, endured, ageless and unchanged. But it didn't know the pain of losing your family, of being left alone in the world with a heartache that seemingly would never end. He looked down at the flowers laid on the graves of his family members, the petals fluttering in the breeze. They too will wither and die, he thought, while I remain.

Chapter 40
Florence, Italy, December 1348

The months after losing Angelina formed a grey, lifeless blur in his memory. It was later that same year that Daddi decided it was time for him to move on. Estancia and Christiano, Margharita's former husband, gradually made their way through the grief of losing half of their family. Sharing a common bond of sorrow, they became closer and ultimately decided to become husband and wife.

Daddi was heartbroken at the loss of Angelina, as well as his daughter, Constanzia, and four of his grandchildren. His desire to paint had faded away and he spent long days by himself aimlessly walking the countryside. Being outside, among the olive trees, grape vineyards and rolling grasslands covered with sheep was where he felt most at peace. He decided at that point that Daddi the painter would cease to exist.

After dinner one night, he brought out a bottle of grappa and set it on the large, wooden table in the courtyard. He poured glasses for Christiano and Estancia, as well as himself, and asked them to be seated.

"I am going to ask you to help me with something that I know you will find odd. Perhaps you will even think that I have gone mad. But I assure you that I know exactly what I am doing and it is the right decision for me to make. I will need your help and your promise to never speak of this to anyone else. Can you make me that solemn promise on the souls of your mother and your lost children?"

They both looked at him in silence. Estancia was the first to speak.

"Father, you can trust me with anything. I will do whatever is in my power to help you in any way you can. You just need to ask and I am ready to serve."

Christiano heard how earnest his new bride was. While he had not planned on making promises on the souls of his dead children, he had always trusted and respected Daddi, and felt that it was his obligation to assist him. He looked Daddi in the eyes and gave his reply.

"I also will serve you in any way that I can. Whatever you tell me will go to my grave, if that is what you wish."

For the first time in months, Daddi's face warmed into something close to a smile. "I apologize for putting such a heavy burden onto you both. Once I tell you what I have planned, you will understand why I need such a vow of silence."

He patiently explained to them that he had lost his will to paint and to continue the life of the well-respected and renowned artist. If Bernardo Daddi remained, even if he lived in seclusion, he would be hounded by the wealthy and powerful to commission paintings for them. There would be no escape for him. He also realized, although he did not explain to them at that time, that being famous had the additional disadvantage of focusing people's attention on him and inevitably raising questions about how it was possible for the great artist to live so long and look so young. He wasn't ready for that level of scrutiny. It was easier to take this opportunity to put an end to that life and start a new, more reclusive one.

"I have decided that Bernardo Daddi must die, and I must take on a new identity. I have chosen the name Giuseppe di Bernardi."

While Christiano remained impassive, Estancia was unable to hold back her emotions. She cried out, amid tears, "Father, what do you mean that Bernardo Daddi must die? I have already lost my mother, my sister, and my children. I do not want to now lose my father!"

Daddi held her hand. "I know this is difficult to understand. You will not be losing me. I will be here with you always. Only my name will change, which will allow me to live here in peace."

Estancia nodded, apparently comforted by his words. Daddi turned to Christiano, who worked in one of the large banks in Florence.

"Christiano, I will need your help and influence at the bank and in the city government. We will need to make a new identity for Giuseppe di Bernardi and start transferring Daddi's assets to him. Can you help me with that?"

Christiano nodded. "As I said, I will help you in whatever way I can. I believe that I know who to talk to in order to make this happen. Of course, we will need to pay off some government officials to get a new name registered."

"Of course," replied Daddi, glad that Christiano was already approaching this from a logistical perspective. He was a serious young man who knew how to get things done. "You have my blessing to use whatever money you need to make this a reality."

They finished the evening talking about their plans and drinking grappa. It was the most animated that any of them had been since the loss of their family. It felt good to be talking about the future and this seemed to give them something to focus on other than their grief.

Over the next several months, with Christiano managing everything on the financial and legal side, Daddi gradually slowed down his painting, not taking on new projects, and working hard with his apprentices to wrap up the ones that they had in the works. They quietly transferred Bernardo Daddi's assets, including his country villa and the lands that went with it, over to Giuseppe di Bernardi. They had papers created to establish his new identity. Because he would be recognized in Florence as Bernardo Daddi, Christiano brought the papers to the villa for him to sign and to record all transactions.

He began building a new, smaller villa on the estate, choosing a hilltop location that gave him clear views of the valleys and hillsides of his property. It was out of sight of the main house but within reasonable walking distance so he could visit Christiano and Estancia and vice versa. He gave his main building to Estancia and Christiano, to live in and raise a family. He planned on spending the next several decades walking the countryside, overseeing the harvests and the wine making, and traveling throughout Italy and beyond. He wished to remove himself from his old life, which was full of memories of Angelina and the people he loved and had lost.

The most emotionally taxing part of the entire process was planning Daddi's funeral. While Estancia knew that her father would remain, albeit with a new alias, it still pained her to think of losing Bernardo Daddi. Nonetheless, they persevered together, making preparations throughout the summer. Daddi publicly complained of feeling ill and then disappeared to his villa. Because the plague ran its course so quickly, and because Florence and the rest of Europe were still in the heaviest throes of an epidemic that would last for three more years, no one thought it odd when they heard the news that the great artist had succumbed, like his wife and children, to the plague.

Daddi, through Christiano, had ordered a coffin to be brought to the villa. In the month prior to this, Daddi had made a life-size plaster casting of himself and went so far as to paint the entire statue in his image. This they carefully dressed in fine clothing, including a hood, and then wrapped the entire statue in layers of blankets. Daddi had experimented with various plaster mixtures and thicknesses and had come up with a statue that weighed approximately as much as himself. Thus, to the casual and even to the modestly careful observer, this facsimile would easily pass muster. Besides, with the plague raging, people were less than enthusiastic about wanting to look at another dead body up close, even the body of a famous artist.

Although not as large as Giotto's funeral, the city mourned the passing of the great artist with a large ceremony and feast. Daddi's remains were buried in the church of Santa Croce, where a number of his triptychs and wood panels were already part of the church's elaborate decorations. Christiano and Estancia attended the ceremonies and did an admirable job of expressing their loss. After all, even though they knew that Daddi was in fact still alive, it was a moving and emotional experience to see over a thousand well wishers, many from the greatest families in Florence, greater Tuscany, and as far away as Rome and Venice, at his funeral.

When they returned to the villa that evening, they shared the experience with Daddi. He had seriously contemplated showing up to the ceremonies in disguise, but decided in the end that it would be better for him to stay out of Florence for a while, no matter how well camouflaged. He was pleased to hear that the ceremony was well attended and of all the warm comments from former patrons, apprentices, clergy and admirers of his work.

After Christiano and Estancia had gone to bed for the evening, Daddi sat alone by the fire and reflected on his life and where it would take him. He was tired of painting. He had lived the life of a famous painter two times over. He loved the beauty of art and the dedication to the craftsmanship that it entailed. He had enjoyed building his wealth and his fame, but now wondered what it was all for. He also enjoyed sharing his knowledge and skills with younger artists, much like he had with his sons one hundred and fifty years earlier. But the loss of Angelina and his daughter, Constanzia, had hit him hard. He had had everything a man could ask for, but he hadn't appreciated it at the time. He was tired of losing the people he cared for the most. It was one thing to lose a loved one to old age. It was something quite different to lose them to a sudden and terrible illness. He didn't know exactly what the next few years held in store for him, but he knew that they at least did not involve painting. When he retired for the evening, Bernardo Daddi was officially dead. The next morning Giuseppe di Bernardi began his journey in the world.

≪∞ Chapter 41 ∞≫
New York, March 2010

Mackenzie and Anthony had met a number of times since he had disclosed his secret to her. She was full of questions and he was more than willing to answer them. He hadn't thought so at first, but it felt good, after all these years, to share himself with another person. He hadn't done that for hundreds of years, and even then less than a handful of times.

They liked to meet at the small diner in midtown where Mackenzie had initially told him of her suspicions. It made it easy to grab the train to the Cloisters afterwards. They tried to sit in a corner in the back and always got there early before the morning crowds started rolling in. The place was mostly filled with cops who had either just got off duty or were just about to start, as well as a mix of service workers, construction workers, and business people. Anthony loved places like this.

Anthony looked around the diner, cradling his coffee mug with both hands. "You know the great thing about New York diners is that they remain a point of convergence for an entire city."

"What do you mean a point of convergence?" asked Mackenzie.

"It is a place where rich and poor alike can enjoy a bagel with cream cheese or eggs with corn beef hash and freshly brewed coffee and orange juice. If you want to start your day with a Bloody Mary, so be it."

"My father has always loved diners. I guess I've always been drawn to them as well. There's a certain unpolished charm to them," agreed Mackenzie. "No one orders a double skinny macchiato with an extra shot. You order a coffee and they bring it to you in a white, ceramic mug. You're responsible for adding anything else to it."

"Exactly," responded Anthony. "There is a casual grace, a beautiful simplicity to a diner. It is one of the few timeless fragments of society that has not changed much since the 1920s."

Mackenzie sat back and reflected on the time she had spent with Anthony and how close they had grown over the past several months. She had observed and unconsciously catalogued his eating habits, which at least for breakfast were on a pretty regimented rotation at the diner. He cycled through four breakfasts: oatmeal with fruit and cream, coffee, no juice; bagel with cream cheese, lox, tomato, onion and capers with coffee and orange juice; two eggs sunny side up with corn beef hash, whole wheat toast, coffee and orange juice; and buckwheat pancakes with butter and maple syrup, bacon, home fries and coffee. He drank his coffee black. She made it a personal game to try and guess his order before he made it. So far she was batting about .700. Her father would be proud.

She hadn't disclosed Anthony's secret to her father, which weighed on her conscience terribly. They never kept secrets from each other and he knew she was keeping something important from him. She had promised Anthony not to say anything and she was true to her word. She thought about broaching the subject with him on several occasions but it never seemed like the right time. Or maybe she didn't want him to specifically say no to her request.

"I'm sorry to change the subject," she said after a few moments of mutual silence. "But this has been bugging me. Fra. Lippi was a monk. He started his life in a monastery. Wasn't it hard to follow the monastic life after being married and having families?" asked Mackenzie between bites of her muffin.

"No, actually it was perfect for me at the time. My daughter, Estancia, and her husband, Christiano, had both passed away. Their two daughters, Maria Constanzia and Christiana Angelina, were married and starting families of their own. It was odd that I was around at that point. I enjoyed working on the farm and in the vineyard, but I was ready for a change. I wanted to get closer to God, to learn the secrets that I thought the Dominicans could either teach me, or at least direct me towards. Most of the time I enjoyed being a monk. Having a regimented routine and a lot of time to just sit and think and pray were good things for me at that point in my life, at least for a while."

"Yeah, you didn't exactly follow all the tenants of the Dominican order, did you? Especially the one related to celibacy?" Mackenzie said with a sly smile as she blew on her tea.

"I said that a lot of the monastic life was good for me. Not all of it." Anthony winked, with what she detected as a hint of a blush. "Outside of having an affair with a nun and having a child, I think I was an exemplary monk." They both laughed at how absurd that statement sounded.

"Given the time period, they were pretty cool about the whole thing, don't you think? I mean they could have burned you both at the stake or tortured you into renouncing your affair and returning to the 'true' path."

"You could probably say that I was mature for my age," he said with a knowing grin. "Even though I was a relatively junior monk, I was very good friends with the Prior and some of the other monks higher in the order. I knew that they had had their own, shall we say, inappropriate liaisons, and not always with women." He paused as the waiter refilled his coffee mug. Another waitress in a matching gray dress and white apron passed by with an omelet that looked like it could feed a small family, along with a side of crisp fragrant bacon.

"The Catholic Church was an immensely powerful and wealthy institution at that point in time. There was no shortage of eager young men from wealthy families who were willing to join the priesthood and donate a sizable portion of their families' wealth to the church. Having a son in the clergy was not a bad move financially or politically for a wealthy merchant or even a nobleman. A bishop in those days was more powerful than all but the wealthiest merchants, and a cardinal was as powerful as most kings. Remember that two members of the powerful Medici family, Giovanni and Giulio, eventually became Popes Leo X and Clement VII. That would be like two Rockefellers or Rothschilds becoming popes, although the Medici were more powerful than either of those two families. So they really did not need the distraction caused by a disgraced monk and nun hanging around the cloister or in the community. Better to release them from their vows and let them remain friends of the church, especially since my artwork was already well known both within and outside of the church. I attribute it more to sound business decision-making than forgiveness."

Two policemen in crisp blue uniforms walked into the diner and sat down at the counter. The waiter working behind the counter brought them two cups of coffee without asking for their order and welcomed them casually. Mackenzie always felt a kinship towards police officers, having grown up with them her entire life. She imagined that her father spent a good deal of his early career just like these two, walking the beat, stopping in the local diner for breakfast. She often wondered, if her father could, would he go back and do it all over again? If it meant having her mother back, she thought he definitely would.

Mackenzie paused, then asked, "Up until this point we've covered your progression from Berlinghiero Berlinghieri to Bernardo Daddi to Fra Lippi. Who came next? Did you take a hiatus and emerge as Rembrandt, Sisler, or someone else?"

Anthony sipped his coffee and thought for a moment.

"No, I quit painting professionally for almost five hundred years. I paint privately and work as a restorer, but I have not painted as a professional artist since about 1470."

"Why not? Why did you stop?"

"Let me answer that by asking you why you became a restorer," responded Anthony.

"Because I love paintings, and restoring old ones that have been damaged is very fulfilling."

"Yes, it is indeed," replied Anthony, "but I doubt that anyone really sets out to be a restorer. What did you want to be when you were a girl, a restorer?"

"I'm still a girl," said Mackenzie, laughing.

"Funny, yes, you are. You know what I mean."

Mackenzie thought for a moment and then said in a more serious tone, "I wanted to be a painter. From the very beginning I wanted to be a painter more than anything. I used to dream that one day I would have my own show in the great galleries in New York and Paris and everyone would know my work." She thought back to how she used to imagine smartly dressed people viewing her exhibit, glasses of champagne in hand, remarking on how exquisitely she had captured something magical with her work.

"So what happened?" asked Anthony quietly. "What stopped you from becoming a painter?"

"Because by the time I got to college, I started to realize that I wasn't good enough to be an artist, or at least good enough to be the artist I dreamed of being. And by the time I got to grad school I knew for sure. My friend, Kat, is ten times the artist I am and she can't make a living at it. I knew I had a good eye for detail and a lot of patience, and thought that being a restorer might be a good fit. I loved all the additional science and history and research involved as well."

"So are you content with the choice you made?"

"Yes, I love what I do."

"Do you ever look back and wish that you were an artist?"

"No, not really," she lied. Mackenzie had always wanted to be a painter. That desire never left her. She told herself she didn't care, but she knew it wasn't true. "I mean, I would love to be good enough to be considered a great artist, but I'm not. But I try to be very good at what I do now and hope that I'll eventually be considered a world class restorer."

"In that case, in many ways you know why I stopped painting, at least professionally, almost half a millennium ago." Anthony smiled. "You know, when I say half a millennium out loud, it sounds ridiculous."

"But that doesn't make sense," said Mackenzie, almost jumping out of her seat. "You were a great artist. You were three great artists, people that art historians study, that art critics write about and respect. You were considered one of the greatest artists of your time—in fact, three of the greatest artists of three different times!" she said.

Anthony took a last bite of his bagel and wiped his mouth with his napkin. He took another sip of his coffee, which the roaming waitress had just topped off for the fourth time.

"Greatness is relative, or I should say that the perception of greatness is relative. True greatness is not relative, it is absolute. I realized that years ago." Anthony paused a moment and then continued, somewhat nostalgically, "You are quite right, I was fortunate to have been considered a successful artist. I loved being an artist. I loved everything about it. I loved mixing pigments, setting *glare*, trimming my brushes and choosing the right piece of wood. I loved working with young apprentices, seeing their enthusiasm and watching them grow. I would never trade those experiences. I loved watching the look on people's faces when they first saw one of my paintings. I would sit quietly in church and watch as people would come and stare in wonder at some of the triptychs or other paintings that I had made. It is a wonderful feeling when people appreciate something that you have poured your heart and soul into."

"Do you know how rare that is?" asked Mackenzie. "Do you know how few people there are who have experienced what you are talking about? I mean, I can only imagine that feeling."

"Yes, you are absolutely right. I was blessed and feel very fortunate to have had those experiences." Anthony paused and sat back in his seat and looked towards the ceiling, almost in a dreamlike state and continued. "I was confident in my skills and comfortable in the world that I created. I had been honored by Lorenzo and Cosimo de' Medici and by popes and royalty alike. They all sang my praises and it was easy to get taken away by that world."

He looked down at his coffee. A sad look crossed his face momentarily before he continued. "I think that the first time I started to feel that perhaps I was being passed and falling behind was when I saw how rapidly Sandro Botticelli was growing as a painter. I knew that he was going to be great from an early age. By the time I decided that Lippi's time had come, in 1469, the same year that my friend Piero de' Medici passed, Botticelli had emerged as the premier artist of Florence, and perhaps even the entire world. I went into seclusion for a little more than twenty years. When I did return as the young Antonio de Bernardi and presented myself to Lorenzo de' Medici with the papers signed by his grandfather, Cosimo, Botticelli had just finished *The Birth of Venus*. At this time Lorenzo was already embroiled in a terrible dispute with Girolamo Savonarola regarding the future of Florence. He proudly showed me a number of Botticelli's works, including his favorite, *The Adoration of the Magi*, which, as you know, placed Lorenzo and his family, as well as Botticelli himself, in the nativity scene and furthered the myth of the Medici that Lorenzo was so keen on creating. He knew that Botticelli's paintings, just like Donatello's sculptures, marked the start of an era, a new age. Of course we now call that the Renaissance, but that term had not yet been coined. Lorenzo introduced me to a young man, a boy, really, whom the family had taken into their household. That young man was named Michelangelo Buonorroti."

Mackenzie had listened quietly, working hard not to let her excitement show. But she couldn't hold it in anymore.

"You mean that you met Michelangelo when he was a young aspiring artist?" she asked excitedly, trying not to speak too loudly in the diner.

"Yes, it was in late 1490. You cannot imagine the thrill and at the same time the gut wrenching feeling of failure that seeing his work had on me. Having just seen Botticelli's greatness, I looked upon the work of a young artist who I knew immediately would become one of the greatest artists the world had ever known. And this was before ever seeing his greatest works. It would be almost ten years before he began carving the statue of David or painting the Sistine Chapel, but I knew. I had seen great art many times over. But I had never actually felt what I did when I saw Michelangelo's work. It moved me in a way that I have never felt before or since. My head was swimming. I thought that I would either faint or throw up. I forced myself to gather my composure and speak intelligently with Lorenzo. But by then I knew. I knew that I could no longer consider myself a great artist and began to doubt if I really ever was one."

To some extent, Mackenzie knew how he had felt. Her own epiphany happened during her senior year at Bryn Mawr. She was putting the finishing touches on the final piece for her show. Every senior art major at Bryn Mawr put on a personal exhibition of their work. She had already received rave reviews from her teachers and fellow students alike. While trying to remain humble, she knew that it was going to be one of the best exhibits anyone had seen in years. Then she ran into Laura Walters, a freshman, who was working in the studio late one evening, which was rare for first year students. Mackenzie walked over to take a look at what she was painting with the intent of giving the underclassman some encouragement. It only took an instant, but she knew that nothing that she had painted, ever, was as good as the painting that this freshman was working on. Of course, Laura Walters was a very nice girl and was very deferential and complimentary to Mackenzie and her work. After all, Mackenzie was a senior and the acknowledged star student of the department. Somehow the fact that Laura was so nice made it worse. In the blink of an eye her entire world had been shattered and this unassuming eighteen-year-old girl was to blame. Mackenzie hated herself for the feelings of anger and jealousy she felt, but she couldn't help it. She would never be as good a painter as Laura Walters. From that moment onward she never looked at herself, at least as a painter, in the same way again.

She wasn't sure what to say. Everything she thought of saying sounded trite, or worse, like pity. For a while they just sat quietly. It was the first time she had ever seen him look sad. After a long pause, she broke the silence.

"You know, if every artist held themselves up to Michelangelo's standard, not a lot of artwork would have been made since the sixteenth century."

"That is very true. It is a ridiculous standard to set for oneself. In fact, it is arrogant to even consider yourself in the same breath as Michelangelo. I have yet to see any artist who reached his level, either in painting or in sculpture. I guess it was less about comparing myself to that standard than realizing that I could never be a 'truly great' artist. I still feel that way. There have certainly been great artists since Michelangelo. Van Gogh and Monet, Picasso, Rembrandt, and a handful of others. They are all truly great. I would never put myself in their company. So if I did create a painting, I would know that it was destined to be something less than great, and that essentially took the winds out of my sails, so to speak."

Mackenzie understood what he was saying, more so than she cared to admit. But at the same time she felt that he was being way too hard on himself. "Five hundred years is a heck of a long time to let a great sailing ship sit in the harbor waiting for the right breeze. Being an artist isn't about being the best and comparing your work to anyone else's. It's about creating something beautiful, of interpreting the world in a unique way, using light, shadow and color to tell a story that hasn't been told before. You obviously have a God-given talent that few people possess. Students in art history classes throughout the world study your work. There are books written about Daddi and Fra Lippi. You have something inside you that few people possess. I can't imagine that it doesn't want to come out and stretch its wings, or test the wind, like you said."

Antonio leaned back and laughed quietly. He ran both hands through his hair and clasped his hands behind his head.

"You would have been good in sales. Perhaps it is you who missed your calling."

"Are you saying I'm not a good restorer?"

They both laughed and went on with their breakfast.

❧ Chapter 42 ❧
Florence, Italy, June 1462

Filippo Lippi, also known as Fra. Lippi, watched as his wealthy patron remained lost in thought, staring through the large windows of a drawing room in the Medici palace onto the courtyard below. After an extended period of silence and contemplation, he turned around and addressed Lippi.

"Filippo, I want to commission two more paintings to place in the palace," said Cosimo de Medici.

Cosimo had always been an enthusiastic observer of Lippi's work and had been a consistent patron, benefactor, and friend. He had also helped smooth things over with the church when Lippi had decided to renounce his vows after a not-so-secret affair with a nun, Lucrezia Buti. Lippi enjoyed the fact that Cosimo was able to effectively and gently prod him to reach greater heights while also turning a blind eye to Lippi's playful indiscretions with the opposite sex. From Lippi's perspective, it was a perfect partnership.

Cosimo had inherited a thriving business from his father, Giovanni di Bicci de' Medici, and turned it into a financial and political empire that had few rivals, but numerous enemies. Despite his enormous wealth and influence, Lippi saw that Cosimo, probably on the advice of his father, preferred to keep a low profile. He was always well-dressed, but not flamboyantly, unlike many wealthy merchants of his day. Lippi couldn't help but think of the contrast between the subtly dressed but enormously wealthy and powerful Cosimo, and the flamboyant, colorfully dressed Giotto of his previous life. He imagined that the two of them would have gotten along well. Cosimo knew talent and Giotto certainly had plenty of it.

Lippi admired Cosimo immensely. He was a steadfast supporter of the arts, and a more loyal friend you could not ask for. But he also knew that Cosimo's support for paintings, sculptures, and buildings was not just for personal reasons. It had much more to do with demonstrating power than for enjoyment.

While still a young priest in the monastery, Lippi had watched, almost a quarter of a century earlier, while Cosimo cemented his family's position within Florence by sponsoring the architect Brunelleschi, who was able to complete the enormous dome of the cathedral of Florence. The cathedral had stood unfinished for almost a century, and served as a constant embarrassment to all of Florence. Cosimo steadfastly stood behind and funded the admittedly unconventional Brunelleschi, despite extreme criticism and ultimately treachery on the part of the Medici's chief rivals, the Albizzi. In the end, the dome was completed in 1436, an achievement that Cosimo celebrated by hosting, and largely funding, the Council of Florence.

Lippi nodded calmly as he stood with his hands clasped calmly behind him and peered out the windows onto the bustling streets of Florence.

"Cosimo, you know that I am always happy to paint for you. It is an honor that I relish. Did you have a particular topic in mind for these paintings?"

Unlike the other wealthy men that Lippi knew, Cosimo was a thoughtful, quiet man who rarely showed his true emotions in public. Cosimo paused and furrowed his brow slightly, which Lippi knew was the sign that he was thinking through the answer carefully before providing a response.

"Perhaps something to do with the adoration of the child. I have always been drawn to people's amazement at viewing the Christ Child. I thought this would be a subject that would interest you."

Lippi nodded. As usual, Cosimo's taste was exceptional. This was a good topic that would indeed be interesting to paint.

"You are right that this is an excellent topic. Please let me think this through and come up with some initial sketches for you to review." Lippi hesitated slightly before continuing, "I will make two paintings for you, but only charge you for one."

Cosimo continued to look out the window with his hands casually crossed behind his back. A slight smirk appeared on his face. Still looking out the window he said, "Filippo, it has always been my experience that free ultimately tends to be the most expensive price of all. What is your reason for only charging me for one painting?"

"This will actually cost you nothing. I ask only for a favor, and not one for me."

"The plot thickens, my friend," said Cosimo warily. "What favor might you be looking for?"

"I seek to set up my nephew and his family as special emissaries to the Medici to assist in the evaluation and acquisition of art. There are many wonderful artists in Rome and Naples, Siena, Venice, and even Brussels and Barcelona that you should know. You will need a trusted person to evaluate these artists and their work in person and decide whether they are worthy of the Medici family's collection. You should also have someone that you can trust implicitly who can monitor the various projects that you have sponsored. As you know, artists can be easily distracted from their work and often need a gentle hand to get them on track."

"I know of such an artist myself. He has often needed more than a gentle hand, as I'm sure you would attest," said Cosimo with a mischievous grin.

"Indeed," continued Filippo, ignoring Cosimo's playful dig. "My nephew, although quite young, has a great eye for art, but lacks the skills to be an artist himself. I have seen flashes of brilliance in his insights regarding some of the finest paintings here in Florence. He has even given me recommendations on my own paintings that have proven to be surprisingly valuable for one so young. He has a keen eye that I am helping develop. I believe he could be of great use to you and your family as your fortunes and influence grow. After all, you of all people know the value of trusted friends."

"So you are asking me to appoint this young man as an artistic emissary to the Medici?"

"That is exactly what I am asking. He still needs grooming and development, which I have committed to providing. After all, I am not a young man anymore. I will not be on this earth forever. As you have done, I feel an obligation to provide for my family when I am no longer here."

After an uncomfortable pause, Cosimo laughed heartily.

"Filippo, I have known you for almost twenty years. You are a wonderful artist and a great teacher. I have also known you to be a man who can't resist chasing every beautiful woman he sees, married or otherwise. However,

I have rarely known you to be such a generous and selfless individual. I am sure there is some angle to your offer but I am at a loss to find it. I will have papers drawn up to appoint this nephew of yours as an official art emissary to the Medici. What is the boy's name?"

"Alas, I feel that as I have aged, so have I felt the pangs of guilt for my selfish lifestyle. Perhaps after all these years the teachings of my Dominican masters are finally sinking in. I thank you for your support and trust. You will not be disappointed. The boy's name is Antonio di Bernardi."

❧ Chapter 43 ❧
Florence, Italy, March 1488

Antonio di Bernardi walked through the expansive Medici Ricardi palace alongside Lorenzo de' Medici. Antonio was now thirty-four years old, five years younger than Lorenzo. He had just returned to Florence after spending ten years traveling throughout Italy, France, Belgium, Spain, Germany and other parts of Europe. As an emissary of the Medici family, he met with and ultimately secured numerous works of art from some of the finest artists in the world. He was particularly captivated by the work of Venetian artists like Giorgio La Castelfranco and his master Giovanni Bellini. Bellini in particular had been influenced by the work of Flemish artists who had started working in oil as opposed to tempera.

While Antonio did not work as an artist himself, he was able to accurately sketch paintings by these Venetian masters along with providing detailed descriptions and recommendations, which he would send by courier to Lorenzo. In most cases, Lorenzo agreed with his suggestions and made numerous purchases to add to his ever-growing collection.

Based on Bellini's suggestion, Antonio made his way to Belgium, where he came to know the revolutionary work of Robert Campin, Rogier van der Weyden, Jan van Eyck and many others. He was impressed not only by the use of oils and the rich colors they provided, but also the minute details shown in the paintings. Intricate landscapes of the town center would appear in the background window of a portrait of a young woman sitting in her house.

As he had seen in Venice as well, these artists had branched out from the traditional focus of biblical subject matter for their paintings. Campin's simple yet elegant portraits of men and women, not kings and queens or princes and princesses, but of merchants and townspeople, and of course wealthy landowners, brought a new life and possibility to what was thought of as art. Antonio himself felt the liberating effect this had on the artists themselves. He enthusiastically shared his excitement with Lorenzo, who purchased many of these masterpieces for his palace.

Antonio had returned to Florence a little over a month prior, after finishing his latest trip to Germany. While there, he had seen the work of a young man who, at thirteen had painted a self-portrait with so much power and striking realism that Antonio knew he was bound for fame. That young man, Albrecht Dürer, the son of a goldsmith, was apprenticing with an accomplished and successful woodcut illustrator named Michael Wohlgemut. Antonio was fascinated by the woodcut artist's skill and came upon Dürer quite by accident while visiting Wohlgemut. He immediately knew that the apprentice would far outpace the master, if he hadn't already. He promised to stay in close contact with the young Dürer and had plans to eventually sponsor a trip to Florence and Venice for the young artist.

They stopped in the palace's private chapel to admire one of Lorenzo's proudest works. As they stood on the geometrically patterned tile floor filled with circles, triangles, and squares that Antonio had always found strangely out of place, they took in the beauty of Gozzoli's exquisite fresco, *The Journey of the Magi*, which adorned every wall of the chapel. Benozzo Gozzoli was a well known artist who had worked with Fra Angelico on several frescoes for the chapel of Pope Nicholas V in the Vatican, as well a fresco cycle of *The Life of St Francis* in the church of San Francesco. Lorenzo's father, Piero, had summoned Gozzoli to Florence in 1459 to create an elaborate fresco that portrayed key members of the Medici family in the procession of the Magi into Bethlehem. Of course, in this version of the procession, the countryside was the lush, rolling hills of Tuscany. The young King Caspar was none other than Lorenzo de' Medici followed by Cosimo with his sons Piero, Giovanni and Carlo, prince Giuliani and even the painter himself. The entourages of each king were enormous and richly decorated with dozens of gold-gilded horses, pack animals loaded with gifts, camels, monkeys, rare felines and falcons, along with wild deer and hounds in the background engaged in an elaborate hunting party. The message was clear and unambiguous. The Medici family was powerful and clearly part of a greater plan. This painting was used by the Medici to help promote the myth and legend of their family's greatness. This was always one of the first places Lorenzo brought important visitors to the palace. Of course, it was important to say a prayer in the chapel, but it was more important to see and feel the power that emanated from every wall.

Antonio had been to the chapel many times. Nonetheless, it had been almost a decade since Antonio had stood in the chapel and seen this beautiful masterpiece. It was glorious. The vibrant color and richness and sheer pageantry of Gozzoli's fresco was something he never tired of experiencing. They stood in silence while Antonio looked closer at the details of the various components of the painting. He thought that a person could look at this fresco a hundred times and still find something new and unique ever time you saw it.

"Tell me," said Lorenzo breaking the silence, "how does this fresco compare with those you have seen in Venice and Brussels?"

Antonio paused and thought about the question.

"It is more playful and not quite as dimensionally sound as many of the more recent paintings. The faces are not as well developed as the newer paintings. Remember, we are talking about a fresco that is almost thirty years old now. Painters now are reaching levels of realism and perspective that were unheard of even twenty years ago. However, those newer works, and especially those in Bruges and Brussels, lack the majesty of this painting. Look at the young king, for instance. The striking jewel encrusted gold medallions in his brilliant blue crown; his golden, flowing locks and the look of calm on his face as he looks at us from inside the painting. Those elements are found nowhere in greater richness than here in Florence, and indeed in this painting. As my uncle Lippi always told me, we are growing ever more realistic in our painting, but with every step we lose a bit of the nobility and magic of the old masters. I think that I agree with him."

"Hmm, interesting insights," responded Lorenzo. "My father told me that your uncle, Fra. Lippi, mentioned on more than one occasion that you had a fine eye for art, and I certainly have found that to be the case. Come, I want you to see some of the most recent works and artists here in our academy. You can tell me how they compare to the other artists you have seen."

Lorenzo led Anthony through a number of wide hallways, elaborate sitting rooms, salons and finally out through a series of open-air walkways and into an enormous artist's studio.

"This," exclaimed Lorenzo proudly, waving a hand in front of him to the expanse of the room, "is the surprise I wanted to show you. I have established an art school where artists from Tuscany and beyond can study, flourish and hone their skill without having to serve any single master. To my knowledge, it is the first of its kind." They continued walking through the immense studio, which turned out to be a series of studios, each dedicated to different styles and techniques. Sculptors were hard at work in one room, painters in another, bronze gilders in another. There was a room neatly filled with pigments, powders, eggs for tempera and glair, gum Arabic, alumina, vermilion, red ochre, cinnabar, azurite, and dozens of other vegetable dyes and raw materials needed for painting. Neatly stacked cypress planks of various sizes stood at the ready, as well as parchment, both for painting and for boiling. There was a small workshop set aside for brush making with ermine tails and hog's bristles, waxed linen, goose quills, and long straight pieces of chestnut, lark and maple for brush handles.

This academy was at least ten times as large as the largest studio either Daddi or Giotto had at the height of their fame. He was amazed at what Lorenzo had put together, but then again, Lorenzo de' Medici never did anything on a small scale.

"In all my travels I have never seen an academy of art as spectacular as this. I believe that there is nowhere in the world where such an academy exists. It is truly remarkable," said Antonio in awe.

"I wanted to have a place where artists could learn from and be inspired by each other. There is freedom here. But I only bring in the finest artists to study and develop here at the academy."

Lorenzo continued to lead Antonio through a series of studios, which seemed to go on without end. They turned right and entered a small room flooded with light from several large windows set high in the walls. There were three artists working on sculptures in various stages of completion. Lorenzo led him to a thin boy who was hard at work chipping away at a block of marble.

"Michelangelo," called Lorenzo. "Stop and meet a friend of mine."

The boy put down his chisel reluctantly and stood before Lorenzo.

"Michelangelo, I want you to meet Antonio de Bernardi, my personal art consultant and buyer."

"A pleasure to meet you sir," said the boy meekly.

"The pleasure is mine, young man. What is it that you are working on?" asked Antonio.

"I am just practicing my work on arms and hands right now. My master, Domenico Ghirlandaio, says that I must master the entire body before I focus on the face of my sculptures."

They moved closer to the block and Antonio was struck by the power that emanated from the unfinished sculpture. The arms were muscular yet sensual, and the hands seemed to reach out longingly to an unseen presence. Most of the sculpture itself was unfinished, but it seemed to Antonio that this young boy was releasing the body from its granite tomb. He wasn't just carving it, he was giving it life. He could literally feel its presence. There was something special, magical even, about his young boy's talent. He had personally met the greatest artists of the past two hundred years and yet they paled in comparison to this boy who was just honing his skills.

Lorenzo added, "Michelangelo just came to us and now lives as part of our family. Ghirlandaio expects much from this young man and I trust that he will emerge as a first rate sculptor in a few years."

"Do you only sculpt or do you also paint?" asked Antonio.

"I prefer sculpture, but I also paint. I feel freer with a chisel in my hand than a brush, but I enjoy the ability to use color that painting provides," answered Michelangelo without hesitation.

"I have only met a few artists who are equally adept at sculpture and painting. Perhaps you will be one of those rare few. I look forward to seeing your work in the years to come," said Antonio. He thought that if this boy's painting was anywhere near as good as his sculpting then Lorenzo would have indeed found the world's greatest artist. He also knew, without a doubt in his mind, that he himself was incapable of making anything that possessed such clear power and force that could move people so strongly. It was a so-bering realization, but one that was becoming ever more common the more he met other great artists. But he had never felt it so clearly as he did with this twelve-year-old boy.

"Thank you, sir," responded Michelangelo and then returned to chipping away at his block of marble.

Lorenzo and Antonio continued their walk.

"Keep an eye on that one," said Lorenzo in a conspiratorial tone. "I expect that he may one day be Florence's greatest artist."

Antonio nodded as they continued their walk. He doubted that even Lorenzo himself knew the potential of this boy.

❧ Chapter 44 ❧
Rome, Italy, October 1514

Antonio di Bernardi, personal art advisor to the Medici family, had been away from Rome for almost a year, traveling through Europe, appraising and acquiring art from some of the world's greatest artists, who at the time were in the Netherlands and, to a lesser extent, Germany. He was by and large pleased with the mounting and layout of the artwork he had last seen months earlier when he had personally selected them for the papal collection. He made some suggestions on rearranging some of the works and also dividing the German and Dutch paintings into separate galleries.

They had already spent the better part of the morning reviewing some of the recent papal acquisitions, which were both extensive and impressive. The group moved slowly through the labyrinth of hallways at the Vatican with three assistants to Pope Leo X. Alessandro Bertolini, a priest from Milan, was the most engaged of the three, and looked towards Antonio like a child seeking his father's approval on where the paintings had been hung, whether they matched the other paintings in the gallery, and noted gaps that the pope hoped to fill with some new acquisitions. The other two assistants, who were at least ten years Alessandro's senior, shuffled along and grunted or made the occasional comment to confirm that they were at least paying attention. Perhaps they thought their time as the pope's assistant would be spent learning secrets of the faith as opposed to ensuring that expensive paintings were hung carefully in halls that would be seen by only a select few. Either way, they were clearly not excited about what they were currently doing and didn't particularly care what young Antonio thought.

Antonio had known Leo X, formerly Giovanni de' Medici, and his cousin, Giuliano de' Medici, since their birth in Florence. Both Giovanni and Giuliano had been forced to flee Florence when the Medici were expelled from the city in 1494.

After his expulsion, Giovanni travelled extensively throughout Germany, France and the Netherlands for six years before heading to Rome. After Pope Julius's death, Giovanni was elected Pope Leo X in March 1513, and was welcomed back into Florence as the first Florentine pope. Within a month after being elected pope, Leo established Giuliano as both cardinal and archbishop of Florence. His extensive travels throughout Europe, his time in Rome, along with his early studies in his father's academies, had instilled in him a great love of art, which was only slightly less voracious than his ruthless ambition and Machiavellian political prowess.

At the end of the hallway a small group of men in clerical vestiges had gathered. There were several cardinals and assistants, as well as the pope himself. They were standing in front of a set of massive, carved wooden doors that lay open. The group of priests he was with, either out of deference, or fear, or a mixture of both, backed away to allow Antonio to reach this most august congregation first. The cardinals greeted Antonio as he made his way to where Leo X was standing. Antonio knew some of them, but most he had never met before. Upon reaching the pope, Antonio dropped to one knee and kissed the extended ringed finger of the pontiff.

"Your eminence. I am blessed by your presence." Antonio knew all too well that Pope Leo thrived on and expected deference and praise. The pope surrounded himself with sycophants and dealt ruthlessly with those who opposed him. Antonio didn't particularly like Pope Leo, nor had he thought highly of his predecessor, Julius, but he did enjoy the opportunities that being the papal art collector afforded him.

"It is good to see you, my old friend. You look well. I hope that being back in Rome is agreeing with you after so much travel abroad," said the pope casually.

"Yes, your excellence. I never tire of returning to the eternal city and tasting all it has to offer."

"Indeed. One tires of sausage and beer after a time and welcomes some real food," laughed Leo.

"Yes, your eminence. You are quite right about that."

"Come, Antonio. I called you here today because I wanted you to see what must be considered one of the wonders of the world. You of course know that Michelangelo Buonorroti was commissioned by my predecessor, Julius II, God rest his soul, to paint the ceiling of the Sistine Chapel. What you perhaps did not know was that he finished it a little over nine months ago. Have you seen the chapel at all during the painting process?"

"No, your excellence. I knew that Michelangelo had been working on it for several years, but I have not seen it at all." He had, in fact, kept a watchful and admiring eye on Michelangelo ever since his first meeting twenty-six years earlier. He was present for the unveiling of the *Pietà* as well as *The Tomb of Pope Julius II*, both of which were breathtaking. It was all he could do to keep himself from fainting as he stood in stunned rapture the first time he saw the statue of *David*. He had visited that statue multiple times since and always found himself speechless, overwhelmed by the sheer emotional force the statue brought out of him. There had of course been rumors throughout the pope's inner circle about the stunning beauty and grandeur of the Sistine Chapel ceiling, but because of his travels he had yet to see it himself.

"Excellent! It is exactly as I had hoped. There is no better way to see its glory than for the first time and in its finished state. Come, let us go in."

With a gentle shift of his hand, Leo led Antonio and the group through the doorway. They entered into an enormous rectangular room with a marble floor that mixed concentric circles with more linear geometric patterns, all below a large domed ceiling. The walls were thick and plastered with regularly spaced tall stained glass windows on both sides that filled the room with light. The chapel itself was not particularly beautiful, especially compared with some of the spectacular gothic cathedrals that had gained prominence throughout Europe. Without question the focal point of the entire chapel was the vast ceiling, which was completely covered by the most beautiful fresco that Antonio, or anyone in the rest of the world, had ever seen.

Leo, never being one to miss a dramatic opportunity, stopped and raised his left hand upwards towards the ceiling.

"Behold, the completed fresco by Michelangelo."

Antonio didn't hear anything. He just stared overhead at the masterwork painted by the same boy he had met in the Medici academy. To think that the same person painted this spectacular fresco and also carved the greatest statue the world had ever known was beyond belief.

The fresco was remarkable not only for its sheer size and grandeur, but for the beauty and the detail of the work itself. This was a painting that any artist at any time in history would look at in awe and realize that they were in the presence of undeniable greatness. They would also be humbled by his talent. The angelic face of the young Delphic Sybil, lips slightly parted, turning gently back to look longingly into the distance. The innocence and beauty in her face belied her massive arms and frame. She was clearly out of proportion because no woman would have such muscular arms, but somehow she lost none of her femininity. You couldn't help falling in love with this woman. In the center of the ceiling was the image of a powerful Zeus-like God reaching out to touch the finger of Adam, extending life to mankind. The image, the color and the detail were so vivid, so real, you could feel the power of creation in His outstretched finger, which did not quite touch the lazily outreached hand of Adam.

Antonio, as well as the others in the group, wandered the room as if in a trance. There were occasional exhalations of emotions and Leo intermittently pointed out individual scenes and described them to the group. But by and large the men moved about in silence, their gaze never leaving the ceiling. They were in the presence of greatness and they all knew it. After what could have been an hour, but was probably much less than half that, the pope spoke.

"So, Antonio. What do you think?"

Antonio, as if awakened from a dream, barely heard the question. He gathered himself as best he could and forced his mouth to vocalize something. He realized that tears were streaming down his face. He turned away and brushed them aside with his sleeve.

"Your eminence. I have never seen anything so beautiful in my life. This is without question the greatest painting in the history of mankind."

The pope smiled approvingly, the smile of a proud father.

"Excellent, I agree with you. I do not have your extensive knowledge of art but it would seem that the art of painting has been elevated to a higher level. You are fortunate. This is the pope's private chapel. Few below the level of cardinal or prince or duke, for that matter, enter this chamber. Outside of conclave, when the College of Cardinals gather to elect the new pope, no one enters without the personal invitation of the pope."

Leo's father would have smiled at his bravado and his grandfather would have grimaced at it, thought Antonio.

"I cannot express my honor and gratitude, your excellence. I am humbled and awed in the presence of such a masterpiece." He knew then that he would never paint again, at least not professionally, and perhaps not at all, after seeing this enormous work, every inch of it better than anything he was capable of painting. He had known for years that there were many artists greater than him. But he had hoped, somewhere deep inside, that perhaps there was still a place for him as an artist. This fresco, immense and at the same time precise, neatly severed that last cord of hope. There was a calmness that somehow wrapped itself around the pain that accompanied the finality of this realization. He would never be a great artist, and he now admitted to himself, that he probably never was.

He moved onward with the remainder of the group as they made their way out of the chapel. He spent the rest of the day and the next month, in fact, in a daze. The image of that fresco was burned in his memory. Over the next several centuries he would return to the chapel, sometimes on his own, with the pope's blessing, and much later with crowds of tourists. But he never forgot the first time that he saw that chapel in its original majesty.

❧ Chapter 45 ❧

Mackenzie spent the better part of the previous month trying to come to grips with her feelings about Anthony. She lay in bed on her back, which inevitably turned out to be the signal for Octavius to climb on top of her chest. His face was so close to hers that she could actually feel his breath. Having fifteen pounds sitting directly on her rib cage didn't promote good sleep, but it was comforting to have him sitting there while she thought. Ever since Anthony had revealed his secret, they had grown closer and, at least from Mackenzie's perspective, their relationship had moved to a different level. She had no idea if Anthony felt the same way.

After playing it over in her head a hundred times, Mackenzie finally decided to say something to Anthony about how she felt. She had never in her life met anyone that captivated her, who made her feel that she was part of something more than just her everyday life. She was comfortable with him, but tense at the same time. She felt pressure to never let him down. It was odd. Other than her father, she had never felt so concerned about letting another person down in her life. It wasn't that Anthony was judgmental. In fact, it was just the opposite. He accepted her as she was, without pointing out her mistakes and making nit-picky comments about what she could do better, like her mother had. No, it wasn't that Anthony ever criticized her or intentionally revealed her weaknesses, even though she was sure that he could clearly see them. It was that she was so—in love, would be the best description, and in awe would be a close second. She just wanted to be the best person she could be whenever she was with him.

She asked him at work if he wanted to have a drink and some dinner that evening, and he accepted. Anthony recommended a small, casual Italian restaurant in midtown within a couple of blocks of Bloomingdales. It was very reasonably priced, especially for Manhattan, and he went there quite often. He enjoyed their simple, fresh pastas. They also had a great selection of Italian wines by the glass that he liked to sample.

It was a drizzly, chilly spring evening and they decided to share a cab from work. During the cab ride they engaged in small talk, mostly about projects they were working on. The restaurant was filling up rapidly. Fortunately she had called ahead for reservations. They were shown to a small table in the back, passing well-dressed couples and businesspeople enjoying a meal after work. Once they were seated, they ordered a glass of a simple, clean Soave from the Veneto region.

Mackenzie was fidgety and found it hard to offer anything more than superficial nods and "*Uh-huhs*," to most of what he said. Anthony was not a particularly talkative, extroverted person and didn't mind sitting in silence. Mackenzie was typically the one who initiated and drove most of their conversations. She was good at getting him to open up and once she got him started, he was more than able to carry the conversation to any number of subjects. After all, he certainly did have a lot of experiences from which to draw.

They spent most of the meal in idle chatter about work, new paintings that were coming in, Broadway shows, good and bad movies that they had seen, etc. She was so nervous. She went through three glasses of water before the entrees arrived. The server now made it a habit of topping off her glass every time he passed the table.

Mackenzie was clearly not her normal bubbly self and Anthony seemed to have noticed.

"Are you all right?" he finally said as they were sipping espressos at the end of the meal, "Is anything wrong?"

This is it, the moment of truth, she thought. *It would have been better if I had initiated the topic, but here goes.*

She took another sip of water, feeling her hands shaking. "Anthony, I feel really strange saying this to you. I enjoy our time together so much, I don't want to say anything that would jeopardize it. But I need to know if there's not something more than just a good friendship here. I've got feelings for you that go beyond friendship and wanted to see if you felt the same way."

There, I've said it! she thought. *Now it's in his court.*

Anthony sat back in his chair and looked thoughtfully at the ceiling for a moment. Then he leaned forward and placed his hands around Mackenzie's, which were folded in front of her on the table.

"I wanted to say something, but wasn't sure how best to say it," he said, warmly looking into her eyes. "I have very strong feelings for you. I just don't know where they should go or what to do about them."

"Why don't we do what other people do when they have strong feelings for each other and see where they take us?" asked Mackenzie, feeling elated to have him holding her hands.

"It is actually not that simple. I know that it never is and that relationships are always more complex than they seem, but our situation is much more complex than you might think."

"Do you mean because you're probably going to live for another thousand years and I won't?" she asked with a hint of sarcasm.

"Certainly, that is part of it. You cannot imagine how much it hurts to lose those that you love, over and over again. It creates sort of a hard outer shell that protects you from getting too attached so that you do not have to feel that pain again."

"I understand. But certainly it's better to love and be loved than to wall yourself off from your feelings." Was he rejecting her? Was this his polite way of saying that he just wants to be friends? Her heart already felt heavy in her chest.

"Yes, that is very true. There is nothing in life that compares with love. Without love, there would be no art or music or great literature. It is something that binds us all together, something universal. It compels us to greatness and at the same time exposes our deepest fears and weaknesses."

"Then what you're saying is that love is worth the effort and the pain, but you're not sure if it's worth it with me?" Despite her best efforts to keep her emotions in check, tears began welling in her eyes.

"No, no, that is not what I am saying at all. I need to show you something that will help explain why I think that our relationship is more difficult and complex than you think and why I do not think that we can pursue a romantic relationship, even though I would love to as much as you would.

Can you come to my apartment and see what I mean?"

"Okay, this is not where I thought this conversation would be going. What in the world could you show me in your apartment that would explain why we can't be together?" she said, both confused and upset.

"I could probably show you here, although I do not have a computer with me. I know it sounds crazy, but I need to show you something and my apartment is relatively close by and it would be easier to show you there than anywhere else. Please, humor me on this."

"If this is your idea of playing hard to get, then you're terrible at it!" said Mackenzie, only half jokingly.

They walked, mostly in silence, the twenty minutes or so it took to get to Anthony's apartment. The rain had stopped. The chill of early spring was still in the air, damp and musty. It only smelled this way when the bitter cold of winter pulled away and the snow turned to rain. Remnants of the winter's snow clung grudgingly to the sides of the street, hard, grey, encrusted and seemingly unwilling to leave. Snow in December is beautiful, thought Mackenzie, fresh light and delicate. Snow in March, however, was dirty and unwelcome. It matched her feelings at the moment, gray and despondent. She had no idea what he was going to show her, but she was sure that it wasn't going to take their relationship to where she wanted it to go.

They came to Anthony's apartment, took off their wet coats and shoes in the entryway. Anthony poured them both a glass of sherry and led Mackenzie to the computer in the main room.

"Have you ever researched your ancestry?" he asked nonchalantly.

"Not really," replied Mackenzie. "I guess I know about as far back as my grandparents, and I do know that my great grandfather on my mother's side was from France and that my dad's family mostly came from Italy. Other than that, not much."

Anthony made his way around the keyboard and quickly got to the page on the screen that he was looking for.

"As you might imagine, I've got a unique interest in genealogies, ancestries and the like."

"I guess so. I wouldn't have thought of it if you hadn't mentioned it, but yeah, I guess you would be pretty interested in that type of thing." She paused a moment. "But in your case, you probably pursue it from a different direction than most people, don't you?"

Anthony laughed. "Very good. Yes, absolutely. Most people who research their ancestors are looking at who came before them, or perhaps more specifically, whom or where they came from. In my case, I am more interested in who came from me. Let me show you something." He directed Mackenzie's attention to the detailed family tree that now appeared on the screen.

The entire computer screen was filled with a genealogical tree showing her entire family. She grabbed the mouse and scrolled down the page. It went back centuries. Strange names from a distant and, up till now, unknown past filled the screen. She felt somehow violated, as if she had walked into the room of a stalker and found hundreds of photos of her plastered on the walls.

"Holy crap, you've mapped my entire genealogy! I don't know whether to be fascinated or freaked out." She took a deep pull on her sherry and then poured herself another from the bottle on the table.

"I mean, seriously, this isn't something that normal people do! This is something that a stalker does! Is this what you wanted to show me?" She grabbed her head with both hands, trying to figure out what was happening. She was confused and a little pissed off.

"I apologize if I have in any way violated your privacy. That was not my intention at all," said Anthony calmly. "I think that you will find some interesting things about your ancestors." He pointed to several of the branches above her and to the right of her parents.

"One of the things that I find quite fascinating about this ancestry program is that you can benefit from genealogical research that has been conducted by others. For instance, it appears that one of your distant relatives, Eric Tellinson, has done a lot research to fill out your family tree. Are you familiar with him?"

Mackenzie looked closely at the part of the broad tree that appeared on the screen.

"No, I can't say that I've even heard of him. I do recognize the names of my cousins that are listed here. How far does this thing go back?"

"One of the advantages of living this long is that I have a vast knowledge about people who have lived, who they were descended from and who descended from them. It is a relatively worthless knowledge base, but it certainly comes in handy when you are trying to fill out a puzzle like this one." He moved backwards several levels on the tree.

"You are correct that your father's family were from Italy. They came here, like many other immigrants at the turn of the twentieth century, when Italy became a country. I am sure if we went back many centuries before that we would find that some of them came from Greece, like most Italians did. But my research did not go back that far. I only went back until the fourteenth century." Anthony turned from the screen and looked at Mackenzie.

"As far as I can tell, and obviously there is some speculation in some of this, but your very, very distant ancestor was a young couple who lived in Florence in the late 1300s. The mother's name was Christina Angelina Garibaldi. She was the daughter of Christiano and Estancia Garibaldi. Estancia's maiden name was Daddi." Anthony paused momentarily and then continued. "Her mother's name was Angelina Antinori and her father was the painter Bernardo Daddi."

The blood drained from Mackenzie's face. She looked from the screen and back at Anthony.

"Do you mean that I am one of your descendants?"

He smiled gently. "It would appear so. Twenty-two generations separate us, but the line is quite distinct. I would not have been able to connect the dots if it were not for the work that this Eric Tellinson fellow had done."

Mackenzie was at a loss for words. She just stared at the complex branches on the screen.

"How long have you known about this?"

"Probably for the past three to four months," replied Anthony.

"Why didn't you say anything to me before now?" asked Mackenzie.

"You must forgive me. I guess that I have become quite secretive over time. I also see time a bit differently than most people. A decade must seem like a long time to you, but it seems like only a few months to me. I am somewhat hesitant in sharing cryptic knowledge until the moment presents itself. You never know when the right time will come. Tonight was the right time." He paused and then continued. "Do you understand now what I meant earlier when I said that our relationship was more complex than you knew?"

It was all a whirlwind to Mackenzie. She didn't know what to think. She actually wasn't sure whether she was going to throw up on Anthony's carpet, right then and there. An hour ago she was essentially telling this man that she was in love with him and now she was faced with the startling fact that she was actually descended from him. It was surreal. It was too much for her to take.

❧ Chapter 46 ❧

J oe sat on the porch drinking coffee and reading the newspaper and looked at Mackenzie. It was a beautiful Saturday morning in May. He had broached the topic of Anthony several times in the past several months and Mackenzie had told him that everything was fine but she couldn't tell him more than that. Being a detective, he didn't like leaving ends loose or mysteries unsolved. As a father, he was most concerned with her well-being. It remained an elephant that sat between them that neither wished to address.

He folded the sports section that he had just finished and set it on the porch. Mackenzie sat on the glider holding her coffee mug in both hands.

"Yankees seem to be on a roll this year, Dad. Could be another repeat of last year."

"Humph" he grunted. He never liked to be too optimistic about the Yankees for fear of jinxing the team. "They're 21-8 right now and crushed the Sox last night, but it's just the beginning of May. We'll see what happens. If A-Rod plays well in the post season like he did last year instead of choking like he normally does, then they stand a pretty good chance."

He took a sip of coffee and then changed topics. "Thought you might be interested to know that they were able to ID some partial prints off of that dagger that found its way onto our porch."

Mackenzie looked at him with surprise. "I thought they ran it, but couldn't find a match."

"That's right," said Joe, clearing his throat. "But they pulled in a guy the other day on a completely unrelated charge and his prints matched those on the dagger." He paused and a knowing smile came to his face. "Guess who Mr. X turns out to be?"

She shook her head.

"Turns out he's the nephew of none other than Stephen Thomas."

She looked at him and her mouth silently formed a, "Wow!"

"Yep," he nodded. "Looks like this young man had somehow kept his nose clean up to this point and had never been printed. But it seems like he might be doing some minor errands for one of the families, probably the Genovese, and got nabbed. Fortunately for us, he was stupid enough not to wipe the dagger clean. You'd be surprised how often that happens."

"So that's pretty incriminating for Stephen Thomas, isn't it?"

"Circumstantially, yes," he replied. "It doesn't really mean anything, but it definitely directs suspicion back to him and might be enough to get some more resources directed at him. I think we're close on this one, Kenz, and he knows we are. This little gesture on his part only helps direct the spotlight a bit more."

She nodded. "It also exonerates Anthony from having anything to do with it."

He rubbed the stubble on his chin and neck. "That it does." He paused. "But you already knew that, didn't you?"

"Yes, I did, but it's still nice to tie up loose ends," she smiled. "Isn't that what you always told me?"

"Yes it is," he agreed. "Unfortunately, because my daughter won't share what she knows with her father, who tirelessly helped her work through this puzzle, it only ties up one of many loose ends as it pertains to Mr. Bataglia." He looked at her with a wry smile. It bothered him more than he cared to admit that Mackenzie was keeping a secret from him. They had always been so close and shared everything with each other, especially after her mother died. He wasn't sure if he was more upset about the fact that she wouldn't share what she knew with him or that this whole Anthony Bataglia mystery remained another unclosed loop just sitting out there, taunting him. He had done everything he could to help her make sense of it. They worked as a team. Then, just when it looked like they were going to crack the case, she betrayed him and closed him out. For some reason she chose to give her allegiance to Anthony as opposed to him. That, more than anything, more than the lack of closure, was what hurt, and he couldn't easily get past it.

"I know, Dad. I wish I could tell you more, but I promised that I wouldn't. Not now at least. Maybe there will be a time when I can. I hate to keep anything from you, but I have to honor my word." She paused, grinning. "That's another thing you taught me, isn't it?"

He grunted to himself. "All I care about is that you are safe. I still have my doubts," he pointed a friendly finger in her direction, "that you helped raise, by the way. But I trust your judgment and I respect your privacy. I'm always here if you need my help."

"I know that, Dad. You know I would never keep anything from you unless there was a good reason. You've always been there for me. I'll be fine." She saw the hurt in his face and hoped that she could share Anthony's story with him at some point. That time was not now, though.

❧ Chapter 47 ❧

Anthony sat at the counter with Mackenzie looking onto the traffic on West 4th Street. Even though it was a bit more of a commute to the Cloisters for him, she had coerced him into joining her for breakfast at Joe Muffin, which she mentioned was a favorite haunt of hers from graduate school. Anthony had never been here, but the dreadlocked chef Jean Paul's roasted red pepper, arugula, and feta quiche seemed to whisper invitingly to him from behind the glass counter when they placed their order. He watched as the owner, Angela, unsuccessfully tried to convince Mackenzie to try something other than a poppy seed muffin and cappuccino.

He sipped a double cappuccino while he ate the quiche with the beautifully crumbly homemade crust. "I am both disappointed and offended that you never brought me here before," he said, feigning an indignant glare.

"Don't feel bad. This is the first time I've ever come here with a guy. I'm pretty sure they were convinced that I was a dyed-in-the-wool lesbian or a desolate loner."

He nodded. "The wonderful thing about great cities is that they can transpose culture and time. I have had incredible quiches in Paris, of course, but I have also had quiches that are just as good and perhaps better in Copenhagen, London, and Tokyo. This one is right up there. A Parisian would be impressed by this quiche." He paused, looked around the café suspiciously, and then whispered to Mackenzie. "Although he would be loath to admit it in public."

She laughed. "I've never tried anything but the poppy seed muffin, but I'm willing to put it against anything Manhattan can offer. I'm not sure if poppy seed muffins are big in France, but I bet this one would hold its own in a Paris bistro as well." He watched Mackenzie nibble around the edges of her muffin and sip her cappuccino. *Such an interesting woman*, he thought, *and at the same time very much a little girl.*

"I want to tell you something and I hope you take it how it's intended," continued Mackenzie.

Anthony turned to look at her. "This sounds pretty serious. Let me have it."

"You need to start painting again."

He looked at her with a playful smile. "I do paint. I am a restorer. I paint every day. I also paint in my studio. You have seen my work, on numerous occasions." He knew what she meant and was trying to get her off the subject.

"You know what I mean. For the past couple hundred years or so you've occupied your time touching up artwork you or one of your friends or family painted six or seven hundred years ago, or making copies of someone else's work. You haven't released a new painting since the Renaissance, for Christ sake."

He calmly looked around the cafe. Fortunately there were very few other customers near them. He gestured to her to keep her voice down, especially when it had to do with talking about being alive for several hundred years. "I told you why I stopped painting." It did not appear that she was going to give up without a fight. He expected nothing less from her.

She leaned in closer to him and in a softer voice continued. "Yeah, and I actually understand why you stopped. But, like I said before, if every great painter decided not to paint because they weren't as good as Michelangelo, then there wouldn't have been a new painting since about 1550. It would be like a musician deciding not to make music because the Beatles or Mozart did it better. Maybe you're not as good as Michelangelo. Let's say that's the case. There's still a lot of room in the realm of great painters who aren't as good as Michelangelo."

Anthony wiped the crumbs of the quiche from his mouth and sipped his cappuccino. She was right, of course. Comparing yourself to geniuses was not only a sign of arrogance, it was a recipe for disappointment. He had lived with that feeling for centuries.

"You know that I have not thought of actually painting something new in ages. I cannot remember the last time that I felt the urge to try to become

242

a painter again. I am not sure if I still have what it takes to be one. You have to *need* to paint to be a great painter, not just *want* to paint." He repeated to her what he had told himself many times over. He wondered how much of it was the truth and how much was an excuse. At this point, he had to admit that it was probably fifty-fifty.

"Then you have to develop that *need* again. Think of what type of painter you could be now, having seen so many great painters throughout the ages. I've seen both your original works and the replicas you've painted, and both are phenomenal. Your style would be something that the world has never seen."

Hmm, he thought, *that is an interesting perspective.* She was a tough person to argue with, not only because of her persistence but because of her spot-on insights. "Perhaps you are right. On the other hand, perhaps I have been so many different painters, and I have seen and copied so many more, that I no longer have a style of my own. It is all such a jumble to me sometimes." Anthony looked down at his folded hands on the table. He had struggled with this so many times in his mind. In some ways, he had to admit, perhaps only to himself, that he was scared. He was scared that he no longer had what was necessary to be an artist.

"You need to find out who you are now. Your style will emerge once you put brush to canvas. There's no one alive who can incorporate more knowledge and experience than you. Think what that would be like!"

Anthony smiled. He had always been attracted to intelligent women who weren't afraid to speak their mind. Mackenzie reminded him of his second wife, Angelina. It was crazy but perhaps Angelina was talking to him through this long distant descendant of theirs, separated by over two dozen generations.

"I will think about what you have said," he said after a thoughtful pause. "But right now, I want to focus on the rest of this quiche. If I do start painting again, and that is a big if, then you need to try one of these."

"It's a deal." Mackenzie went back to work on her muffin with a satisfied smile.

❧ Chapter 48 ❧

Several months had passed since Anthony had shared his finding that Mackenzie was likely his direct descendent. Their relationship had grown even closer, although not necessarily in the romantic sense that Mackenzie had wanted. But she understood and was fine with where it was headed. Anthony was away on business in Italy, but would be returning in the next day or so.

Mackenzie had taken the opportunity to go on a ten-day trip to Cancun with her college friend, Katarina. It had been a wonderful time to sit back, drink beer and tequila and just lounge around in the warm Mexican sun and read Carlos Castaneda novels. The beaches were beautiful, the whitest sand and the clearest aqua blue water she had ever seen, and the snorkeling in Cozumel was amazing. Towards the end, she couldn't wait to get back and tell Anthony all about it. They were putting the finishing touches on Fra. Lippi's *Adoration of the Magi* and were expecting to receive another Lippi, this time Lippi's son, Filippino, sometime in the next week or so. Mackenzie had never really thought of it much, but she now found it strange and oddly surreal that Filippino Lippi was likely a very distant relative of hers.

After a quick breakfast with her dad, she headed to work. She made it to the Cloisters at about 8:30 a.m. where she was met by Simon Davidson just inside the main entrance.

"Hello, Simon, I wasn't expecting an official greeting upon my return, but it's most welcome," said Mackenzie cheerily.

Simon looked far from cheery.

"Mackenzie, I'd like to speak with you in my office, if you have a minute," he said, and without waiting for her reply ushered her downstairs to his office.

Uh oh, she thought. She had never once gotten in trouble in school but this must be what it felt like to be taken down to the principal's office. *I wonder if I did something wrong?*

When they reached his office, he offered her a seat on a straight-backed fourteenth century wooden chair that was beautiful to look at, excellent for your posture, and slightly more comfortable than the rack. He closed the door behind her.

"I didn't want you to hear this from anyone but me." He paused a bit as he sat down behind his desk on what appeared to be a much more modern and much more comfortable chair.

"Late last week we received a report from Italy that there had been an accident. It seems that there was an explosion on a private boat that was sailing between Livorno and Elba," he hesitated. "No survivors were found. The name of the boat's pilot was Anthony Bataglia. The authorities believe that he was sailing alone."

Mackenzie stopped breathing. Her world had just been put on pause.

"Is he," she hesitated, "I mean, is he dead?" she asked, still finding it hard to even breathe let alone form cogent sentences.

"I'm afraid so," replied Simon calmly. "We were contacted by someone in Lucca who said that they were a trustee of the Di Bernardi Family Trust. Apparently, Anthony was a beneficiary of that trust. He had us listed as his current place of work and the trust felt that we should know."

"How did they identify him?" she asked, trying to maintain whatever level of decorum she had left.

Simon looked at her with thoughtful, caring eyes.

"I know this is very hard. It's been hard on all of us. We thought the world of Anthony. I know that you two were very close. The man who called said that the Italian Coast Guard had been notified of an explosion at sea by one of the big cruise ships in the Mediterranean. What they found was the tattered remains of the ship, as well as some documents, a passport, an international certificate of competence in navigation, some credit cards, etc. They all belonged to Anthony. The boat was purchased by the Di Bernardi Trust last month. The man at the Marina where the boat was docked positively identified Anthony as the person who had set sail the previous day. They did not find a body but it was pretty far out at sea and the explosion happened around midnight according to the cruise ship. The Coast Guard searched the area but you can imagine that it's a huge expanse of open ocean. I didn't ask for more than that."

Of course not, who would in such a situation? Mackenzie thought that she probably wouldn't have asked either.

"I—I don't know what to say." She paused as tears filled her eyes and she felt the full force of what she had just heard flow through her body. She thought she might pass out.

Simon poured her a glass of water from a sixteenth century French ewer sitting on a low bookshelf near his desk.

"Here, take a sip of this. I know this is very hard. I'm not a therapist or anything. We don't usually get news like this and I'm not well prepared to convey it. Take as much time as you need. If you would like to take some time off, I totally understand. Everyone here is pretty shaken up about the news."

"Do they know how it happened?" she asked, stumbling over the words.

"The Coast Guard believes that it was most likely a propane tank used in the galley that had a leak and then a spark lit it off. Apparently it's rare but it does happen now and then." Simon was clearly distraught himself, but was trying hard to hold it together for Mackenzie's sake.

Mackenzie sat, tears streaming down her face, trying to come to grips with what had just happened. An explosion on a ship? She didn't even know he owned a boat! He never mentioned a boat or sailing or anything like that to her. *I guess it could happen to anyone*, she thought, *even someone who had been alive since before America had even been discovered.* So many thoughts were going through her head. *Had it been quick? Had he suffered?* He had told her that he needed to go to Italy for a few weeks to take care of some of his affairs there. She hadn't thought anything of it. As natural as anything you could imagine. She would be in Mexico, he would be in Italy, and they would both be back to work today.

She didn't want to go home. Not yet, at least. What was she going to do by herself anyway? She spent the day as if she were sleepwalking. All the other conservators shared her grief and she spent most of the day sitting in front of a worktable talking with colleagues, sobbing or trying not to cry, but unable to hold it back.

She stared at the painting they had worked on together for the past month. It was stunning. Ever since Anthony had revealed his true past, there was something magical about restoring paintings with him. She wasn't just working with a master restorer, she was working with the original artist. She relished every moment they had spent together in front of those marvelous works of art. Now, she thought, with eyes red and sore from constant crying, she would never have that opportunity again. The day ended and she gradually made it back to her father's house, exhausted and heavy hearted.

† † †

The memorial service was Simon's idea. At first Mackenzie was against it because she didn't want to admit that Anthony was really gone. Simon gently convinced her that while it was painful for her especially, many of the other restorers thought highly of Anthony and would appreciate paying their final respects.

Two weeks had passed since Simon had shared the news of Anthony's untimely death with Mackenzie and the rest of the restorers. Because the accident happened so far away from them in Italy, they all had secretly hoped that the news was inaccurate, that there had been a mistake and that Anthony would eventually show up for work like nothing had happened. That didn't happen. In fact, Mackenzie and her father followed the story online. Her father still had some contacts in the Italian police force and they confirmed Mackenzie's worst suspicions. Anthony Bataglia was dead. It was official.

Her father had tried to comfort her as best he could, but she remained in shock. She couldn't believe that he was gone, vanished. How could someone who had survived so long, over half a millennium, die so suddenly? She hadn't even had a chance to really say a proper goodbye to him. They had both been busy getting ready for their trips and had just said a casual goodbye the last time they were together. After all, they would see each other within a couple of weeks. No big deal. Despite her father's efforts to make her favorite dishes, she had no appetite. She felt hollow. There was a part of her that just didn't even exist anymore. Anthony had taken it with him, never to return.

The restorers and Simon gathered in the cloistered garden during their lunch break. It was a warm, sunny spring day. New shoots had already come out on most of the trees and bushes and light green leaves danced in the wind. Simon held a rectangular wooden box in his hand. In the box was one of the paint brushes that Anthony had used on his last restoration, wrapped in a rag that smelled of turpentine. He felt that this was a fitting remembrance for a great artist. Simon had offered the rest of Anthony's supplies, his palette, the rest of the brushes and a few knives to Mackenzie. She accepted them appreciatively, although with little enthusiasm. It was just another sign of his absence, of the finality of it all.

Upon Mackenzie's recommendation, they had dug a small hole next to the Japanese maple in the garden. She told Simon that Anthony was very fond of that particular tree and she felt that it was as good as anyplace to bury his brush. They stood in a semi-circle in front of the small tree, its delicate limbs hanging limp, which seemed to reflect the somber mood of the group. There were six of them in total, Charles, Ariadne, Takeshi, Thomas van Arden, Simon, and Mackenzie. Simon said some words about Anthony. How they had been fortunate to have such a distinguished and talented restorer working with them at the Cloisters. Charles shared a story about how Anthony had given him some advice and historical insights about a cross that he was working on. He was amazed that someone in his thirties would know so much about a thirteenth century cross from Bologna, especially when that wasn't his field of expertise. They were all quiet individuals and predominately worked alone, so there wasn't too much to share. It was all Mackenzie could do to not just burst out crying throughout the entire ceremony, or whatever this was called. She held a handkerchief and blotted the tears from her eyes and tried not to shake uncontrollably. She had nothing to say, nothing that she had wanted to share with the group. She couldn't have spoken anyway, even if she wanted to. She was in love with Anthony. No one else knew how she felt and she wasn't about to share her deepest feelings with them now.

Simon carefully placed the box in the makeshift grave and they each tossed a handful of the moist dirt onto the box. Charles then finished the job and gently tapped down the earth and evened out the grave. They hugged each other with red eyes and headed back into the building. Mackenzie stayed behind staring at the grave and the small maple tree. Could she ever sit out in this garden and eat her lunch like she had done countless times with Anthony? Would this tree and this garden bring her comfort or just pain? She wasn't sure. She turned to make her way back inside and noticed a pigeon perched on the statue of St. Francis. She envied the bird's simple life. He didn't feel pain or loss or heartache. But she did, and it wasn't going away anytime soon.

❧ Chapter 49 ❧

After a quiet dinner during which she had barely spoken to her father and mostly pushed her food around the plate, she went up to her room and sat on her bed beside Octavius, who was curled up in a tight ball. It had been almost a month since Anthony's death. She had lost nearly ten pounds and her clothes hung loosely on her. Her father had gone from concerned to downright upset. He threatened to make her see a counselor if she didn't start eating more. She didn't care. She tried to force herself to eat, to actually care about eating, but she couldn't. She didn't care about anything anymore. She made her way through life in a fog. The past month went by slowly but she couldn't remember much of any of it.

At about 8 p.m. her cell phone rang. It was a strange, long number beginning with *3906*.

"Hello," she answered with some hesitation.

"Hello, Mackenzie, I hope I am not disturbing you."

The voice on the other end. So familiar. *Could it be?* No, it was impossible. It was just Mackenzie's brain playing tricks. She tried to answer, but her voice had left her.

"Mackenzie, are you there?" the caller asked.

"Anthony?" she managed to croak. "Is that you?"

"Yes." A pause, and then, "I apologize for not calling sooner."

She wasn't sure what to believe. Was this some type of horrible prank call? But who would want to make such a call?

"But, Simon told me—he told everyone that you were dead," she said, her voice cracking as tears filled her eyes. She could barely breathe. "My dad even got confirmation from the Italian police!"

"I know. It must have been a terrible shock for you. I am very sorry to have put you through such a thing."

250

"A terrible shock!" she erupted, trying to gain her composure. She wiped her eyes with her sleeve. "That's an understatement! Christ, Anthony, you put me through hell! Does this mean that you are all right? That you didn't die on a boat?" *Stupid question!* "Were you hurt? Are you in a hospital?" The questions just kept coming to her. She couldn't believe she was talking to Anthony again.

"Well, it is sort of a long story. Give me a minute and I will try to explain," he said in a calm, comforting voice. "Anthony Bataglia, the art conservator on loan from the Uffizi, passed away in an explosion on a private yacht off the coast of Livorno. That much is now accepted as fact by the police and the case has been closed. A propane gas leak in the galley of the boat caused the explosion. No survivors and no body found. Freak accident, yes. Raising undue suspicion, no." He continued, "I, however, am not dead, which pretty much goes without saying, given that I am talking with you on the phone right now."

This was too much for her to comprehend at the moment. She'd spent the last month in mourning, dealing with the finality of Anthony's life. She still hadn't really accepted it, but was finally starting to come to grips with losing him. And then, out of the blue comes a phone call from Anthony, or whoever he was now, calmly describing that he had staged the whole thing and that he was fine. Was this some sick joke?

"But why did Anthony have to die?" It was all she could think to ask at this point.

His voice remained calm. "A number of things came together at the right moment in time to make this possible. I told you before that timing these things is a bit challenging and you have to take your opportunities when they present themselves. Ultimately, I was able to do this because of your persistent nudging, which, if you were my wife, might be called *nagging*."

"What are you talking about? I never told you to kill yourself, or I mean, to kill Anthony." She wasn't sure what he was saying. So many conflicting emotions were hitting her all at once, happiness, relief, surprise, confusion, and now most of all, anger. "If you didn't die, then why did you let me go through the worst month of my entire freaking life thinking that you were dead?" She tried not to raise her voice and alarm her father, but it was hard. She was so upset she was visibly shaking.

"I know, and I cannot imagine what you must have felt. Trust me, if there were another way to do it, I would have. It happened very quickly. Besides, you are a terrible liar and I needed to have closure both here in Italy and there in New York. Everyone who knew Anthony needed to think that he was dead. If I had told you ahead of time, you could never have pulled it off. I mean that as a compliment. Being a good liar is not a worthy trait in a person; helpful on occasion, yes, but not admirable. You are one of the most honest and sincere people I have ever met. You could not tell a credible lie if your life depended on it. In this case, my life, or at least my current and future personas, depended on a credible lie. I hope you can at least understand."

The confusion had subsided somewhat, and so had the anger, at least temporarily. She was relieved, certainly. He was alive! Whatever his name was now, he was alive. Their conversation prompted Octavius to wake and begin passing back and forth against her arm, each time pushing harder against her, while she talked.

"What do you mean that I was the reason you did this?" She came back to something he said earlier that struck her as odd.

"You have been telling me for the past six months that I should paint again. Remember our conversation at that little cafe in the Village, the one with the great quiche? Well, I have decided to do just that. I am starting a new chapter in my life, and for the first time in about five hundred years, thanks to you, I am going to be a painter again. David Giacomo will begin his painting career in Venice. If not for you, I would never have decided to do this. The time is right. I am excited again. I have not been excited to be doing anything for longer than I can remember. I owe that to you."

Great, she thought, blowing her nose with a tissue. I'm the reason he decided to break my heart and throw me into full clinical depression. She hadn't cared about anything for the past month and now it suddenly seemed like a bad dream from which she had just woken. While she understood why he had done this, she was still so emotionally raw from what she went through that it was hard to process everything without breaking down. She realized that she had been standing for most of the conversation and made herself sit down before she passed out.

"What about us? Will I be able to see you again? Will you be coming back to New York?"

"I will be with you for as long as you live. You are the most important person in the world to me. I have a beautiful place in Venice that you are welcome to visit, or to live, any time. We can talk, Skype, or whatever, anytime you like. As far as coming to New York, it is probably better for me to keep a low profile for a while. Too many people know Anthony and you would be surprised how people react when they see a dead person walking the streets. But I do have a favor to ask of you, if that is all right."

"I'm not sure if I feel like doing you any favors after what you put me through, but what is it?" she said, trying to sound angry, but that particular emotion was gradually being replaced by relief and even elation. She gently rubbed Octavius under the chin while he raised his head towards the ceiling in casual delight.

"The di Bernardi Family Trust still owns a very nice apartment on the upper west side of Manhattan. You have been there a number of times, I am sure you remember the place. I hate to leave it empty and I cannot imagine selling it either. Besides, moving all of those paintings is a logistical nightmare. Would you be willing to live there rent free for as long as you like? It is completely paid for and the trust pays all maintenance fees. I can have papers drawn up next week to officially have you listed as the primary tenant. Is that something you are comfortable with?"

Living for free in a luxury four bedroom condo, filled with original masterpieces dating from the fourteenth century, with a view of Central Park didn't require a lot of thought.

"I'll do it on one condition. Octavius will be coming with me and walking all over your Persian carpets."

"I would not have it any other way. I hope the place will be to the little Emperor's liking."

They both laughed. After all the emotions she had experienced, she was able to laugh for the first time in a month. She hadn't lost him. He was still here. She would be living in his place, he would be painting again and they could be together, maybe not every day, but whenever possible. Making a few trips to Venice wasn't such a bad thing either.

"Mackenzie, I want you to know how much I love you. I have not felt like this about anyone for longer than you can imagine. You have made me feel alive again. I can never thank you enough."

"I love you, too," she said as her eyes filled with joyous tears. "I'm sure David Giacomo is going to do his predecessors proud. Please promise to stay in touch. I will hunt you down if you don't."

"It is a deal. Now try not to look too happy when you go to work and blow the whole thing. Remember, you need to be in mourning for a couple days more." He paused, "Oh, and there is just one more thing; you can call it fulfilling a promise if you like."

"You're starting to push your luck, Signore Giacomo," she said, trying to sound stern.

"Yes, I know. But I remember distinctly that you said if I were to paint again, you would try something other than the poppy seed muffin at your café. I would personally suggest the quiche."

She couldn't help but laugh, wiping back her tears. "Sounds fair to me."

❧ Chapter 50 ❧
Venice, Italy, October 2010

Fortunately, the summer with its pounding sun and unrelenting crowds had forgotten how hot it actually got here in the summer. One would think that being completely engulfed by water would help moderate the temperature of the archipelago. But that didn't seem to be the case. After all, Venice was originally created by draining swampland, which tended to be associated with high humidity. Having lived in New York for so long, he had forgotten about the unrelenting intensity of the Italian summer. It was hard for him to imagine a place that was worse than Florence during the height of tourist season, but Venice was making a strong push for the title.

He shivered as he remembered the summer; hordes of tourists from all over the globe jamming the streets, taking pictures in front of St. Marc's Basilica, cruise ships unloading gaggles of middle aged adventurers in khaki shorts and Tommy Bahama shirts, all carrying large bottles of water to guard against the dreaded possibility of being caught without clean drinking water, as if they were crossing the Sahara as opposed to touring a city with nearly a thousand cafés.

Venice's weather was both interesting and predictable. The winters were cold and the summers were hot. It often dropped below freezing in January and February and got up into the nineties in July and August. Both extremes posed their own challenges. October and November were nice, much like in New York. Sweater weather, as they say.

David Giacomo walked into one of the small cafes just a few streets down from his apartment, ordered a croissant and a cappuccino, and sat outside in front of the cafe. He casually nibbled on his croissant and sipped his coffee as he watched the city come to life. It was just after 7:00 a.m. He always relished watching a city slowly come to life. It didn't matter which city he was in. After all, you really didn't see an entire city come to life, per se; you saw a small sliver of that city spring to life. You could be in central London or the lower east side of Manhattan or Trastevere in Rome, Aoyama in Tokyo, Le Marais in Paris. It really didn't matter, because you were always watching a micro-sector of a major metropolis awake. It always started out slowly. The bigger the city, the earlier it rose. New York at five a.m. was as lively as Stockholm at six, actually more so. They were all pretty busy by seven. Just watching them shake off their overnight hibernation was always a pleasure. It was like you were eavesdropping on a private conversation, but without the guilt. No one noticed you. You were just another part of the cityscape. They went on with their normal routines uninterrupted and unbothered by the man in the corner sipping his coffee, nibbling on his croissant, reading a newspaper.

He had spent the better part of the past two months getting his place in shape, buying painting supplies, shipping some personal effects from Florence and purchasing some new furniture here in Venice. He wasn't in a huge hurry, which was good, because nothing was easy in Venice. You could ultimately acquire almost anything you wanted here, just like in any other city, but it took time and you more than likely had to get off the islands to make any significant purchases. Then those had to be brought onto the islands, carried through the narrow streets, up the even narrower staircases and installed into apartments with electrical and plumbing systems that typically were several generations past their prime. Fortunately, having done this more than a few times, he had instructed the broker he used to find an apartment that had recently been renovated and fitted with new HVAC, electricity, plumbing, and a modern kitchen.

The things you could get in Venice, if you knew where to look, knew what you wanted, and had patience and money, were treasures that could only be found here. You could find beautiful draperies of damask, silk, and velvet, and spectacular Turkish rugs that could have proudly adorned the Doge's palace. Murano glass chandeliers and sconces that threw a spectrum of color throughout the room, Venetian mirrors with elaborate frames made of etched or beveled pieces of mirror accented in black and vibrant red and yellow jewels, or gracefully shaped Fortuny lamps with fine silk shades were all easily available.

Venetian planning regulations required that you keep the outer walls of gray trachyte intact. But what you did behind those walls was virtually carte blanche. The choices were endless, from sixteenth century Venetian or Ottoman to twenty-first century Scandinavian contemporary. So behind the dingy gray walls that hadn't changed in centuries and looked as if they would crumble and fall at any minute lay palaces of unbelievable splendor. In some cases they truly were palaces, twenty to thirty room luxury estates that would have made Louis XIII proud. More often than not, those palaces had been divided up over time into eight-room mini-estates that were still spectacular in their own right.

David had found a six-room *Piano Nobile*, which in Venice meant the second floor, with larger windows and better views away from the dampness and inevitable flooding of the ground floor, in the Castello neighborhood, or *Sestieri*, of Venice. Castello was the largest of the six *Sestieri* that made up the Venetian island and was far away from the hustle and bustle of San Marco square, the Rialto Bridge, and the train station. His apartment on the Riva dei Sette Martin looked out onto the lagoon and to the open sea and gave him stunning views of the Campanile of San Marco, the Salute, San Giorgio Maggiore, and San Clemente.

In a word, his apartment was breathtaking. The ceilings were fifteen feet high, which, along with the tall wood framed windows, made the large rooms seem even more spacious. The walls and ceilings were covered in Venetian plaster, which was a mixture of plaster and marble dust, in this case pink marble, which was applied in multiple thin layers. These were then polished to a smooth finish. The marble dust gave a unique depth and sheen to the plaster. The floors were also pink granite, with generous appointments of Turkish rugs. The large French windows opened to a long balcony that ran the length of three entire rooms and looked out onto the sea.

David made one of the largest rooms his new studio. It was spacious and airy and filled with natural light. His current project involved painting a series of large frescoes that would cover the walls and ceilings of every room in his new home. The fresco would flow, appearing out of the plaster and then disappearing back into it. The edges would be undefined and the scenes would seem to drop off, as if complete sections had been plastered over. This was to be his new style, both for himself and for other patrons who might be interested in his talents.

When he wasn't getting his apartment and personal affairs in order, he spent most of his time wandering through the streets of Venice, taking photos of places and scenes that interested him. Venice at dawn and at dusk had two completely different color palettes. The vibrant early morning light contrasted sharply with the long shadows and tired light of the fading sunset. The canals themselves were a spectrum of colors ranging from a frothy pale green to a deep indigo. The sky and the water framed the spectacular silhouette of this magical place. Whatever you added beyond these could be either incidental or central to the scene. These would serve as the inspirations for his new paintings and frescoes. Gone were the limitations of having to paint interpretations of biblical scenes or portraits of saints, noblemen or wealthy merchants that he had labored for over two centuries to capture. Art in the past two hundred years had shown him that everyday life was a worthy subject with infinite possibilities. Just as importantly, he was confident in his ability to transmit this beauty to canvas or plaster and he was excited to be painting again. Where better than the timeless city of Venice to begin anew? David Giacomo had begun painting. Whether future art historians or critics would mark this time period and single out his work for study as they had done in the past was something that did not concern him. He was no longer obsessed with fame, as he had been for much of his career. He would likely never be another Michelangelo. But he had come to accept the simple truth that no one would. No one would be Van Gogh, or Da Vinci, or Monet, or Dürer, or in fact anyone else. He painted because he *needed* to paint. It was who he was, who he was meant to be, an artist.

He looked at his watch and then finished his cappuccino and wiped the crumbs of the croissant from his lips. He made his way to a nearby canal, flagged a water taxi, and directed the driver to take him to the airport. After winding his way through a labyrinth of canals they came to the open lagoon and on towards the mainland where Marco Polo airport sat beside the water. He paid the driver and made his way into the international arrivals area. He looked on the screen, awaiting British Airways flight 578 from Heathrow.

After approximately twenty minutes, he saw Mackenzie making her way out of customs. She flashed a warm, travel-weary smile when she saw him. They hugged and then headed out towards the lagoon to grab a water taxi.

"Did you have a nice flight?" he asked, rolling her luggage by his side.

"Yeah, it was pretty uneventful. I've never flown first class before. It was awesome. Thank you so much, it must have cost a fortune!"

"Glad you enjoyed it."

They climbed onto the water taxi and made their way towards the archipelago.

"You look great," she said admiringly.

"Thank you. You too. Your hair is a mess, but otherwise you look beautiful." They both laughed. "How is everything at the Cloisters?"

"Oh, it's good. I just finished up a Conrad von Soest. It's the second restoration I did from beginning to end," she said with obvious pride. "I think it turned out well."

They passed the tall smoke stacks on the island of Murano, where glass making had been moved from Venice in 1291 to reduce the risk of fire in the more populated areas.

"Of course it did. You are very good at what you do. I expect that you will be hitting Simon up for a raise in no time." They didn't say anything for a few moments as the taxi ferried them closer to the main islands, through the deep green and blue waters.

"Mackenzie, I have been thinking about something for a while," he said, breaking the silence. "You have not told your father about my situation, is that correct?"

"No, of course not. I promised that I wouldn't tell anyone and I haven't. Why?"

"I expected that to be the case. I also know that you are very close to your father and it must be difficult to keep something like this from him."

"It's been terrible, really. I've never kept anything from my dad and he helped me so much in piecing things together. I know that he respects my promise, but I also know that he feels hurt and there's something between us now that was never there before."

He could sense that this was something that had been on her mind for some time.

"As you can imagine, I have had to keep secrets from people I loved all my life. It is a terrible burden to carry and one that I do not wish to place on anyone, especially someone I care about as much as you." He paused, and then looked directly at her. "When you go back home, feel free to share my secret with your father. But, and you have to promise me this, the secret must stay with the two of you and no one else."

Her face glowed with joy in the warm Venetian sun. She wrapped her arms around Anthony in a big hug. "Thank you so much! You can't imagine how happy this makes me! I promise that we won't share your secret with anyone."

He placed his hands over hers. "Do you think he will believe you? Detectives are not really known for accepting incredible stories."

"Are you saying that I am more gullible than my father?" They both laughed. "I'm not sure whether he'll believe it or not, but he's always preached the old adage from Sherlock Holmes, 'once every other possibility has been ruled out, then the one that remains, however unlikely, must be the truth.' So, yeah, I think he'll believe me. I can be pretty persuasive when I need to."

"That you can," replied Anthony with a deepening grin.

The taxi plowed onward. The wind blew his hair back on his tan face, as he squinted into in the sun. He caught her staring at him. "Is something wrong?"

She pulled back the hair towards his temple. "I just noticed that you have some grey in your hair. I never noticed it before. Is it makeup?"

He turned towards her and smiled. "No, it is real grey." He paused for a moment as the main islands approached across the light green chop in the lagoon. "I guess you could say that it is just a natural part of growing old." He smiled at her.

She stared at him, momentarily taking in what he had just said. "Does that mean what I think it does?"

He just smiled and looked forward towards the Campanile in the distance. They turned into the Grand Canal and made their way into the center of Venice. Soft white clouds floated across the blue sky as centuries'-old buildings formed one of the most beautiful passageways in the world.

*H*ISTORICAL *F*ACTS

While the dialogue of all characters in this book is completely fictitious, a number of the main characters actually did exist.

BERLINGHIERO BERLINGHIERI was a well-known Byzantine painter from Lucca who was active from 1200 –1240. He had three sons who also worked as artists: **Bonaventura** (active 1228–1274); **Marco** (active 1222 – 1259); and **Barone** (active 1228 – 1282). There is a beautiful mosaic on the façade of the San Martino Cathedral in Lucca that remains today. Bonaventura's *St. Francis and His Life* altarpiece (1235) still resides in the church of San Francesco in Pescia, Italy. Berlinghiero's wife Ilaria is a created name.

BERNARDO DADDI was a Florentine painter (1280 – 1348). He was also likely an apprentice of Giotto. His birth date actually remains unknown, and in fact his death is estimated to be 1348 because his last painting was dated as 1347. After Giotto's death he became Florence's leading painter. His children's names, as well as his wife Angelina, are all fictitious.

GIOTTO DI BONDONE (1267 – 1337), known as Giotto, was a Florentine painter and architect. He is credited with making a break from the Byzantine style and bringing more accurate depictions of life in his artwork. There remains some debate with regard to who actually painted all of the Life of St. Francis frescoes in the Basilica of St. Francis of Assisi. It is widely acknowledged that Giotto and the Florentine painter Cimabue, who was a teacher of Giotto, painted the frescoes. However, in the absence of firm documentation the entire cycle of frescoes has been attributed to Giotto, mostly because of his prestige.

FILIPPO LIPPI, aka **FRA LIPPI** (1406 – 1469) was a Florentine painter, who was brought up as an unwanted child in a Carmelite friary, where he took his vows in 1421. He wasn't particularly successful as a friar and had an affair with a nun, Lucrezia Buti, who bore him a son, Filippino, and a daughter, Alessandra. They were released from their vows and allowed to marry. His son Filippino actually went on to become a successful painter himself. He was a highly regarded painter during his lifetime and was patronized by the Medici family.

THE MEDICI. The Medici family was one of the most powerful families in Florence, Italy, and indeed the world. It would be hard to compare another family's breadth of influence and power to that of the Medici.

COSIMO DE MEDICI (1389-1464) was an astute businessman fascinated by the secrets of ancient Rome and Greece and paid to have lost teachings, sculptures, and other artifacts brought back to Florence, which he envisioned would emerge as the next Rome or Athens. Despite fierce opposition, he supported the architect Filippo Brunelleschi in building the largest unsupported dome in the Christian world for the unfinished Duomo. He built his father's relatively small bank into an international powerhouse with offices reaching from Brussels to Cairo. At the time of his death, the Medici bank was the most profitable organization in Europe. He was the most sought after patron of the arts and can rightly be considered the father of the Renaissance.

LORENZO DE MEDICI (1449-1492) continued his father's support of the arts and founded the first art academy in the world, which would support, among others, Michelangelo, Botticelli and Leonardo Da Vinci. Known as Lorenzo the Magnificent, he was instrumental in pushing art into a more secular realm, much to the dismay of the church, and in particular an influential Dominican monk named Girolamo Savonarola who would continue to serve as an enemy of Lorenzo, the entire Medici family, and ultimately the foundation of the Renaissance itself.

POPE LEO X (elected 1513) was originally born Giovanni di Lorenzo de Medici (1475-1521), and was the second son of Lorenzo. His reign as pope (as well as that of his cousin Guillio, who was elected Pope Clement VII in 1523) was highlighted by political intrigue and conspicuous excesses. Leo X is also associated with granting indulgences to those who donated to the reconstruction of St. Peter's Basilica, which partly led to Martin Luther's 95 Theses. Despite Pope Leo's efforts to fight against Luther's premises, his reign saw the growth of Lutheranism throughout Scandinavia and Northern Europe.

POPE CLEMENT VII's reign (1523-1534) may best be remembered for his denial of King Henry VIII's request for an annulment from his first wife

Catherine of Aragon, which then led to the formation of the Anglican church in England.

Every painting described in *The Painter of Time* actually exists and the description of each, including the artist and the year that each was unveiled is accurate.

The description of the Cloisters is largely accurate. It is a beautiful Medieval building set in Fort Tryon Park on the northern edge of Central Park along the Hudson River. John D. Rockefeller, Jr., not only donated most of his private art collection and bought the land where the Cloisters now sits, he also did in fact purchase several hundred acres of the New Jersey Palisades on the other side of the Hudson River and donated them to the state of New Jersey to help preserve the view of the museum. There are several cloistered gardens, although I doubt that there is a Japanese maple anywhere within those gardens. I also am not sure that there is a statue of St. Francis in the garden. Those both served allegorical purposes in the story and seemed to be acceptable embellishments.

The Sherman Fairchild Center for Objects Conservation at the Cloisters did indeed open in 2002 to go along with the larger Sherman Fairchild Center at the Metropolitan Museum of Art. The description of the layout of center and the workspaces, however, is based in my imagination.